the sword in the stone

T. H. White

the sword in the stone

With Decorations and a New Introduction

by the Author

TIME Reading Program Special Edition

TIME INCORPORATED, NEW YORK

TIME-LIFE BOOKS
EDITOR *Norman P. Ross*
TEXT DIRECTOR *William Jay Gold*
ART DIRECTOR *Edward A. Hamilton*
CHIEF OF RESEARCH *Beatrice T. Dobie*
ASSISTANT TEXT DIRECTOR *Jerry Korn*

EDITOR, TIME READING PROGRAM *Max Gissen*
RESEARCHER *Ann S. Lang*
DESIGNER *Lore Levenberg*

PUBLISHER *Rhett Austell*
GENERAL MANAGER *John A. Watters*

TIME MAGAZINE
EDITOR *Roy Alexander*
MANAGING EDITOR *Otto Fuerbringer*
PUBLISHER *Bernhard M. Auer*

COVER DESIGN *Alan E. Cober*

for
Sir Thomas Maleore,
Knight

editors' preface

Part 1 of a trilogy (3 books) called "The Once and Future King." Merlyn lived backwards in time, remember

Terence Hanbury White can be compared with no other writer of the 20th Century. He belonged to no school, preached no fashionable creed, spoke for no class or generation. He was an original, a man of prodigious accomplishments, encyclopedic learning and poetic imagination. Because he defied easy classification, his books never earned him the effusive critical acclaim that was lavished on many a lesser writer. Yet when Tim White died in January 1964, a week or so after completing his introduction to this special edition of *The Sword in the Stone,* the novel had long been accepted as one of the few incontestable classics of modern English literature.

White was endowed in rare measure with qualities that seem curiously old-fashioned in today's world. He deeply loved his native England. As a scholar he immersed himself in its past; as naturalist and sportsman he had a metaphysical understanding of the land and its birds and beasts. Himself the master of many difficult skills, from falconry to flying, he hated the synthetic or slipshod, revering craftsmanship as a form of truth. In an age that sometimes seems to celebrate immorality and maladjustment, White was bold enough to exalt the chivalric virtues of goodness and valor, honesty, loyalty and kindliness. "I don't very much believe in the modern theory that the whole object of life is gratified desire," he once said. It was his achievement as a writer to make honor seem not only a worthier quest but a far more engrossing one.

Of all his 25-odd books, *The Sword in the Stone* always remained the one that was closest to White's heart. First published in 1938, it was to lead to three other novels, all of them together comprising *The Once and Future King,* White's great, glowing panoply of Arthurian legend. This first novel, about the young King Arthur, nicknamed "the Wart," is by far the sunniest, most exuberant book of this heroic and complex tetralogy. It is also the one that most nearly reflects White's own experience, as he explains in his introduction. Like Merlyn, the absent-minded magician who was chosen to tutor the King-to-be, White was a delightful, irresistible teacher. But he liked to think that there was much of himself also in the Wart, in the boy's loneliness and physical prowess and in the quickening excitement of learning that he likened to the "glee of the porpoise, pouring and leaping through strange seas."

White is often brilliantly funny in this book, notably in the chapter describing a joust between two elderly knights in armor whose charges sound "like a motor omnibus in collision with a smithy." But it is not for comic effect that his characters use modern slang and refer to such wild anachronisms as Eton and Red propaganda; the reason is that to White the people of this book are not sirrahs or varlets from a creaky costume drama but living, freshly relevant people speaking to the 20th Century. Their relationships reflect the author's profound humanity and his respect for the responsible, well-ordered society. Even such broadly comic figures as the officious sergeant at arms or the blimpish Sir Grummore Grummursum do not lack dignity. The humblest of his characters, from the Dog Boy who lives in the kennels to the hedgehog who croons *Sweet Genevieve,* are useful and likable. Each creature on wing or foot or fin has his just place, his unique lesson.

The book opens in an England where Might is Right and dragons still hiss like teakettles in the great jungles of the Forest Sauvage. It is a land of sylvan innocence, of roughshod ways and rural graces. For a boy, particularly a nobleman's child, Old England was an Eden. This idyll is shadowed, for the Wart, by the awareness that he is not the true son of Sir Ector, the jolly old squire who insists that "the battle of Crécy was won upon the playing fields of Camelot." The King-to-be has no inkling of his destiny, or why it is that a magician of Merlyn's caliber has been sent to give him and his unamiable foster brother, Kay, "a first rate eddication," as Sir Ector calls it.

Since Merlyn lives backward in time the wise, white-bearded magician is understandably often confused. He cannot always remember whether the *Encyclopaedia Britannica* in his wondrously cluttered cottage has been published yet, nor can he explain exactly what psychoanalysis is when he uses it to treat a village idiot. But he is incomparably the most exciting teacher a boy ever had. For in addition to giving routine lessons, mostly Summulae Logicales and the astrolabe, he has the power to turn the Wart into any kind of beast or insect, fish or fowl from which the boy may acquire the extracurricular learning he will need as England's King.

As a perch, deep in the castle moat, the Wart narrowly escapes being devoured by a monstrous pike. He learns courage and self-discipline by becoming a falcon—a merlin, of course—and spending a night among the hawks in the castle mews. The Wart is exposed to the 20th Century totalitarian state by becoming Worker 42436/WD in an ant colony where loudspeakers blare "Antland, Antland Over All" and posters proclaim: "EVERYTHING NOT FORBIDDEN IS COMPULSORY." Later, by contrast, he joins a flight of white-fronted geese, those "sailors of the air," whose unerring odysseys above the clouds teach Merlyn's pupil the meaning of true freedom and unenvious peace.

The young Arthur learns also from all manner of men and women: from bumbling King Pellinore, who is forever questing after the ludicrous Beast Glatisant; from Robin Wood (as he was known in those days); from Nurse, a medieval Malaprop; from Hob the Falconer. But thanks to Merlyn's magic, it is the creatures of sky and field and water, the true "lovers and helpers of the Wart," who flock to his aid when he stands before Excalibur. Rising before him "like the Punch and Judy ghosts of remembered days," they coach and cheer the Wart until, on his third try, he slips the great sword from the stone "as gently as from a scabbard." After his coronation, he asks Merlyn: "Will you stay with me for a long time?" "Yes, Wart" the magician replies. "Or rather, as I should say (or is it have said?), Yes, King Arthur."

In every age, of course, legend is not merely inherited but reshaped as well, and this has been particularly true in the case of the Arthurian epic. T. H. White's Once and Future King lived in the Sixth Century and had become a musty figure of folklore when, nine centuries later, Sir Thomas Malory took the story "out of certeyn books of frensshe, and reduced it into Englysshe," making the Knights of the Round Table

live again for his time. To Tennyson in the romantic
19th Century, they seemed like proper Victorians; to
Mark Twain, they were fitting figures for satire.

It was T. H. White's achievement to rediscover the
wonder and nobility of Arthur's age, finding in the con-
flict between Might and Right a telling parallel with
our own darkened era. No less than those people who
lived amid "the great jungle of Old England," he sug-
gests, modern man inhabits a Forest Sauvage. In the
late 1950s White extensively revised *The Sword in the
Stone* in preparation for the publication of *The Once
and Future King*. In the process he inserted several
chapters—notably those about Antland and the wild
geese—that reflected a more somber view of our time
than he had taken two decades earlier.

Indeed, it is hard to believe that White was barely
30 when he wrote his first Arthurian novel. Even at
that age, however, he was a man of remarkable achieve-
ments. He had already published a volume of poems,
two thrillers, a panoramic review of the Victorian Age,
a hilarious pair of books on sporting life, and, most
successfully, *England Have My Bones,* an intimate, rambling, beautifully told chronicle of the English country-
side and White's experiences while learning to pilot a
plane. "One of my private curses as an author," he
once wrote, "is that readers expect authors to write the
same book over and over again." But it was a curse to
which White never yielded. After *The Sword in the
Stone,* he published books as varied in subject matter as
The Goshawk, a minor classic about falconry; a science-
fiction novel reminiscent of Jules Verne; the first English translation of a medieval bestiary; and *Mistress
Masham's Repose,* an enchanting fantasy about a 10-
year-old girl who inherits a huge country estate and
finds that her tenants include a colony of Lilliputians.

And, of course, there were the three other books about King Arthur—which would have been followed, had White lived, by a fifth and final volume for which he had compiled ledgers full of notes, writing in green ink with a goose quill pen. He also had plans for a travel book on the United States, which he crisscrossed in late 1963 on a lecture tour and found, somewhat to his surprise, endlessly fascinating.

Though he called himself a "nostalgic Tory" and bitterly lamented Britain's decline from greatness, Tim White was the least stuffy man alive. On the tiny Channel island of Alderney, where the white-haired, blue-eyed author lived for the last 15 years of his life, he was known not only as a genuine English eccentric but also as an unfailingly magnanimous neighbor who would ungrudgingly give his time and money—when he had any—to help others in distress. As he himself hints in his introduction, Tim White was a lonely, love-crossed man who adored children and bitterly regretted his own bachelorhood.

Yet, in fact, every reader of *The Sword in the Stone* is his ward, a Wart to White's Merlyn. His tender and magical book is, above all, a paean to excellence, whether in hunting, haymaking or scholarship.

In the life of every man and woman, White believed, there is a sword locked in stone. With honor and kindness and courage, with diligence and knowledge, it can come as swiftly and cleanly free as it did for the young King Arthur.

—THE EDITORS OF TIME

RP introduction

So far as I can make out, the Arthurian interest has been knocking about in my family for a long time. I have been told that my father was going to be christened Gaseth, but the nurse who took him to be baptized forgot the name on the way to the church and he got called Garrick instead. I also had a great-uncle called Arthur. At all events, I was writing what I hoped was poetry about knights-in-armor from the age of 16 or so and I still have one poem of that period which begins "Sir Gringamour in shining mail. . . ." The names enchanted me. Sir Gringamour, really! And there was Sir Ozanna le Cure Hardy, probably the nicest name of the lot. I can't find the poem, but I have a vague recollection that it had something to do with La Belle Dame Sans Merci.

My thesis for an honors degree at Cambridge University, when I was about 22 years old, and that is very long ago, was about the Arthurian cycle.

People who are going to be writers or painters or musicians or artists of any sort can hardly ever support themselves as such from the beginning, so they have to be moonlighters with a secondary occupation on which they depend for a living. I am a natural-born teacher like Merlyn in *The Sword in the Stone,* and I therefore earned my bread and butter as a school-master for the first seven years, while trying to estab-lish some sort of reputation as an author. It meant teaching for two thirds of the year and writing the rest of the time, with no holidays. I adored teaching, was devoted to young people, and I wish in a way that I was with them still.

At the age of 30 I was living rather an extravagant life—flying airplanes, driving a Bentley, fishing for salmon and riding to foxhounds with a hunter of my own—but it suddenly dawned on me, on that birthday, that if I didn't look sharp and get out of the teaching profession it would be a case of Good-bye, Mr. Chips. Schoolmasters in England—although they are the salt of the earth and belong to the second most important profession (after doctors)—tend to suffer from one de-fect. They are Tritons among minnows. They have nev-er severed the umbilical cord from their Alma Mater. They have gone first as boarders to their private schools, then as boarders to what the English call public schools, then as boarders to the University, and there they are back again as teachers in similar schools—as grown-up schoolboys surrounded by smaller ones who have to re-gard them as being infallible.

I did not want to be always in the right, always in authority over my inferiors in age, always protected by and suckling from the Alma Mater. I wanted to get out into the real, wild world as an adult, where nature was red in tooth and claw, and there I wanted to compete with my equals. I don't know whether I really wanted to—for I was as fond of my pupils as Merlyn, too—but I felt it would be better for my own character. It was a moral compulsion of the kind which activated people like Sir Lancelot. Moralists are prone to make themselves miserable by trying to do what seems to be right.

So I sold the horse and the Bentley and the top hat and everything else, and paid my debts, and found I had $300 (or more accurately the equivalent in pounds) in my pocket to last the rest of my life. I also had a contract with my publisher to pay me about a thousand dollars a year for two years, in return, practically speaking, for an option on all my books forever.

I found a gamekeeper's cottage, at a dollar a week, in a wood near the school which I could hardly bear to leave, and I bought myself a secondhand bicycle instead of the Bentley, and I did not think it was difficult for a single man to live on five or six dollars a week. You could do pretty well on bread and cheese and milk and eggs and the rabbits which lived in the woodland, and there was even something over for a few pints of beer on Saturday evenings at the pub. This was getting on for 30 years ago.

What I had not bargained for was that I was free.

There are few free people in the world. Probably the least free man on earth is the Pope—think of his engagement book—and after him the President of the United States. The moment you have a public profession, or a family, or a wife, or even any property of your own like a house and its furniture, or a job which you have to hold down—at that moment you have lost your freedom and have become the servant of other people or things. The only free man I can think of is a hobo. Millionaires are far from free—they have to spend the whole time clutching their millions. Even monks or nuns who own nothing personally are not free. They have to serve their communities and observe a schedule of their own.

But I had nothing. Even the cottage was rented. There was no reason why I should get up at any particular time in the morning or go to bed at any particular time at night. I could eat when I was hungry and sleep when I was tired. I had no wife or children or responsibilities—except one very great one, a red setter bitch —and there was no reason why I should not walk straight out of the cottage door if I wanted to and thumb a lift to Timbuktu.

This is a rare circumstance, and it is also difficult. It is much easier to be a tram than an automobile. Trams have grooves to run on and do not have to make decisions. If you have no grooves and the world is one vast freeway as broad as it is long and you are an automobile —that is, a thing that moves itself—then you have got to make decisions all the time. You must not only decide when to have breakfast and when to go to bed, you must also decide which is the right direction—you must distinguish between right and wrong.

As is usual with things that are difficult, the freedom was incredibly rewarding. The more difficult a thing is to do, the more wonderful it is to do it well.

I was wild with freedom. I was a hawk, a falcon, which had slipped its jesses. The wide air was mine again, as it ought to be in boyhood, and that year— which seems in retrospect to have passed like a flash— was one of the only seven consciously happy years I have had in all my life.

I spent it writing *The Sword in the Stone.*

It seems to me now that the book was a happy one because I was happy. Merlyn's cottage in the book is a fairly close description of the cottage I was living in. The Forest Sauvage is the woodland which was round it. The Wart is a mixture of the boys I had liked as a teacher. And I was doing in real life the very things which occupy the Wart. (Perhaps I was the Wart as well as Merlyn?) I was training a couple of goshawks to hunt rabbits, I was helping farmers to make hay, I was out with the poachers at night as much as I was out in the daytime of the miraculous summer, I was fishing for tench before dawn, and most of the time I was looking after small animals which needed help. I really did have an owl called Archimedes—he had been rescued from a pond as a baby—and the small badgers really did nip my ankles with their needle teeth until I hopped. The book wrote itself, much as Merlyn's dishes did their own washing up.

People have sometimes asked me whether I do things so as to write about them. Do you go down in an old-fashioned diving suit, they ask, so as to describe it? Did you learn to fly those ancient airplanes so as to write a book about them?

Well, the answer is that I get involved in airplanes or owls or diving suits because of their own challenge, and soon after—when I have found out how to do it— I suddenly want to turn round, because I am the sort of teacher I was telling you about, and tell everybody else. It is like a swimmer who gets into rather a cold sea and turns round, puffing, and says, "Come in! Come in! It's wonderful!"

The later history of *The Sword in the Stone* was wonderful, too.

I had hardly written it when a large book club pounced upon it. Don't forget that I was a sort of game-warden and that something like a thousand books get published every month. How and why on earth did they pick on me? Who read the thing? Mathematically speaking—since there can only be a certain number of judges in the club—the odds were that it would not even get read. But evidently somebody did happen to read it, and then the lucky series of chances was on. Later it and its sequels became the basis for a Broadway musical, *Camelot*. I have fallen deeply in love with the stage version of my book—and of all things with the music. It is wonderful music—but that is not surprising. It is just like everything else which came out of that happy, lucky, free year.

—T. H. WHITE

*"I pray you all, gentlemen and gentlewomen that read-
eth this book, from the beginning to the ending, pray for me
while I am on live, that God send me good deliverance, and
when I am dead, I pray you all pray for my soul."*

—SIR THOMAS MALEORE, KNIGHT

July 31st, 1485

*"And now it is all gone—like an insubstantial pageant
faded; and between us and the old English there lies a gulf of
mystery which the prose of the historian will never adequately
bridge. They cannot come to us, and our imaginations can but
feebly penetrate to them. Only among the aisles of the cathe-
dral, only as we gaze upon their silent figures sleeping on
their tombs, some faint conceptions float before us of what
these men were when they were alive."*

chapter one

On Mondays, Wednesdays and Fridays it was Court Hand and Summulae Logicales, while the rest of the week it was the Organon, Repetition and Astrology. The governess was always getting muddled with her astrolabe, and when she got specially muddled she would take it out of the Wart by rapping his knuckles. She did not rap Kay's knuckles, because when Kay grew older he would be Sir Kay, the master of the estate. The Wart was called the Wart because it more or less rhymed with Art, which was short for his real name. Kay had given him the nickname. Kay was not called anything but Kay, as he was too dignified to have a nickname and would have flown into a passion if anybody had tried to give him one. The governess had red hair and some mysterious wound from which she derived a lot of prestige by showing it to all the women of the castle, behind closed doors. It was believed to be where she sat down, and to have been caused by sitting on some armour at a picnic by mistake. Eventually she offered to show it to Sir Ector, who was Kay's father, had hysterics and was sent away. They found out afterwards that she had been in a lunatic hospital for three years.

In the afternoons the programme was: Mondays and Fridays, tilting and horsemanship; Tuesdays, hawking;

Wednesdays, fencing; Thursdays, archery; Saturdays, the theory of chivalry, with the proper measures to be blown on all occasions, terminology of the chase and hunting etiquette. If you did the wrong thing at the mort or the undoing, for instance, you were bent over the body of the dead beast and smacked with the flat side of a sword. This was called being bladed. It was horseplay, a sort of joke like being shaved when crossing the line. Kay was not bladed, although he often went wrong.

When they had got rid of the governess, Sir Ector said, "After all, damn it all, we can't have the boys runnin' about all day like hooligans—after all, damn it all? Ought to be havin' a first-rate eddication, at their age. When I was their age I was doin' all this Latin and stuff at five o'clock every mornin'. Happiest time of me life. Pass the port."

Sir Grummore Grummursum, who was staying the night because he had been benighted out questin' after a specially long run, said that when he was their age he was swished every mornin' because he would go hawkin' instead of learnin'. He attributed to this weakness the fact that he could never get beyond the Future Simple of Utor. It was a third of the way down the left-hand leaf, he said. He thought it was leaf ninety-seven. He passed the port.

Sir Ector said, "Had a good quest today?"

Sir Grummore said, "Oh, not so bad. Rattlin' good day, in fact. Found a chap called Sir Bruce Saunce Pité choppin' off a maiden's head in Weedon Bushes, ran him to Mixbury Plantation in the Bicester, where he doubled back, and lost him in Wicken Wood. Must have been a good twenty-five miles as he ran."

"A straight-necked 'un," said Sir Ector.

"But about these boys and all this Latin and that," added the old gentleman. "Amo, amas, you know, and runnin' about like hooligans: what would you advise?"

"Ah," said Sir Grummore, laying his finger by his nose and winking at the bottle, "that takes a deal of thinkin' about, if you don't mind my sayin' so."

"Don't mind at all," said Sir Ector. "Very kind of you to say anythin'. Much obliged, I'm sure. Help yourself to port."

"Good port this."

"Get it from a friend of mine."

"But about these boys," said Sir Grummore. "How many of them are there, do you know?"

"Two," said Sir Ector, "counting them both, that is."

"Couldn't send them to Eton, I suppose?" inquired Sir Grummore cautiously. "Long way and all that, we know."

It was not really Eton that he mentioned, for the College of Blessed Mary was not founded until 1440, but it was a place of the same sort. Also they were drinking Metheglyn, not Port, but by mentioning the modern wine it is easier to give you the feel.

"Isn't so much the distance," said Sir Ector, "but that giant What's-'is-name is in the way. Have to pass through his country, you understand."

"What is his name?"

"Can't recollect it at the moment, not for the life of me. Fellow that lives by the Burbly Water."

"Galapas," said Sir Grummore.

"That's the very chap."

"The only other thing," said Sir Grummore, "is to have a tutor."

"You mean a fellow who teaches you."

"That's it," said Sir Grummore. "A tutor, you know, a fellow who teaches you."

"Have some more port," said Sir Ector. "You need it after all this questin'."

"Splendid day," said Sir Grummore. "Only they never seem to kill nowadays. Run twenty-five miles and then mark to ground or lose him altogether. The worst is when you start a fresh quest."

"We kill all our giants cubbin'," said Sir Ector. "After that they give you a fine run, but get away."

"Run out of scent," said Sir Grummore, "I dare say. It's always the same with these big giants in a big country. They run out of scent."

"But even if you was to have a tutor," said Sir Ector, "I don't see how you would get him."

"Advertise," said Sir Grummore.

"I have advertised," said Sir Ector. "It was cried by the *Humberland Newsman and Cardoile Advertiser*."

"The only other way," said Sir Grummore, "is to start a quest."

"You mean a quest for a tutor," explained Sir Ector.

"That's it."

"Hic, Haec, Hoc," said Sir Ector. "Have some more of this drink, whatever it calls itself."

"Hunc," said Sir Grummore.

So it was decided. When Grummore Grummursum had gone home next day, Sir Ector tied a knot in his handkerchief to remember to start a quest for a tutor as soon as he had time to do so, and, as he was not sure how to set about it, he told the boys what Sir Grummore had suggested and warned them not to be hooligans meanwhile. Then they went hay-making.

It was July, and every able-bodied man and woman on the estate worked during that month in the field, under Sir Ector's direction. In any case the boys would have been excused from being eddicated just then.

Sir Ector's castle stood in an enormous clearing in a still more enormous forest. It had a courtyard and a moat with pike in it. The moat was crossed by a fortified stone bridge which ended half-way across it. The other half was covered by a wooden drawbridge which was wound up every night. As soon as you had crossed the drawbridge you were at the top of the village street —it had only one street—and this extended for about half a mile, with thatched houses of wattle and daub on either side of it. The street divided the clearing into two huge fields, that on the left being cultivated in hundreds of long narrow strips, while that on the right ran down to a river and was used as pasture. Half of the right-hand field was fenced off for hay.

It was July, and real July weather, such as they had in Old England. Everybody went bright brown, like Red Indians, with startling teeth and flashing eyes. The dogs moved about with their tongues hanging out, or lay panting in bits of shade, while the farm horses sweated through their coats and flicked their tails and tried to kick the horse-flies off their bellies with their great hind hoofs. In the pasture field the cows were on the gad, and could be seen galloping about with their tails in the air, which made Sir Ector angry.

Sir Ector stood on the top of a rick, whence he could see what everybody was doing, and shouted commands all over the two-hundred-acre field, and grew purple in the face. The best mowers mowed away in a line where the grass was still uncut, their scythes roaring in the strong sunlight. The women raked the dry hay together in long strips with wooden rakes, and the two boys with pitchforks followed up on either side of the strip, turning the hay inwards so that it lay well for picking up. Then the great carts followed, rumbling with their spiked wooden wheels, drawn by horses or slow white oxen. One man stood on top of the cart to receive the hay and direct operations, while one man walked on either side picking up what the boys had prepared and throwing it to him with a fork. The cart was led down the lane between two lines of hay, and was loaded in strict rotation from the front poles to the back, the man on top calling out in a stern voice where he wanted each fork to be pitched. The loaders grumbled at the boys for not having laid the hay properly and threatened to tan them when they caught them, if they got left behind.

When the wagon was loaded, it was drawn to Sir Ector's rick and pitched to him. It came up easily because it had been loaded systematically—not like modern hay—and Sir Ector scrambled about on top, getting in the way of his assistants, who did the real work, and stamping and perspiring and scratching about with his fork and trying to make the rick grow straight and shouting that it would all fall down as soon as the west winds came.

The Wart loved hay-making, and was good at it. Kay, who was two years older, generally stood on the edge of the bundle which he was trying to pick up, with the result that he worked twice as hard as the Wart for only half the result. But he hated to be beaten at anything, and used to fight away with the wretched hay—which he loathed like poison—until he was quite sick.

The day after Sir Grummore's visit was sweltering for the men who toiled from milking to milking and then again till sunset in their battle with the sultry element. For the hay was an element to them, like sea or air, in which they bathed and plunged themselves and which they even breathed in. The seeds and small scraps stuck in their hair, their mouths, their nostrils, and worked, tickling, inside their clothes. They did not wear many clothes, and the shadows between their sliding muscles were blue on the nut-brown skins. Those who feared thunder had felt ill that morning.

In the afternoon the storm broke. Sir Ector kept them at it till the great flashes were right overhead, and then, with the sky as dark as night, the rain came hurling against them so that they were drenched at once and could not see a hundred yards. The boys lay crouched under the wagons, wrapped in hay to keep their wet bodies warm against the now cold wind, and all joked with one another while heaven fell. Kay was shivering, though not with cold, but he joked like the others because he would not show he was afraid. At the last and greatest thunderbolt every man startled involuntarily, and each saw the other startle, until they laughed away their shame.

But that was the end of the hay-making and the beginning of play. The boys were sent home to change their clothes. The old dame who had been their nurse fetched dry jerkins out of a press, and scolded them for catching their deaths, and denounced Sir Ector for keeping on so long. Then they slipped their heads into the laundered shirts, and ran out to the refreshed and sparkling court.

"I vote we take Cully and see if we can get some rabbits in the chase," cried the Wart.

"The rabbits will not be out in this wet," said Kay sarcastically, delighted to have caught him over natural history.

"Oh, come on. It will soon be dry."

"I must carry Cully, then."

Kay insisted on carrying the goshawk and flying her, when they went hawking together. This he had a right to do, not only because he was older than the Wart but also because he was Sir Ector's proper son. The Wart was not a proper son. He did not understand this, but it made him feel unhappy, because Kay seemed to regard it as making him inferior in some way. Also it was different not having a father and mother, and Kay had taught him that being different was wrong. Nobody talked to him about it, but he thought about it when he was alone, and was distressed. He did not like people to bring it up. Since the other boy always did bring it up when a question of precedence arose, he had got into the habit of giving in at once before it could be mentioned. Besides, he admired Kay and was a born follower. He was a hero-worshipper.

"Come on, then," cried the Wart, and they scampered off toward the Mews, turning a few cartwheels on the way.

The Mews was one of the most important parts of the castle, next to the stables and the kennels. It was opposite to the solar, and faced south. The outside windows had to be small, for reasons of fortification, but the windows which looked inward to the courtyard were big and sunny. The windows had close vertical slats nailed down them, but no horizontal ones. There was no glass, but to keep the hawks from draughts there was horn in the small windows. At one end of the Mews there was a little fireplace and a kind of snuggery, like the place in a saddle-room where the grooms sit to clean their tack on wet nights after fox-hunting. Here there were a couple of stools, a cauldron, a bench with all sorts of small knives and surgical instruments, and some shelves with pots on them. The pots were labelled Cardamum, Ginger, Barley Sugar, Wrangle, For a Snurt, For the Craye, Vertigo, etc. There were leather skins hanging up, which had been snipped about as pieces were cut out of them for jesses, hoods or leashes. On a neat row of nails there were Indian bells and swivels and silver varvels, each with Ector cut on. A special shelf, and the most beautiful of all, held the hoods: very old cracked rufter hoods which had been made for birds before Kay was born, tiny hoods for the merlins, small hoods for tiercels, splendid new hoods which had been knocked up to pass away the long winter evenings. All the hoods, except the rufters, were made in Sir Ector's colours: white leather with red baize at the sides and a bunch of blue-grey plumes on top, made out of the hackle feathers of herons. On the bench there was a jumble of oddments such as are to be found in every workshop, bits of cord, wire, metal, tools, some bread and cheese which the mice had been at, a leather bottle, some frayed gauntlets for the left hand, nails, bits of sacking, a couple of lures and some rough tallies scratched on the wood. These read: Conays ɪɪɪɪɪɪɪ, Harn ɪɪɪ, etc. They were not spelled very well.

Right down the length of the room, with the afternoon sun shining full on them, there ran the screen perches to which the birds were tied. There were two little merlins which had only just been taking up from hacking, an old peregrine who was not much use in this wooded country but who was kept for appearances, a kestrel on which the boys had learned the rudiments of falconry, a spar-hawk which Sir Ector was kind enough to keep for the parish priest, and, caged off in a special apartment of his own at the far end, there was the tiercel goshawk Cully.

The Mews was neatly kept, with sawdust on the floor to absorb the mutes, and the castings taken up every day. Sir Ector visited the place each morning at seven o'clock and the two austringers stood at attention outside the door. If they had forgotten to brush their hair he confined them to barracks. They took no notice.

Kay put on one of the left-hand gauntlets and called Cully from the perch—but Cully, with all his feathers close-set and malevolent, glared at him with a mad marigold eye and refused to come. So Kay took him up.

"Do you think we ought to fly him?" asked the Wart doubtfully. "Deep in the moult like this?"

"Of course we can fly him, you ninny," said Kay. "He only wants to be carried a bit, that's all."

So they went out across the hay-field, noting how the carefully raked hay was now sodden again and losing its goodness, into the chase where the trees began to grow, far apart as yet and parklike, but gradually crowding into the forest shade. The conies had hundreds of buries under these trees, so close together that the problem was not to find a rabbit, but to find a rabbit far enough away from its hole.

"Hob says that we must not fly Cully till he has roused at least twice," said the Wart.

"Hob does not know anything about it. Nobody can tell whether a hawk is fit to fly except the man who is carrying it.

"Hob is only a villein anyway," added Kay, and began to undo the leash and swivel from the jesses.

When he felt the trappings being taken off him, so that he was in hunting order, Cully did make some movements as if to rouse. He raised his crest, his shoulder coverts and the soft feathers of his thighs. But at the last moment he thought better or worse of it and subsided without the rattle. This movement of the hawk's made the Wart itch to carry him. He yearned to take him away from Kay and set him to rights himself. He felt certain that he could get Cully into a good temper by scratching his feet and softly teasing his breast feathers upward, if only he were allowed to do it himself, instead of having to plod along behind with the stupid lure. But he knew how annoying it must be for the elder boy to be continually subjected to advice, and so he held his peace. Just as in modern shooting, you must never offer criticism to the man in command, so in hawking it was important that no outside advice should be allowed to disturb the judgment of the aus-tringer.

"So-ho!" cried Kay, throwing his arm upward to give the hawk a better take-off, and a rabbit was scoot-ing across the close-nibbled turf in front of them, and Cully was in the air. The movement had surprised the Wart, the rabbit and the hawk, all three, and all three hung a moment in surprise. Then the great wings of the aerial assassin began to row the air, but reluctant and undecided. The rabbit vanished in a hidden hole. Up went the hawk, swooping like a child flung high in a swing, until the wings folded and he was sitting in a tree. Cully looked down at his masters, opened his beak in an angry pant of failure, and remained motion-less. The two hearts stood still.

chapter two

A good while later, when they had been whistling and luring and following the disturbed and sulky hawk from tree to tree, Kay lost his temper.

"Let him go, then," he said. "He is no use anyway."

"Oh, we could not leave him," cried the Wart. "What would Hob say?"

"It is my hawk, not Hob's," exlaimed Kay furiously. "What does it matter what Hob says? He is a servant."

"But Hob made Cully. It is all right for us to lose him, because we did not have to sit up with him three nights and carry him all day and all that. But we can't lose Hob's hawk. It would be beastly."

"Serve him right, then. He is a fool and it is a rotten hawk. Who wants a rotten stupid hawk? You had better stay yourself, if you are so keen on it. I am going home."

"I will stay," said the Wart sadly, "if you will send Hob when you get there."

Kay began walking off in the wrong direction, raging in his heart because he knew that he had flown the bird when he was not properly in yarak, and the Wart had to shout after him the right way. Then the latter sat down under the tree and looked up at Cully like a cat watching a sparrow, with his heart beating fast.

It was well enough for Kay, who was not really keen on hawking except in so far as it was the proper occupation for a boy in his station of life, but the Wart had some of the falconer's feelings and knew that a lost hawk was the greatest possible calamity. He knew that Hob had worked on Cully for fourteen hours a day to teach him his trade, and that his work had been like Jacob's struggle with the angel. When Cully was lost a part of Hob would be lost too. The Wart did not dare to face the look of reproach which would be in the falconer's eye, after all that he had tried to teach them.

What was he to do? He had better sit still, leaving the lure on the ground, so that Cully could settle down and come in his own time. But Cully had no intention of doing this. He had been given a generous gorge the night before, and he was not hungry. The hot day had put him in a bad temper. The waving and whistling of the boys below, and their pursuit of him from tree to tree, had disturbed his never powerful brains. Now he did not quite know what he wanted to do, but it was not what anybody else wanted. He thought perhaps it would be nice to kill something, from spite.

A long time after that, the Wart was on the verge of the true forest, and Cully was inside it. In a series of infuriating removes they had come nearer and nearer, till they were further from the castle than the boy had ever been, and now they had reached it quite.

Wart would not have been frightened of an English forest nowadays, but the great jungle of Old England was a different matter. It was not only that there were wild boars in it, whose sounders would at this season be furiously rooting about, nor that one of the surviving wolves might be slinking behind any tree, with pale eyes and slavering chops. The mad and wicked animals were not the only inhabitants of the crowded gloom. When men themselves became wicked they took refuge there, outlaws cunning and bloody as the gore-crow, and as persecuted. The Wart thought particularly of a man named Wat, whose name the cottagers used to frighten their children with. He had once lived in Sir Ector's village and the Wart could remember him. He squinted, had no nose, and was weak in his wits. The children threw stones at him. One day he turned on the children and caught one and made a snarly noise and bit off his nose too. Then he ran into the forest. They threw stones at the child with no nose, now, but Wat was supposed to be in the forest still, running on all fours and dressed in skins.

There were magicians in the forest also in those legendary days, as well as strange animals not known to modern works of natural history. There were regular bands of Saxon outlaws—not like Wat—who lived together and wore green and shot with arrows which never missed. There were even a few dragons, though these were small ones, which lived under stones and could hiss like a kettle.

Added to this, there was the fact that it was getting dark. The forest was trackless and nobody in the village knew what was on the other side. The evening hush had fallen, and the high trees stood looking at the Wart without a sound.

He felt that it would be safer to go home, while he still knew where he was—but he had a stout heart, and did not want to give in. He understood that once Cully had slept in freedom for a whole night he would be wild again and irreclaimable. Cully was a passager. But if the poor Wart could only mark him to roost, and if Hob would only arrive then with a dark lantern, they might still take him that night by climbing the tree, while he was sleepy and muddled with the light. The boy could see more or less where the hawk had perched, about a hundred yards within the thick trees, because the home-going rooks of evening were mobbing that place.

He made a mark on one of the trees outside the forest, hoping that it might help him to find his way back, and then began to fight his way into the undergrowth as best he might. He heard by the rooks that Cully had immediately moved further off.

The night fell still as the small boy struggled with the brambles. But he went on doggedly, listening with all his ears, and Cully's evasions became sleepier and shorter until at last, before the utter darkness fell, he could see the hunched shoulders in a tree above him against the sky. Wart sat down under the tree, so as not to disturb the bird any further as it went to sleep, and Cully, standing on one leg, ignored his existence.

"Perhaps," said the Wart to himself, "even if Hob does not come, and I do not see how he can very well follow me in this trackless woodland now, I shall be able to climb up by myself at about midnight, and bring Cully down. He might stay there at about midnight because he ought to be asleep by then. I could speak to him softly by name, so that he thought it was just the usual person coming to take him up while hooded. I shall have to climb very quietly. Then, if I do get him, I shall have to find my way home, and the drawbridge will be up. But perhaps somebody will wait for me, for Kay will have told them I am out. I wonder which way it was? I wish Kay had not gone."

He snuggled down between the roots of the tree, trying to find a comfortable place where the hard wood did not stick into his shoulder-blades.

"I think the way was behind that big spruce with the spike top. I ought to try to remember which side of me the sun is setting, so that when it rises I may keep it on the same side going home. Did something move under that spruce tree, I wonder? Oh, I wish I may not meet that old wild Wat and have my nose bitten off! How aggravating Cully looks, standing there on one leg as if there was nothing the matter."

At this there was a quick whirr and a smack and the Wart found an arrow sticking in the tree between the fingers of his right hand. He snatched his hand away, thinking he had been stung by something, before he noticed it was an arrow. Then everything went slow. He had time to notice quite carefully what sort of an arrow it was, and how it had driven three inches into the solid wood. It was a black arrow with yellow bands round it, like a wasp, and its cock feather was yellow. The two others were black. They were dyed goose feathers.

The Wart found that, although he was frightened of the danger of the forest before it happened, once he was in it he was not frightened any more. He got up quickly—but it seemed to him slowly—and went behind the other side of the tree. As he did this, another arrow came whirr and frump, but this one buried all except its feathers in the grass, and stayed still, as if it had never moved.

On the other side of the tree he found a waste of bracken, six foot high. This was splendid cover, but it betrayed his whereabouts by rustling. He heard another arrow hiss through the fronds, and what seemed to be a man's voice cursing, but it was not very near. Then he heard the man, or whatever it was, running about in the bracken. It was reluctant to fire any more arrows because they were valuable things and would certainly get lost in the undergrowth. Wart went like a snake, like a coney, like a silent owl. He was small and the creature had no chance against him at this game. In five minutes he was safe.

The assassin searched for his arrows and went away grumbling—but the Wart realized that, even if he was safe from the archer, he had lost his way and his hawk. He had not the faintest idea where he was. He lay down for half an hour, pressed under the fallen tree where he had hidden, to give time for the thing to go right away and for his own heart to cease thundering. It had begun beating like this as soon as he knew that he had got away.

"Oh," thought he, "now I am truly lost, and now there is almost no alternative except to have my nose bitten off, or to be pierced right through with one of those waspy arrows, or to be eaten by a hissing drag-on or a wolf or a wild boar or a magician—if magicians do eat boys, which I expect they do. Now I may well wish that I had been good, and not angered the governess when she got muddled with her astrolabe, and had loved my dear guardian Sir Ector as much as he deserved."

At these melancholy thoughts, and especially at the recollection of kind Sir Ector with his pitchfork and his red nose, the poor Wart's eyes became full of tears and he lay most desolate beneath the tree.

The sun finished the last rays of its lingering good-bye, and the moon rose in awful majesty over the silver tree-tops, before he dared to stand. Then he got up, and dusted the twigs out of his jerkin, and wandered off forlorn, taking the easiest way and trusting himself to God. He had been walking like this for about half an hour, and sometimes feeling more cheerful—because it really was very cool and lovely in the summer forest by moonlight—when he came upon the most beautiful thing that he had seen in his short life so far.

There was a clearing in the forest, a wide sward of moonlit grass, and the white rays shone full upon the tree trunks on the opposite side. These trees were beeches, whose trunks are always more beautiful in a pearly light, and among the beeches there was the smallest movement and a silvery clink. Before the clink there were just the beeches, but immediately afterward there was a knight in full armour, standing still and silent and unearthly, among the majestic trunks. He was mounted on an enormous white horse that stood as rapt as its master, and he carried in his right hand, with its butt resting on the stirrup, a high, smooth jousting lance, which stood up among the tree stumps, higher and higher, till it was outlined against the velvet sky. All was moonlit, all silver, too beautiful to describe.

The Wart did not know what to do. He did not know whether it would be safe to go up to this knight, for there were so many terrible things in the forest that even the knight might be a ghost. Most ghostly he looked, too, as he hoved meditating on the confines of the gloom. Eventually the boy made up his mind that even if it were a ghost, it would be the ghost of a knight, and knights were bound by their vows to help people in distress.

"Excuse me," he said, when he was right under the mysterious figure, "but can you tell me the way back to Sir Ector's castle?"

At this the ghost jumped, so that it nearly fell off its horse, and gave out a muffled baaa through its visor, like a sheep.

"Excuse me," began the Wart again, and stopped, terrified, in the middle of his speech.

For the ghost lifted up its visor, revealing two enormous eyes frosted like ice; exclaimed in an anxious voice, "What, what?"; took off its eyes—which turned out to be horn-rimmed spectacles, fogged by being inside the helmet; tried to wipe them on the horse's mane—which only made them worse; lifted both hands above its head and tried to wipe them on its plume; dropped its lance; dropped the spectacles; got off the horse to search for them—the visor shutting in the process; lifted its visor; bent down for the spectacles; stood up again as the visor shut once more, and exclaimed in a plaintive voice, "Oh, dear!"

The Wart found the spectacles, wiped them, and gave them to the ghost, who immediately put them on (the visor shut at once) and began scrambling back on its horse for dear life. When it was there it held out its hand for the lance, which the Wart handed up, and, feeling all secure, opened the visor with its left hand, and held it open. It peered at the boy with one hand up—like a lost mariner searching for land—and exclaimed, "Ah-hah! Whom have we here, what?"

"Please," said the Wart, "I am a boy whose guardian is Sir Ector."

"Charming fellah," said the Knight. "Never met him in me life."

"Can you tell me the way back to his castle?"

"Faintest idea. Stranger in these parts meself."

"I am lost," said the Wart.

"Funny thing that. Now I have been lost for seventeen years.

"Name of King Pellinore," continued the Knight. "May have heard of me, what?" The visor shut with a pop, like an echo to the What, but was opened again immediately. "Seventeen years ago, come Michaelmas, and been after the Questing Beast ever since. Boring, very.''

"I should think it would be," said the Wart, who had never heard of King Pellinore, nor of the Questing Beast, but he felt that this was the safest thing to say in the circumstances.

"It is the Burden of the Pellinores," said the King proudly. "Only a Pellinore can catch it—that is, of course, or his next of kin. Train all the Pellinores with that idea in mind. Limited eddication, rather. Fewmets, and all that."

"I know what fewmets are," said the boy with interest. "They are the droppings of the beast pursued. The harborer keeps them in his horn, to show to his master, and can tell by them whether it is a warrantable beast or otherwise, and what state it is in."

"Intelligent child," remarked the King. "Very. Now I carry fewmets about with me practically all the time.

"Insanitary habit," he added, beginning to look dejected, "and quite pointless. Only one Questing Beast, you know, so there can't be any question whether she is warrantable or not."

Here his visor began to droop so much that the Wart decided he had better forget his own troubles and try to cheer his companion, by asking questions on the one subject about which he seemed qualified to speak. Even talking to a lost royalty was better than being alone in the wood.

"What does the Questing Beast look like?"

"Ah, we call it the Beast Glatisant, you know," replied the monarch, assuming a learned air and beginning to speak quite volubly. "Now the Beast Glatisant, or, as we say in English, the Questing Beast—you may

call it either,'' he added graciously—''this Beast has
the head of a serpent, ah, and the body of a libbard,
the haunches of a lion, and he is footed like a hart.
Wherever this beast goes he makes a noise in his belly
as it had been the noise of thirty couple of hounds
questing.

''Except when he is drinking, of course,'' added
the King.

''It must be a dreadful kind of monster,'' said the
Wart, looking about him anxiously.

''A dreadful monster,'' repeated the King. ''It is
the Beast Glatisant.''

''And how do you follow it?''

This seemed to be the wrong question, for
Pellinore began to look even more depressed.

''I have a brachet,'' he said sadly. ''There she is,
over there.''

The Wart looked in the direction which had been
indicated with a despondent thumb, and saw a lot of
rope wound round a tree. The other end of the rope
was tied to King Pellinore's saddle.

''I do not see her very well.''

''Wound herself round the other side, I dare say.
She always goes the opposite way from me.''

The Wart went over to the tree and found a large
white dog scratching herself for fleas. As soon as she
saw the Wart, she began wagging her whole body, grin-
ning vacuously, and panting in her efforts to lick his
face, in spite of the cord. She was too tangled up to
move.

''It's quite a good brachet,'' said King Pellinore,
''only it pants so, and gets wound round things, and
goes the opposite way. What with that and the visor,
what, I sometimes don't know which way to turn.''

"Why don't you let her loose?" asked the Wart. "She would follow the Beast just as well like that."

"She goes right away then, you see, and I don't see her sometimes for a week.

"Gets a bit lonely without her," added the King, "following the Beast about, and never knowing where one is. Makes a bit of company, you know."

"She seems to have a friendly nature."

"Too friendly. Sometimes I doubt whether she is really chasing the Beast at all."

"What does she do when she sees it?"

"Nothing."

"Oh, well," said the Wart. "I dare say she will get to be interested in it after a time."

"It is eight months, anyway, since we saw the Beast at all."

The poor fellow's voice had grown sadder and sadder since the beginning of the conversation, and now he definitely began to snuffle. "It is the curse of the Pellinores," he exclaimed. "Always mollocking about after that beastly Beast. What on earth use is she, anyway? First you have to stop to unwind the brachet, then your visor falls down, then you can't see through your spectacles. Nowhere to sleep, never know where you are. Rheumatism in the winter, sunstroke in the summer. All this horrid armour takes hours to put on. When it is on it's either frying or freezing, and it gets rusty. You have to sit up all night polishing the stuff. Oh, how I do wish I had a nice house of my own to live in, a house with beds in it and real pillows and sheets. If I was rich that's what I would buy. A nice bed with a nice pillow and a nice sheet that you could lie in, and then I would put this beastly horse in a meadow and tell that beastly brachet to run away and play, and throw all this beastly armour out of the window, and let the beastly Beast go and chase himself—that I would.''

"If you could show me the way home,'' said the Wart craftily, ''I am sure Sir Ector would put you up in a bed for the night.''

"Do you really mean it?'' cried the King. ''In a bed?''

"A feather bed.''

King Pellinore's eyes grew round as saucers. ''A feather bed!'' he repeated slowly. ''Would it have pillows?''

"Down pillows.''

"Down pillows!'' whispered the King, holding his breath. And then, letting it out in one rush, ''What a lovely house your gentleman must have!''

"I do not think it is more than two hours away,'' said the Wart, following up his advantage.

"And did this gentleman really send you out to invite me in?'' (He had forgotten about the Wart being lost.) ''How nice of him, how very nice of him, I do think, what?''

"He will be pleased to see us,'' said the Wart truthfully.

"Oh, how nice of him,'' exclaimed the King again, beginning to bustle about with his various trappings. ''And what a lovely gentleman he must be, to have a feather bed!

"I suppose I should have to share it with somebody?'' he added doubtfully.

"You could have one of your own.''

"A feather bed of one's very own, with sheets and a pillow—perhaps even two pillows, or a pillow and a bolster—and no need to get up in time for breakfast! Does your guardian get up in time for breakfast?''

"Never,'' said the Wart.

"Fleas in the bed?"

"Not one."

"Well!" said King Pellinore. "It does sound too nice for words, I must say. A feather bed and none of those fewmets for ever so long. How long did you say it would take us to get there?"

"Two hours," said the Wart—but he had to shout the second of these words, for the sounds were drowned in his mouth by a noise which had that moment arisen close beside them.

"What was that?" exclaimed the Wart.

"Hark!" cried the King.

"Mercy!"

"It is the Beast!"

And immediately the loving huntsman had forgotten everything else, but was busied about his task. He wiped his spectacles upon the seat of his trousers, the only accessible piece of cloth about him, while the belling and bloody cry arose all around. He balanced them on the end of his long nose, just before the visor automatically clapped to. He clutched his jousting lance in his right hand, and galloped off in the direction of the noise. He was brought up short by the rope which was wound round the tree—the vacuous brachet meanwhile giving a melancholy yelp—and fell off his horse with a tremendous clang. In a second he was up again —the Wart was convinced that the spectacles must be broken—and hopping round the white horse with one foot in the stirrup. The girths stood the test and he was in the saddle somehow, with his jousting lance between his legs, and then he was galloping round and round the tree, in the opposite direction to the one in which the brachet had wound herself up. He went round three times too often, the brachet meanwhile running and yelping the other way, and then, after four or five back casts, they were both free of the obstruction. "Yoicks, what!" cried King Pellinore, waving his lance in the air, and swaying excitedly in the saddle. Then he disappeared into the gloom of the forest, with the unfortunate hound trailing behind him at the other end of the cord.

chapter three

The boy slept well in the woodland nest where he had laid himself down, in that kind of thin but refreshing sleep which people have when they begin to lie out of doors. At first he only dipped below the surface of sleep, and skimmed along like a salmon in shallow water, so close to the surface that he fancied himself in air. He thought himself awake when he was already asleep. He saw the stars above his face, whirling on their silent and sleepless axis, and the leaves of the trees rustling against them, and he heard small changes in the grass. These little noises of footsteps and soft-fringed wing-beats and stealthy bellies drawn over the grass blades or rattling against the bracken at first frightened or interested him, so that he moved to see what they were (but never saw), then soothed him, so that he no longer cared to see what they were but trusted them to be themselves, and finally left him altogether as he swam down deeper and deeper, nuzzling into the scented turf, into the warm ground, into the unending waters under the earth.

It had been difficult to go to sleep in the bright summer moonlight, but once he was there it was not difficult to stay. The sun came early, causing him to **turn over in protest, but in going to sleep he had learned** to vanquish light, and now the light could not rewake him. It was nine o'clock, five hours after daylight, before he rolled over, opened his eyes, and was awake at once. He was hungry.

The Wart had heard about people who lived on berries, but this did not seem practical at the moment, because it was July, and there were none. He found two wild strawberries and ate them greedily. They tasted nicer than anything, so that he wished there were more. Then he wished it was April, so that he could find some birds' eggs and eat those, or that he had not lost his goshawk Cully, so that the hawk could catch him a rabbit which he would cook by rubbing two sticks together like the base Indian. But he had lost Cully, or he would not have lost himself, and probably the sticks would not have lighted in any case. He decided that he could not have gone more than three or four miles from home, and that the best thing he could do would be to sit still and listen. Then he might hear the noise of the haymakers, if he were lucky with the wind, and he could hearken his way to the castle by that.

What he did hear was a faint clanking noise, which made him think that King Pellinore must be after the Questing Beast again, close by. Only the noise was so regular and single in intention that it made him think of King Pellinore doing some special action, with great patience and concentration—trying to scratch his back without taking off his armour, for instance. He went toward the noise.

There was a clearing in the forest, and in this clearing there was a snug cottage built of stone. It was a cottage, although the Wart could not notice this at the time, which was divided into two bits. The main bit was the hall or every-purpose room, which was high because it extended from floor to roof, and this room had a fire on the floor whose smoke came out eventually from a hole in the thatch of the roof. The other half of the cottage was divided into two rooms by a horizontal floor which made the top half into a bedroom and study, while the bottom half served for a larder, storeroom, stable and barn. A white donkey lived in this down-stairs room, and a ladder led to the one upstairs.

There was a well in front of the cottage, and the metallic noise which the Wart had heard was caused by a very old gentleman who was drawing water out of it by means of a handle and chain.

Clank, clank, clank, went the chain, until the bucket hit the lip of the well, and "Drat the whole thing!" said the old gentleman. "You would think that after all these years of study you could do better for yourself than a by-our-lady well with a by-our-lady bucket, whatever the by-our-lady cost.

"By this and by that," added the old gentleman, heaving his bucket out of the well with a malevolent glance, "why can't they get us the electric light and company's water?"

He was dressed in a flowing gown with fur tippets which had the signs of the zodiac embroidered over it, with various cabalistic signs, such as triangles with eyes in them, queer crosses, leaves of trees, bones of birds and animals, and a planetarium whose stars shone like bits of looking-glass with the sun on them. He had a pointed hat like a dunce's cap, or like the headgear worn by ladies of that time, except that the ladies were accustomed to have a bit of veil floating from the top of it. He also had a wand of lignum vitae, which he had laid down in the grass beside him, and a pair of horn-rimmed spectacles like those of King Pellinore.

They were unusual spectacles, being without ear pieces, but shaped rather like scissors or like the antennae of the tarantula wasp.

"Excuse me, sir," said the Wart, "but can you tell me the way to Sir Ector's castle, if you don't mind?"

The aged gentleman put down his bucket and looked at him.

"Your name would be the Wart."

"Yes, sir, please, sir."

"My name," said the old man, "is Merlyn."

"How do you do?"

"How do."

When these formalities had been concluded, the Wart had leisure to look at him more closely. The magician was staring at him with a kind of unwinking and benevolent curiosity which made him feel that it would not be at all rude to stare back, no ruder than it would be to stare at one of his guardian's cows who happened to be thinking about his personality as she leaned her head over a gate.

Merlyn had a long white beard and long white moustaches which hung down on either side of it. Close inspection showed that he was far from clean. It was not that he had dirty fingernails, or anything like that, but some large bird seemed to have been nesting in his hair. The Wart was familiar with the nests of spar-hawk and Gos, the crazy conglomerations of sticks and oddments which had been taken over from squirrels or crows, and he knew how the twigs and the tree foot were splashed with white mutes, old bones, muddy feathers and castings. This was the impression which he got from Merlyn. The old man was streaked with droppings over his shoulders, among the stars and triangles of his gown, and a large spider was slowly lowering itself from the tip of his hat, as he gazed and slowly blinked at the little boy in front of him. He had a worried expression, as though he were trying to remember some name which began with Chol but which was pronounced in quite a different way, possibly Menzies or was it Dalziel? His mild blue eyes, very big and round under the tarantula spectacles, gradually filmed and clouded over as he gazed at the boy, and then he turned his head away with a resigned expression, as though it was all too much for him after all.

"Do you like peaches?"

"Very much indeed," said the Wart, and his mouth began to water so that it was full of sweet, soft liquid.

"They are scarcely in season," said the old man reprovingly, and he walked off in the direction of the cottage.

The Wart followed after, since this was the simplest thing to do, and offered to carry the bucket (which seemed to please Merlyn, who gave it to him) and waited while he counted the keys—while he muttered and mislaid them and dropped them in the grass. Finally, when they had got their way into the black and white home with as much trouble as if they were burgling it, he climbed up the ladder after his host and found himself in the upstairs room.

It was the most marvellous room that he had ever been in.

There was a real corkindrill hanging from the rafters, very lifelike and horrible with glass eyes and scaly tail stretched out behind it. When its master came into the room it winked one eye in salutation, although it was stuffed. There were thousands of brown books in leather bindings, some chained to the book-shelves and others propped against each other as if they had had too much to drink and did not really trust themselves. These gave out a smell of must and solid brownness which was most secure. Then there were stuffed birds, pop-injays, and maggot-pies and kingfishers, and peacocks with all their feathers but two, and tiny birds like bee-tles, and a reputed phoenix which smelt of incense and cinnamon. It could not have been a real phoenix, be-cause there is only one of these at a time. Over by the mantelpiece there was a fox's mask, with GRAFTON, BUCKINGHAM TO DAVENTRY, 2 HRS 20 MINS written under it, and also a forty-pound salmon with AWE, 43 MIN., BULLDOG written under it, and a very life-like basilisk with CROWHURST OTTER HOUNDS in Roman print. There were several boars' tusks and the claws of tigers and libbards mounted in symmetrical patterns, and a big head of Ovis Poli, six live grass snakes in a kind of aquarium, some nests of the solitary wasp nicely set up in a glass cylinder, an ordinary beehive whose inhabitants went in and out of the window unmolested, two young hedgehogs in cot-ton wool, a pair of badgers which immediately began to cry Yik-Yik-Yik-Yik in loud voices as soon as the ma-gician appeared, twenty boxes which contained stick caterpillars and sixths of the puss-moth, and even an oleander that was worth sixpence—all feeding on the appropriate leaves—a guncase with all sorts of weapons which would not be invented for half a thousand years, a rod-box ditto, a chest of drawers full of salmon flies which had been tied by Merlyn himself, another chest whose drawers were labelled Mandragora, Mandrake, Old Man's Beard, etc., a bunch of turkey feathers and goose-quills for making pens, an astrolabe, twelve pairs of boots, a dozen purse-nets, three dozen rabbit wires, twelve corkscrews, some ants' nests between two glass plates, ink-bottles of every possible colour from red to violet, darning-needles, a gold medal for being the best scholar at Winchester, four or five recorders, a nest of field mice all alive-o, two skulls, plenty of cut glass, Venetian glass, Bristol glass and a bottle of Mastic varnish, some satsuma china and some cloisonné, the fourteenth edition of the Encyclopaedia Britannica (marred as it was by the sensationalism of the popular plates), two paint-boxes (one oil, one water-colour), three globes of the known geographical world, a few fossils, the stuffed head of a cameleopard, six pismires, some glass retorts with cauldrons, bunsen burners, etc., and a complete set of cigarette cards depicting wild fowl by Peter Scott.

Merlyn took off his pointed hat when he came into this chamber, because it was too high for the roof, and immediately there was a scamper in one of the dark corners and a flap of soft wings, and a tawny owl was sitting on the black skull-cap which protected the top of his head.

"Oh, what a lovely owl!" cried the Wart.

But when he went up to it and held out his hand, the owl grew half as tall again, stood up as stiff as a poker, closed its eyes so that there was only the smallest slit to peep through—as you are in the habit of doing when told to shut your eyes at hide-and-seek—and said in a doubtful voice:

"There is no owl."

Then it shut its eyes entirely and looked the other way.

"It is only a boy," said Merlyn.

"There is no boy," said the owl hopefully, without turning round.

The Wart was so startled by finding that the owl could talk that he forgot his manners and came closer still. At this the bird became so nervous that it made a mess on Merlyn's head—the whole room was quite white with droppings—and flew off to perch on the farthest tip of the corkindrill's tail, out of reach.

"We see so little company," explained the magician, wiping his head with half a worn-out pair of pyjamas which he kept for that purpose, "that Archimedes is a little shy of strangers. Come, Archimedes, I want you to meet a friend of mine called Wart."

Here he held out his hand to the owl, who came waddling like a goose along the corkindrill's back—he waddled with this rolling gait so as to keep his tail from being damaged—and hopped down to Merlyn's finger with every sign of reluctance.

"Hold out your finger and put it behind his legs. No, lift it up under his train."

When the Wart had done this, Merlyn moved the owl gently backward, so that the boy's finger pressed against its legs from behind, and it either had to step back on the finger or get pushed off its balance altogether. It stepped back. The Wart stood there delighted, while the furry feet held tight on his finger and the sharp claws prickled his skin.

"Say how d'you do properly," said Merlyn.

"I will not," said Archimedes, looking the other way and holding tight.

"Oh, he *is* lovely," said the Wart again. "Have you had him long?"

"Archimedes has stayed with me since he was small, indeed since he had a tiny head like a chicken's."

"I wish he would talk to me."

"Perhaps if you were to give him this mouse here, politely, he might learn to know you better."

Merlyn took a dead mouse out of his skull-cap— "I always keep them there, and worms too, for fishing. I find it most convenient"—and handed it to the Wart, who held it out rather gingerly toward Archimedes. The nutty curved beak looked as if it were capable of doing damage, but Archimedes looked closely at the mouse, blinked at the Wart, moved nearer on the finger, closed his eyes and leaned forward. He stood there with closed eyes and an expression of rapture on his face, as if he were saying Grace, and then, with the absurdest sideways nibble, took the morsel so gently that he would not have broken a soap bubble. He remained leaning forward with closed eyes, with the mouse suspended from his beak, as if he were not sure what to do with it. Then he lifted his right foot—he was right-handed, though people say only men are—and took hold of the mouse. He held it up like a boy holding a stick of rock or a constable with his truncheon, looked at it, nibbled its tail. He turned it round so that it was head first, for the Wart had offered it the wrong way round, and gave one gulp. He looked round at the company with the tail hanging out of the corner of his mouth—as much as to say, "I wish you would not all stare at me so" —turned his head away, politely swallowed the tail, scratched his sailor's beard with his left toe, and began to ruffle out his feathers.

"Let him alone," said Merlyn. "Perhaps he does not want to be friends with you until he knows what you are like. With owls, it is never easy-come and easy-go."

"Perhaps he will sit on my shoulder," said the Wart, and with that he instinctively lowered his hand, so that the owl, who liked to be as high as possible, ran up the slope and stood shyly beside his ear.

"Now breakfast," said Merlyn.

The Wart saw that the most perfect breakfast was laid out neatly for two, on a table before the window. There were peaches. There were also melons, strawberries and cream, rusks, brown trout piping hot, grilled perch which were much nicer, chicken devilled enough to burn one's mouth out, kidneys and mushrooms on toast, fricassee, curry, and a choice of boiling coffee or best chocolate made with cream in large cups.

"Have some mustard," said the magician, when they had got to the kidneys.

The mustard-pot got up and walked over to his plate on thin silver legs that waddled like the owl's. Then it uncurled its handles and one handle lifted its lid with exaggerated courtesy while the other helped him to a generous spoonful.

"Oh, I love the mustard-pot!" cried the Wart. "Wherever did you get it?"

At this the pot beamed all over its face and began to strut a bit, but Merlyn rapped it on the head with a teaspoon, so that it sat down and shut up at once.

"It is not a bad pot," he said grudgingly. "Only it is inclined to give itself airs."

The Wart was so much impressed by the kindness of the old man, and particularly by the lovely things which he possessed, that he hardly liked to ask him personal questions. It seemed politer to sit still and to speak when he was spoken to. But Merlyn did not speak much, and when he did speak it was never in questions, so that the Wart had little opportunity for conversation. At last his curiosity got the better of him, and he asked something which had been puzzling him for some time.

"Would you mind if I ask you a question?"

"It is what I am for."

"How did you know to set breakfast for two?"

The old gentleman leaned back in his chair and lighted an enormous meerschaum pipe—Good gracious, he breathes fire, thought the Wart, who had never heard of tobacco—before he was ready to reply. Then he looked puzzled, took off his skull-cap—three mice fell out—and scratched in the middle of his bald head.

"Have you ever tried to draw in a looking-glass?" he asked.

"I don't think I have."

"Looking-glass," said Merlyn, holding out his hand. Immediately there was a tiny lady's vanity-glass in his hand.

"Not that kind, you fool," he said angrily. "I want one big enough to shave in."

The vanity-glass vanished, and in its place there was a shaving mirror about a foot square. He then demanded pencil and paper in quick succession; got an unsharpened pencil and the *Morning Post;* sent them back; got a fountain pen with no ink in it and six reams of brown paper suitable for parcels; sent them back; flew into a passion in which he said by-our-lady quite often, and ended up with a carbon pencil and some cigarette papers which he said would have to do.

He put one of the papers in front of the glass and made five dots.

o   o

o

o   o

"Now," he said, "I want you to join those five dots up to make a W, looking only in the glass."

The Wart took the pen and tried to do as he was bid.

"Well, it is not bad," said the magician doubt-fully, "and in a way it does look a bit like an M."

Then he fell into a reverie, stroking his beard, breathing fire, and staring at the paper.

"About the breakfast?"

"Ah, yes. How did I know to set breakfast for two? That was why I showed you the looking-glass. Now ordinary people are born forwards in Time, if you understand what I mean, and nearly everything in the world goes forward too. This makes it quite easy for the ordinary people to live, just as it would be easy to join those five dots into a W if you were allowed to look at them forwards, instead of backwards and inside out. But I unfortunately was born at the wrong end of time, and I have to live backwards from in front, while surrounded by a lot of people living forwards from be-hind. Some people call it having second sight."

He stopped talking and looked at the Wart in an anxious way.

"Have I told you this before?"

"No, we only met about half an hour ago."

"So little time to pass?" said Merlyn, and a big tear ran down to the end of his nose. He wiped it off with his pyjamas and added anxiously, "Am I going to tell it you again?"

"I do not know," said the Wart, "unless you have not finished telling me yet."

"You see, one gets confused with Time, when it is like that. All one's tenses get muddled, for one thing. If you know what is *going* to happen to people, and not what *has* happened to them, it makes it difficult to prevent it happening, if you don't want it to have happened, if you see what I mean? Like drawing in a mirror."

The Wart did not quite see, but was just going to say that he was sorry for Merlyn if these things made him unhappy, when he felt a curious sensation at his ear. "Don't jump," said the old man, just as he was going to do so, and the Wart sat still. Archimedes, who had been standing forgotten on his shoulder all this time, was gently touching himself against him. His beak was right against the lobe of the ear, which its bristles made to tickle, and suddenly a soft hoarse voice whispered, "How d'you do," so that it sounded right inside his head.

"Oh, owl!" cried the Wart, forgetting about Merlyn's troubles instantly. "Look, he has decided to talk to me!"

The Wart gently leaned his head against the smooth feathers, and the tawny owl, taking the rim of his ear in its beak, quickly nibbled right round it with the smallest nibbles.

"I shall call him Archie!"

"I trust you will do nothing of the sort," exclaimed Merlyn instantly, in a stern and angry voice, and the owl withdrew to the farthest corner of his shoulder.

"Is it wrong?"

"You might as well call me Wol, or Olly," said the owl sourly, "and have done with it.

"Or Bubbles," it added in a bitter voice.

Merlyn took the Wart's hand and said kindly, "You are young, and do not understand these things. But you will learn that owls are the most courteous, single-hearted and faithful creatures living. You must never be familiar, rude or vulgar with them, or make them look ridiculous. Their mother is Athene, the goddess of wisdom, and, although they are often ready to play the buffoon to amuse you, such conduct is the prerogative of the truly wise. No owl can possibly be called Archie."

"I am sorry, owl," said the Wart.

"And I am sorry, boy," said the owl. "I can see that you spoke in ignorance, and I bitterly regret that I should have been so petty as to take offence where none was intended."

The owl really did regret it, and looked so remorseful that Merlyn had to put on a cheerful manner and change the conversation.

"Well," said he, "now that we have finished breakfast, I think it is high time that we should all three find our way back to Sir Ector.

"Excuse me a moment," he added as an afterthought, and, turning round to the breakfast things, he pointed a knobbly finger at them and said in a stern voice, "Wash up."

At this all the china and cutlery scrambled down off the table, the cloth emptied the crumbs out of the window, and the napkins folded themselves up. All ran off down the ladder, to where Merlyn had left the bucket, and there was such a noise and yelling as if a lot of children had been let out of school. Merlyn went to the door and shouted, "Mind, nobody is to get broken." But his voice was entirely drowned in shrill squeals, splashes, and cries of "My, it is cold," "I shan't stay in long," "Look out, you'll break me," or "Come on, let's duck the teapot."

"Are you really coming all the way home with me?" asked the Wart, who could hardly believe the good news.

"Why not? How else can I be your tutor?"

At this the Wart's eyes grew rounder and rounder, until they were about as big as the owl's who was sitting on his shoulder, and his face got redder and redder, and a breath seemed to gather itself beneath his heart.

"My!" exclaimed the Wart, while his eyes sparkled with excitement at the discovery. "I must have been on a Quest!"

chapter four

The Wart started talking before he was half-way over the drawbridge. "Look who I have brought," he said. "Look! I have been on a Quest! I was shot at with three arrows. They had black and yellow stripes. The owl is called Archimedes. I saw King Pellinore. This is my tutor, Merlyn. I went on a Quest for him. He was after the Questing Beast. I mean King Pellinore. It was terrible in the forest. Merlyn made the plates wash up. Hallo, Hob. Look, we have got Cully."

Hob just looked at the Wart, but so proudly that the Wart went quite red. It was such a pleasure to be back home again with all his friends, and everything achieved.

Hob said gruffly, "Ah, master, us shall make an austringer of 'ee yet."

He came for Cully, as if he could not keep his hands off him longer, but he patted the Wart too, fondling them both because he was not sure which he was gladder to see back. He took Cully on his own fist, re-assuming him like a lame man putting on his accustomed wooden leg, after it had been lost.

"Merlyn caught him," said the Wart. "He sent Archimedes to look for him on the way home. Then

Archimedes told us that he had been and killed a pigeon and was eating it. We went and frightened him off. After that, Merlyn stuck six of the tail feathers round the pigeon in a circle, and made a loop in a long piece of string to go round the feathers. He tied one end to a stick in the ground, and we went away behind a bush with the other end. He said he would not use magic. He said you could not use magic in Great Arts, just as it would be unfair to make a great statue by magic. You have to cut it out with a chisel, you see. Then Cully came down to finish the pigeon, and we pulled the string, and the loop slipped over the feathers and caught him round the legs. He was angry! But we gave him the pigeon.''

Hob made a duty to Merlyn, who returned it courteously. They looked upon one another with grave affection, knowing each other to be masters of the same trade. When they could be alone together they would talk about falconry, although Hob was naturally a silent man. Meanwhile they must wait their time.

''Oh, Kay,'' cried the Wart, as the latter appeared with their nurse and other delighted welcomers. ''Look, I have got a magician for our tutor. He has a mustard-pot that walks.''

''I am glad you are back,'' said Kay.

''Alas, where did you sleep, Master Art?'' exclaimed the nurse. ''Look at your clean jerkin all muddied and torn. Such a turn as you gave us, I really don't know. But look at your poor hair with all them twigs in it. Oh, my own random, wicked little lamb.''

Sir Ector came bustling out with his greaves on back to front, and kissed the Wart on both cheeks. ''Well, well, well,'' he exclaimed moistly. ''Here we are again, hey? What the devil have we been doin', hey? Settin' the whole household upside down.''

But inside himself he was proud of the Wart for staying out after a hawk, and prouder still to see that he had got it, for all the while Hob held the bird in the air for everybody to see.

"Oh, sir," said the Wart, "I have been on that quest you said for a tutor, and I have found him. Please, he is this gentleman here, and he is called Merlyn. He has got some badgers and hedgehogs and mice and ants and things on this white donkey here, because we could not leave them behind to starve. He is a great magician, and can make things come out of the air."

"Ah, a magician," said Sir Ector, putting on his glasses and looking closely at Merlyn. "White magic, I hope?"

"Assuredly," said Merlyn, who stood patiently among the throng with his arms folded in his necromantic gown, while Archimedes sat very stiff and elongated on the top of his head.

"Ought to have some testimonials," said Sir Ector doubtfully. "It's usual."

"Testimonials," said Merlyn, holding out his hand.

Instantly there were some heavy tablets in it, signed by Aristotle, a parchment signed by Hecate, and some typewritten duplicates signed by the Master of Trinity, who could not remember having met him. All these gave Merlyn an excellent character.

"He had 'em up his sleeve," said Sir Ector wisely. "Can you do anything else?"

"Tree," said Merlyn. At once there was an enormous mulberry growing in the middle of the courtyard, with its luscious blue fruits ready to patter down. This was all the more remarkable, since mulberries only became popular in the days of Cromwell.

"They do it with mirrors," said Sir Ector.

"Snow," said Merlyn. "And an umbrella," he added hastily.

Before they could turn round, the copper sky of summer had assumed a cold and lowering bronze, while the biggest white flakes that ever were seen were floating about them and settling on the battlements. An inch of snow had fallen before they could speak, and all were trembling with the wintry blast. Sir Ector's nose was blue, and had an icicle hanging from the end of it, while all except Merlyn had a ledge of snow upon their shoulders. Merlyn stood in the middle, holding his umbrella high because of the owl.

"It's done by hypnotism," said Sir Ector, with chattering teeth. "Like those wallahs from the Indies.

"But that'll do," he added hastily, "that'll do very well. I'm sure you'll make an excellent tutor for teachin' these boys."

The snow stopped immediately and the sun came out—"Enough to give a body a pewmonia," said the nurse, "or to frighten the elastic commissioners"— while Merlyn folded up his umbrella and handed it back to the air, which received it.

"Imagine the boy doin' a quest like that by himself," exclaimed Sir Ector. "Well, well, well! Wonders never cease."

"I do not think much of it as a quest," said Kay. "He only went after the hawk, after all."

"And got the hawk, Master Kay," said Hob reprovingly.

"Oh, well," said Kay, "I bet the old man caught it for him."

"Kay," said Merlyn, suddenly terrible, "thou wast ever a proud and ill-tongued speaker, and a misfortunate one. Thy sorrow will come from thine own mouth."

At this everybody felt uncomfortable, and Kay, instead of flying into his usual passion, hung his head. He was not at all an unpleasant person really, but clever, quick, proud, passionate and ambitious. He was one of those people who would be neither a follower nor a leader, but only an aspiring heart, impatient in the failing body which imprisoned it. Merlyn repented of his rudeness at once. He made a little silver hunting-knife come out of the air, which he gave him to put things right. The knob of the handle was made of the skull of a stoat, oiled and polished like ivory, and Kay loved it.

chapter five

Sir Ector's home was called The Castle of the Forest Sauvage. It was more like a town or a village than any one man's home, and indeed it was the village during times of danger: for this part of the story is one which deals with troubled times. Whenever there was a raid or an invasion by some neighbouring tyrant, everybody on the estate hurried into the castle, driving the beasts before them into the courts, and there they remained until the danger was over. The wattle and daub cottages nearly always got burned, and had to be rebuilt afterwards with much profanity. For this reason it was not worth while to have a village church, as it would constantly be having to be replaced. The villagers went to church in the chapel of the castle. They wore their best clothes and trooped up the street with their most respectable gait on Sundays, looking with vague and dignified looks in all directions, as if reluctant to disclose their destination, and on week-days they came to Mass and vespers in their ordinary clothes, walking much more cheerfully. Everybody went to church in those days, and liked it.

The Castle of the Forest Sauvage is still standing, and you can see its lovely ruined walls with ivy on them,

standing broached to the sun and wind. Some lizards
live there now, and the starving sparrows keep warm
on winter nights in the ivy, and a barn owl drives it
methodically, hovering outside the frightened congregations and beating the ivy with its wings, to make them
fly out. Most of the curtain wall is down, though you
can trace the foundations of the twelve round towers
which guarded it. They were round, and stuck out
from the wall into the moat, so that the archers could
shoot in all directions and command every part of the
wall. Inside the towers there are circular stairs. These
go round and round a central column, and this column
is pierced with holes for shooting arrows. Even if the
enemy had got inside the curtain wall and fought their
way into the bottom of the towers, the defenders could
retreat up the bends of the stairs and shoot at those
who followed them up, inside, through these slits.

The stone part of the drawbridge with its barbican
and the bartizans of the gatehouse are in good repair.
These have many ingenious arrangements. Even if ene-
mies got over the wooden bridge, which was pulled
up so that they could not, there was a portcullis
weighted with an enormous log which would squash
them flat and pin them down as well. There was a large
hidden trapdoor in the floor of the barbican, which
would let them into the moat after all. At the other
end of the barbican there was another portcullis, so
that they could be trapped between the two and an-
nihilated from above, while the bartizans, or hanging
turrets, had holes in their floors through which the defenders could drop things on their heads. Finally, inside the gatehouse, there was a neat little hole in
the middle of the vaulted ceiling, which had painted
tracery and bosses. This hole led to the room above,

where there was a big cauldron, for boiling lead or oil.

So much for the outer defences. Once you were inside the curtain wall, you found yourself in a kind of wide alley-way, probably full of frightened sheep, with another complete castle in front of you. This was the inner shell-keep, with its eight enormous round towers which still stand. It is lovely to climb the highest of them and to lie there looking out toward the Marches, from which some of these old dangers came, with nothing but the sun above you and the little tourists trotting about below, quite regardless of arrows and boiling oil. Think for how many centuries that unconquerable tower has withstood. It has changed hands by secession often, by siege once, by treachery twice, but never by assault. On this tower the look-out hoved. From here he kept the guard over the blue woods towards Wales. His clean old bones lie beneath the floor of the chapel now, so you must keep it for him.

If you look down and are not frightened of heights (the Society for the Preservation of This and That have put up some excellent railings to preserve you from tumbling over), you can see the whole anatomy of the inner court laid out beneath you like a map. You can see the chapel, now quite open to its god, and the windows of the great hall with the solar over it. You can see the shafts of the huge chimneys and how cunningly the side flues were contrived to enter them, and the little private closets now public, and the enormous kitchen. If you are a sensible person, you will spend days there, possibly weeks, working out for yourself by detection which were the stables, which the mews, where were the cow byres, the armoury, the lofts, the well, the smithy, the kennel, the soldiers' quarters, the priest's room, and my lord's and lady's chambers. Then

it will all grow about you again. The little people—
they were smaller than we are, and it would be a job
for most of us to get inside the few bits of their armour
and old gloves that remain—will hurry about in the
sunshine, the sheep will baa as they always did, and perhaps from Wales there will come the ffff-putt of the
triple-feathered arrow which looks as if it had never
moved.

This place was, of course, a paradise for a boy to
be in. The Wart ran about it like a rabbit in its own
complicated labyrinth. He knew everything, everywhere, all the special smells, good climbs, soft lairs,
secret hiding-places, jumps, slides, nooks, larders and
blisses. For every season he had the best place, like a cat,
and he yelled and ran and fought and upset people and
snoozed and daydreamed and pretended he was a Knight,
without stopping. Just now he was in the kennel.

People in those days had rather different ideas
about the training of dogs to what we have today. They
did it more by love than strictness. Imagine a modern
M.F.H. going to bed with his hounds, and yet Flavius
Arrianus says that it is ''Best of all if they can sleep
with a person because it makes them more human and
because they rejoice in the company of human beings:
also if they have had a restless night or been internally
upset, you will know of it and will not use them to
hunt next day.'' In Sir Ector's kennel there was a special boy, called the Dog Boy, who lived with the hounds
day and night. He was a sort of head hound, and it
was his business to take them out every day for walks,
to pull thorns out of their feet, keep cankers out of
their ears, bind the smaller bones that got dislocated,
dose them for worms, isolate and nurse them in distemper, arbitrate in their quarrels and to sleep curled

up among them at night. If one more learned quotation may be excused, this is how, later on, the Duke of York who was killed at Agincourt described such a boy in his Master of Game: "Also I will teach the child to lead out the hounds to scombre twice in the day in the morning and in the evening, so that the sun be up, especially in winter. Then should he let them run and play long in a meadow in the sun, and then comb every hound after the other, and wipe them with a great wisp of straw, and this he shall do every morning. And then he shall lead them into some fair place where tender grass grows as corn and other things, that therewith they may feed themselves as it is medicine for them." Thus, since the boy's "heart and his business be with the hounds," the hounds themselves become "goodly and kindly and clean, glad and joyful and playful, and goodly to all manner of folks save to the wild beasts to whom they should be fierce, eager and spiteful."

Sir Ector's dog boy was none other than the one who had his nose bitten off by the terrible Wat. Not having a nose like a human, and being, moreover, subjected to stone-throwing by the other village children, he had become more comfortable with animals. He talked to them, not in baby-talk like a maiden lady, but correctly in their own growls and barks. They all loved him very much, and revered him for taking thorns out of their toes, and came to him with their troubles at once. He always understood immediately what was wrong, and generally he could put it right. It was nice for the dogs to have their god with them, in visible form.

The Wart was fond of the Dog Boy, and thought him very clever to be able to do these things with animals—for he could make them do almost anything just by moving his hands—while the Dog Boy loved the

Wart in much the same way as his dogs loved him, and thought the Wart was almost holy because he could read and write. They spent much of their time together, rolling about with the dogs in the kennel.

The kennel was on the ground floor, near the mews, with a loft above it, so that it should be cool in summer and warm in winter. The hounds were alaunts, gaze-hounds, lymers and braches. They were called Clumsy, Trowneer, Phoebe, Colle, Gerland, Talbot, Luath, Luffra, Apollon, Orthros, Bran, Gelert, Bounce, Boy, Lion, Bungey, Toby, and Diamond. The Wart's own special one was called Cavall, and he happened to be licking Cavall's nose—not the other way about—when Merlyn came in and found him.

"That will come to be regarded as an insanitary habit," said Merlyn, "though I cannot see it myself. After all, God made the creature's nose just as well as he made your tongue.

"If not better," added the philosopher pensively.

The Wart did not know what Merlyn was talking about, but he liked him to talk. He did not like the grown-ups who talked down to him, but the ones who went on talking in their usual way, leaving him to leap along in their wake, jumping at meanings, guessing, clutching at known words, and chuckling at complicated jokes as they suddenly dawned. He had the glee of the porpoise then, pouring and leaping through strange seas.

"Shall we go out?" asked Merlyn. "I think it is about time we began lessons."

The Wart's heart sank at this. His tutor had been there a month, and it was now August, but they had done no lessons so far. Now he suddenly remembered that this was what Merlyn was for, and he thought with dread of Summulae Logicales and the filthy astrolabe. He knew that it had to be borne, however, and got up obediently enough, after giving Cavall a last reluctant pat. He thought that it might not be so bad with Merlyn, who might be able to make even the old Organon interesting, particularly if he would do some magic.

They went into the courtyard, into a sun so burning that the heat of hay-making seemed to have been nothing. It was baking. The thunder-clouds which usually go with hot weather were there, high columns of cumulus with glaring edges, but there was not going to be any thunder. It was too hot even for that. "If only," thought the Wart, "I did not have to go into a stuffy classroom, but could take off my clothes and swim in the moat."

They crossed the courtyard, having almost to take deep breaths before they darted across it, as if they were going quickly through an oven. The shade of the gatehouse was cool, but the barbican, with its close walls, was hottest of all. In one last dash across the desert they had reached the drawbridge—could Merlyn have guessed what he was thinking?—and were staring down into the moat.

It was the season of water-lilies. If Sir Ector had not kept one section free of them for the boys' bathing, all the water would have been covered. As it was, about twenty yards on each side of the bridge were cut each year, and one could dive in from the bridge itself. The moat was deep. It was used as a stew, so that the inhabitants of the castle could have fish on Fridays, and for this reason the architects had been careful not to let the drains and sewers run into it. It was stocked with fish every year.

"I wish I was a fish," said the Wart.

"What sort of fish?"

It was almost too hot to think about this, but the Wart stared down into the cool amber depths where a school of small perch were aimlessly hanging about.

"I think I should like to be a perch," he said. "They are braver than the silly roach, and not quite so slaughterous as the pike are."

Merlyn took off his hat, raised his staff of lignum vitae politely in the air, and said slowly, "Snylrem stnemilpmoc ot enutpen dna lliw eh yldnik tpecca siht yob sa a hsif?"

Immediately there was a loud blowing of sea-shells, conches and so forth, and a stout, jolly-looking gentleman appeared seated on a well-blown-up cloud above the battlements. He had an anchor tattooed on his stomach and a handsome mermaid with Mabel written under her on his chest. He ejected a quid of tobacco, nodded affably to Merlyn and pointed his trident at the Wart. The Wart found he had no clothes on. He found that he had tumbled off the drawbridge, landing with a smack on his side in the water. He found that the moat and the bridge had grown hundreds of times bigger. He knew that he was turning into a fish.

"Oh, Merlyn," he cried, "please come too."

"For this once," said a large and solemn tench beside his ear, "I will come. But in future you will have to go by yourself. Education is experience, and the essence of experience is self-reliance."

The Wart found it difficult to be a new kind of creature. It was no good trying to swim like a human being, for it made him go corkscrew and much too slowly. He did not know how to swim like a fish.

"Not like that," said the tench in ponderous tones. "Put your chin on your left shoulder and do jack-knives. Never mind about the fins to begin with.''

The Wart's legs had fused together into his back-bone and his feet and toes had become a tail fin. His arms had become two more fins—of a delicate pink—and he had sprouted some more somewhere about his stomach. His head faced over his shoulder, so that when he bent in the middle his toes were moving toward his ear instead of toward his forehead. He was a beautiful olive-green, with rather scratchy plate-armour all over him, and dark bands down his sides. He was not sure which were his sides and which were his back and front, but what now appeared to be his belly had an attractive whitish colour, while his back was armed with a splendid great fin that could be erected for war and had spikes in it. He did jack-knives as the tench directed and found that he was swimming vertically downward into the mud.

''Use your feet to turn to left or right,'' said the tench, ''and spread those fins on your tummy to keep level. You are living in two planes now, not one.''

The Wart found that he could keep more or less level by altering the inclination of his arm fins and the ones on his stomach. He swam feebly off, enjoying himself very much.

''Come back,'' said the tench. ''You must learn to swim before you can dart.''

The Wart returned to his tutor in a series of zig-zags and remarked, ''I do not seem to keep quite straight.''

''The trouble with you is that you do not swim from the shoulder. You swim as if you were a boy, bending at the hips. Try doing your jack-knives right from the neck downward, and move your body exactly the same amount to the right as you are going to move it to the left. Put your back into it.''

Wart gave two terrific kicks and vanished altogether in a clump of mare's tail several yards away.

"That's better," said the tench, now out of sight in the murky olive water, and the Wart backed himself out of his tangle with infinite trouble, by wriggling his arm fins. He undulated back toward the voice in one terrific shove, to show off.

"Good," said the tench, as they collided end to end. "But direction is the better part of valour.

"Try if you can do this one," it added.

Without apparent exertion of any kind it swam off backward under a water-lily. Without apparent exertion—but the Wart, who was an enterprising learner, had been watching the slightest movement of its fins. He moved his own fins anti-clockwise, gave the tip of his tail a cunning flick, and was lying alongside the tench.

"Splendid," said Merlyn. "Let us go for a little swim."

The Wart was on an even keel now, and reasonably able to move about. He had leisure to look at the extraordinary universe into which the tattooed gentleman's trident had plunged him. It was different from the universe to which he had been accustomed. For one thing, the heaven or sky above him was now a perfect circle. The horizon had closed to this. In order to imagine yourself into the Wart's position, you would have to picture a round horizon, a few inches about your head, instead of the flat horizon which you usually see. Under this horizon of air you would have to imagine another horizon of under water, spherical and practically upside down—for the surface of the water acted partly as a mirror to what was below it. It is difficult to imagine. What makes it a great deal more difficult to imagine is that everything which human beings would consider to be above the water level was fringed with all the colours of the spectrum. For instance, if you had happened to be fishing for the Wart, he would have seen you, at the rim of the tea saucer which was the upper air to him, not as one person waving a fishing-rod, but as seven people, whose outlines were red, orange, yellow, green, blue, indigo and violet, all waving the same rod whose colours were as varied. In fact, you would have been a rainbow man to him, a beacon of flashing and radiating colours, which ran into one another and had rays all about. You would have burned upon the water like Cleopatra in the poem.

The next most lovely thing was that the Wart had no weight. He was not earth-bound any more and did not have to plod along on a flat surface, pressed down by gravity and the weight of the atmosphere. He could do what men have always wanted to do, that is, fly. There is practically no difference between flying in the water and flying in the air. The best of it was that he did not have to fly in a machine, by pulling levers and sitting still, but could do it with his own body. It was like the dreams people have.

Just as they were going to swim off on their tour of inspection, a timid young roach appeared from between two waving bottle bushes of mare's tail and hung about, looking pale with agitation. It looked at them with big, apprehensive eyes and evidently wanted something, but could not make up its mind.

"Approach," said Merlyn gravely.

At this the roach rushed up like a hen, burst into tears, and began stammering its message.

"If you p-p-p-please, doctor," stammered the poor creature, gabbling so that they could scarcely understand what it said, "we have such a d-dretful case of s-s-s-something or other in our family, and we w-w-w-wondered if you could s-s-s-spare the time? It's our d-d-d-dear Mamma, who w-w-w-will swim a-a-all the time upside d-d-d-down, and she d-d-d-does look so horrible and s-s-s-speaks so strange, that we r-r-r-really thought she ought to have a d-d-d-doctor, if it w-w-w-wouldn't be too much? C-C-C-Clara says to say so, Sir, if you s-s-s-see w-w-w-what I m-m-m-mean?''

Here the poor roach began fizzing so much, what with its stammer and its tearful disposition, that it became quite inarticulate and could only stare at Merlyn with mournful eyes.

''Never mind, my little man,'' said Merlyn. ''There, there, lead me to your dear Mamma, and we shall see what we can do.''

They all three swam off into the murk under the drawbridge, upon their errand of mercy.

''Neurotic, these roach,'' whispered Merlyn, behind his fin. ''It is probably a case of nervous hysteria, a matter for the psychologist rather than the physician.''

The roach's Mamma was lying on her back as he had described. She was squinting, had folded her fins on her chest, and every now and then she blew a bubble. All her children were gathered round her in a circle, and every time she blew they nudged each other and gasped. She had a seraphic smile on her face.

''Well, well, well,'' said Merlyn, putting on his best bed-side manner, ''and how is Mrs. Roach today?''

He patted the young roaches on the head and advanced with stately motions toward his patient. It should perhaps be mentioned that Merlyn was a ponderous, deep-beamed fish of about five pounds, leather coloured, with small scales, adipose in his fins, rather slimy, and having a bright marigold eye—a respectable figure.

Mrs. Roach held out a languid fin, sighed emphatically and said, "Ah, doctor, so you've come at last?"

"Hum," said the physician, in his deepest tone.

Then he told everybody to close their eyes—the Wart peeped—and began to swim round the invalid in a slow and stately dance. As he danced he sang. His song was this:

> Therapeutic,
> Elephantic,
> Diagnosis,
> Boom!
> Pancreatic,
> Microstatic,
> Anti-toxic,
> Doom!
> With a normal catabolism,
> Gabbleism and babbleism,
> Snip, Snap, Snorum,
> Cut out his abdonorum.
> Dyspepsia,
> Anaemia,
> Toxaemia.
> One, two, three,
> And out goes He,
> With a fol-de-rol-derido for the Five Guinea Fee.

At the end of the song he was swimming round his patient so close that he actually touched her, stroking his brown smooth-scaled flanks against her more rattly pale ones. Perhaps he was healing her with his slime —for all the fishes are said to go to the Tench for medicine—or perhaps it was by touch or massage or hypnotism. In any case, Mrs. Roach suddenly stopped squinting, turned the right way up, and said, "Oh, doctor, dear doctor, I feel I could eat a little lob-worm now."

"No lob-worm," said Merlyn, "not for two days. I shall give you a prescription for a strong broth of algae every two hours, Mrs. Roach. We must build up your strength, you know. After all, Rome was not built in a day."

Then he patted all the little roaches once more, told them to grow up into brave little fish, and swam off with an air of importance into the gloom. As he swam, he puffed his mouth in and out.

"What did you mean by that about Rome?" asked the Wart, when they were out of earshot.

"Heaven knows."

They swam along, Merlyn occasionally advising him to put his back into it when he forgot, and the strange under-water world began to dawn about them, deliciously cool after the heat of the upper air. The great forests of weed were delicately traced, and in them there hung motionless many schools of sticklebacks learning to do their physical exercises in strict unison. On the word One they all lay still; at Two they faced about; at Three they all shot together into a cone, whose apex was a bit of something to eat. Water snails slowly ambled about on the stems of the lilies or under their leaves, while fresh-water mussels lay on the bottom doing nothing in particular. Their flesh was salmon pink, like a very good strawberry cream ice. The small congregations of perch—it was a strange thing, but all the bigger fish seemed to have hidden themselves—had delicate circulations, so that they blushed or grew pale as easily as a lady in a Victorian novel. Only their blush was a deep olive colour, and it was the blush of rage. Whenever Merlyn and his companion swam past them, they raised their spiky dorsal fins in menace, and only lowered them when they saw that Merlyn was a tench.

The black bars on their sides made them look as if they had been grilled, and these also could become darker or lighter. Once the two travellers passed under a swan. The white creature floated above like a Zeppelin, all indistinct except what was under the water. The latter part was quite clear and showed that the swan was floating slightly on one side with one leg cocked over its back.

"Look," said the Wart, "it is the poor swan with the deformed leg. It can only paddle with one leg, and the other side of it is hunched."

"Nonsense," said the swan snappily, putting its head into the water and giving them a frown with its black nares. "Swans like to rest in this position, and you can keep your fishy sympathy to yourself, so there." It continued to glare at them from up above, like a white snake suddenly let down through the ceiling, until they were out of sight.

"You swim along," said the tench, "as if there was nothing to be afraid of in the world. Don't you see that this place is exactly like the forest which you had to come through to find me?"

"Is it?"

"Look over there."

The Wart looked, and at first saw nothing. Then he saw a small translucent shape hanging motionless near the surface. It was just outside the shadow of a water-lily and was evidently enjoying the sun. It was a baby pike, absolutely rigid and probably asleep, and it looked like a pipe stem or a sea-horse stretched out flat. It would be a brigand when it grew up.

"I am taking you to see one of those," said the tench, "the Emperor of these purlieus. As a doctor I have immunity, and I dare say he will respect you as my companion as well—but you had better keep your tail bent in case he is feeling tyrannical."

"Is he the King of the Moat?"

"He is. Old Jack they call him, and some call him Black Peter, but for the most part they do not mention him by name at all. They just call him Mr. P. You will see what it is to be a king."

The Wart began to hang behind his conductor a little, and perhaps it was as well that he did, for they were almost on top of their destination before he noticed it. When he did see the old despot he started back in horror, for Mr. P. was four feet long, his weight incalculable. The great body, shadowy and almost invisible among the stems, ended in a face which had been ravaged by all the passions of an absolute monarch—by cruelty, sorrow, age, pride, selfishness, loneliness and thoughts too strong for individual brains. There he hung or hoved, his vast ironic mouth permanently drawn downward in a kind of melancholy, his lean clean-shaven chops giving him an American expression, like that of Uncle Sam. He was remorseless, disillusioned, logical, predatory, fierce, pitiless—but his great jewel of an eye was that of a stricken deer, large, fearful, sensitive and full of griefs. He made no movement, but looked upon them with his bitter eye.

The Wart thought to himself that he did not care for Mr. P.

"Lord," said Merlyn, not paying attention to his nervousness, "I have brought a young professor who would learn to profess."

"To profess what?" asked the King of the Moat slowly, hardly opening his jaws and speaking through his nose.

"Power," said the tench.

"Let him speak for himself."

"Please," said the Wart, "I don't know what I ought to ask."

"There is nothing," said the monarch, "except the power which you pretend to seek: power to grind and power to digest, power to seek and power to find, power to await and power to claim, all power and pitilessness springing from the nape of the neck."

"Thank you."

"Love is a trick played on us by the forces of evolution. Pleasure is the bait laid down by the same. There is only power. Power is of the individual mind, but the mind's power is not enough. Power of the body decides everything in the end, and only Might is Right.

"Now I think it is time that you should go away, young master, for I find this conversation uninteresting and exhausting. I think you ought to go away really almost at once, in case my disillusioned mouth should suddenly determine to introduce you to my great gills, which have teeth in them also. Yes, I really think you might be wise to go away this moment. Indeed, I think you ought to put your back into it. And so, a long farewell to all my greatness."

The Wart had found himself almost hypnotized by the big words, and hardly noticed that the tight mouth was coming closer and closer to him. It came imperceptibly, as the lecture distracted his attention, and suddenly it was looming within an inch of his nose. On the last sentence it opened, horrible and vast, the skin stretching ravenously from bone to bone and tooth to tooth. Inside there seemed to be nothing but teeth, sharp teeth like thorns in rows and ridges everywhere, like the nails in labourers' boots, and it was only at the last second that he was able to regain his own will, to pull himself together, to recollect his instructions and to escape. All those teeth clashed behind him at the tip of his tail, as he gave the heartiest jack-knife he had ever given.

In a second he was on dry land once again, standing beside Merlyn on the piping drawbridge, panting in his stuffy clothes.

chapter six

One Thursday afternoon the boys were doing their archery as usual. There were two straw targets fifty yards
apart, and when they had shot their arrows at one, they
had only to go to it, collect them, and shoot back at the
other, after facing about. It was still the loveliest summer weather, and there had been chicken for dinner, so
that Merlyn had gone off to the edge of their shooting-
ground and sat down under a tree. What with the
warmth and the chicken and the cream he had poured
over his pudding and the continual repassing of the boys
and the tock of the arrows in the targets—which was as
sleepy to listen to as the noise of a lawn-mower or of a
village cricket match—and what with the dance of the
egg-shaped sunspots between the leaves of his tree, the
aged man was soon fast asleep.

Archery was a serious occupation in those days. It
had not yet been turned over to Indians and small boys.
When you were shooting badly you got into a bad temper, just as the wealthy pheasant shooters do today. Kay
was shooting badly. He was trying too hard and plucking
on his loose, instead of leaving it to the bow.

"Oh, come on," he said. "I am sick of these
beastly targets. Let's have a shot at the popinjay."

They left the targets and had several shots at the popinjay—which was a large, bright-coloured artificial bird stuck on the top of a stick, like a parrot—and Kay missed these also. First he had the feeling of, "Well, I will hit the filthy thing, even if I have to go without my tea until I do it." Then he merely became bored.

The Wart said, "Let's play Rovers then. We can come back in half an hour and wake Merlyn up."

What they called Rovers, consisted in going for a walk with their bows and shooting one arrow each at any agreed mark which they came across. Sometimes it would be a molehill, sometimes a clump of rushes, sometimes a big thistle almost at their feet. They varied the distance at which they chose these objects, sometimes picking a target as much as 120 yards away—which was about as far as these boys' bows could carry—and sometimes having to aim actually below a close thistle because the arrow always leaps up a foot or two as it leaves the bow. They counted five for a hit, and one if the arrow was within a bow's length, and they added up their scores at the end.

On this Thursday they chose their targets wisely. Besides, the grass of the big field had been lately cut, so that they never had to search for their arrows for long, which nearly always happens, as in golf, if you shoot ill-advisedly near hedges or in rough places. The result was that they strayed further than usual and found themselves near the edge of the savage forest where Cully had been lost.

"I vote," said Kay, "that we go to those buries in the chase, and see if we can get a rabbit. It would be more fun than shooting at these hummocks."

They did this. They chose two trees about a hundred yards apart, and each boy stood under one of them waiting for the conies to come out again. They stood still, with their bows already raised and arrows fitted, so that they would make the least possible movement to disturb the creatures when they did appear. It was not difficult for either of them to stand thus, for the first test which they had had to pass in archery was standing with the bow at arm's length for half an hour. They had six arrows each and would be able to fire and mark them all before they needed to frighten the rabbits back by walking about to collect. An arrow does not make enough noise to upset more than the particular rabbit that it is shot at.

At the fifth shot Kay was lucky. He allowed just the right amount for wind and distance, and his point took a young coney square in the head. It had been standing up on end to look at him, wondering what he was.

"Oh, well shot!" cried the Wart, as they ran to pick it up. It was the first rabbit they had ever hit, and luckily they had killed it dead.

When they had carefully gutted it with the hunting knife which Merlyn had given—to keep it fresh—and passed one of its hind legs through the other at the hock, for convenience in carrying, the two boys prepared to go home with their prize. But before they unstrung their bows they used to observe a ceremony. Every Thursday afternoon, after the last serious arrow had been shot, they were allowed to fit one more nock to their strings and to shoot the arrow straight up into the air. It was partly a gesture of farewell, partly of triumph, and it was beautiful. They did it now as salute to their first prey.

The Wart watched his arrow go up. The sun was already westing toward evening, and the trees where they were had plunged them into a partial shade. So, as the arrow topped the trees and climbed into sunlight, it began to burn against the evening like the sun itself. Up and up it went, not weaving as it would have done with a snatching loose, but soaring, swimming, aspiring to heaven, steady, golden and superb. Just as it had spent its force, just as its ambition had been dimmed by destiny and it was preparing to faint, to turn over, to pour back into the bosom of its mother earth, a portent happened. A gore-crow came flapping wearily before the approaching night. It came, it did not waver, it took the arrow. It flew away, heavy and hoisting, with the arrow in its beak.

Kay was frightened by this, but the Wart was furious. He had loved his arrow's movement, its burning ambition in the sunlight, and, besides, it was his best one. It was the only one which was perfectly balanced, sharp, tight-feathered, clean-nocked, and neither warped nor scraped.

"It was a witch," said Kay.

chapter seven

Tilting and horsemanship had two afternoons a week, because they were the most important branches of a gentleman's education in those days. Merlyn grumbled about athletics, saying that nowadays people seemed to think that you were an educated man if you could knock another man off a horse and that the craze for games was the ruin of scholarship—nobody got scholarships like they used to do when he was a boy, and all the public schools had been forced to lower their standards —but Sir Ector, who was an old tilting blue, said that the battle of Crécy had been won upon the playing fields of Camelot. This made Merlyn so furious that he gave Sir Ector rheumatism two nights running before he relented.

Tilting was a great art and needed practice. When two knights jousted they held their lances in their right hands, but they directed their horses at one another so that each man had his opponent on his near side. The base of the lance, in fact, was held on the opposite side of the body to the side at which the enemy was charging. This seems rather inside out to anybody who is in the habit, say, of opening gates with a hunting-crop, but it had its reasons. For one thing, it meant that the shield was on the left arm, so that the opponents charged shield to shield, fully covered. It also meant that a man could be unhorsed with the side or edge of the lance, in a kind of horizontal swipe, if you did not feel sure of hitting him with your point. This was the humblest or least skilful blow in jousting.

A good jouster, like Lancelot or Tristram, always used the blow of the point, because, although it was liable to miss in unskilful hands, it made contact sooner. If one knight charged with his lance held rigidly sideways, to sweep his opponent out of the saddle, the other knight with his lance held directly forward would knock him down a lance length before the sweep came into effect.

Then there was how to hold the lance for the point stroke. It was no good crouching in the saddle and clutching it in a rigid grip preparatory to the great shock, for if you held it inflexibly like this its point bucked up and down to every movement of your thundering mount and you were practically certain to miss the aim. On the contrary, you had to sit loosely in the saddle with the lance easy and balanced against the horse's motion. It was not until the actual moment of striking that you clamped your knees into the horse's sides, threw your weight forward in your seat, clutched the lance with the whole hand instead of with the finger and thumb, and hugged your right elbow to your side to support the butt.

There was the size of the spear. Obviously a man with a spear one hundred yards long would strike down an opponent with a spear of ten or twelve feet before the latter came anywhere near him. But it would have been impossible to make a spear one hundred yards long and, if made, impossible to carry it. The jouster had to find out the greatest length which he could manage with the greatest speed, and he had to stick to that. Sir Lancelot, who came some time after this part of the story, had several sizes of spear and would call for his Great Spear or his Lesser Spear as occasion demanded.

There were the places on which the enemy should be hit. In the armoury of The Castle of the Forest Sauvage there was a big picture of a knight in armour with circles round his vulnerable points. These varied with the style of armour, so that you had to study your opponent before the charge and select a point. The good armourers—the best lived at Warrington, and still live near there—were careful to make all the forward or entering sides of their suits convex, so that the spear point glanced off them. Curiously enough, the shields of Gothic suits were more inclined to be concave. It was better that a spear point should stay on the shield, rather than glance off upward or downward, and perhaps hit a more vulnerable point of the body armour. The best place of all for hitting people was on the very crest of the tilting helm, that is, if the person in question were vain enough to have a large metal crest in whose folds and ornaments the point would find a ready lodging. Many were vain enough to have these armorial crests, with bears and dragons or even ships or castles on them, but Sir Lancelot always contented himself with a bare helmet, or a bunch of feathers which would not hold spears, or, on one occasion, a soft lady's sleeve.

It would take too long to go into all the interesting details of proper tilting which the boys had to learn, for in those days you had to be a master of your craft from the bottom upward. You had to know what wood was best for spears, and why, and even how to turn them so that they would not splinter or warp. There were a thousand disputed questions about arms and armour, all of which had to be understood.

Just outside Sir Ector's castle there was a jousting field for tournaments, although there had been no tournaments in it since Kay was born. It was a green meadow, kept short, with a broad grassy bank raised round it on which pavilions could be erected. There was an old wooden grandstand at one side, lifted on stilts for the ladies. At present the field was only used as a practice-ground for tilting, so a quintain had been erected at one end and a ring at the other. The quintain was a wooden saracen on a pole. He was painted with a bright blue face and red beard and glaring eyes. He had a shield in his left hand and a flat wooden sword in his right. If you hit him in the middle of his forehead all was well, but if your lance struck him on the shield or on any part to left or right of the middle line, then he spun round with great rapidity, and usually caught you a wallop with his sword as you galloped by, ducking. His paint was somewhat scratched and the wood picked up over his right eye. The ring was just an ordinary iron ring tied to a kind of gallows by a thread. If you managed to put your point through the ring, the thread broke, and you could canter off proudly with the ring round your spear.

The day was cooler than it had been for some time, for the autumn was almost within sight, and the two boys were in the tilting yard with the master armourer and Merlyn. The master armourer, or sergeant-at-arms, was a stiff, pale, bouncy gentleman with waxed moustaches. He always marched about with his chest stuck out like a pouter pigeon, and he called out ''On the word One—'' on every possible occasion. He took great pains to keep his stomach in, and often tripped over his feet because he could not see them over his chest. He was generally making his muscles ripple, which annoyed Merlyn.

Wart lay beside Merlyn in the shade of the grand-stand and scratched himself for harvest bugs. The saw-like sickles had only lately been put away, and the wheat stood in stooks of eight among the tall stubble of those times. The Wart still itched. He was also sore about the shoulders and had a burning ear, from making bosh shots at the quintain—for, of course, practice tilting was done without armour. Wart was pleased that it was Kay's turn to go through it now and he lay drowsily in the shade, snoozing, scratching, twitching like a dog and partly attending to the fun.

Merlyn, sitting with his back to all the athleticism, was practising a spell which he had forgotten. It was a spell to make the sergeant's moustaches uncurl, but at present it only uncurled one of them, and the sergeant had not noticed it. He absent-mindedly curled it up again every time Merlyn did the spell, and Merlyn said, "Drat it!" and began again. Once he made the sergeant's ears flap by mistake, and the latter gave a startled look at the sky.

From far off at the other side of the tilting ground the sergeant's voice came floating on the still air.

"Nah, Nah, Master Kay, that ain't it at all. Has you were. Has you were. The spear should be 'eld between the thumb and forefinger of the right 'and, with the shield in line with the seam of the trahser leg. . . ."

The Wart rubbed his sore ear and sighed.

"What are you grieving about?"

"I was not grieving; I was thinking."

"What were you thinking?"

"Oh, it was not anything. I was thinking about Kay learning to be a knight."

"And well you may grieve," exclaimed Merlyn hotly. "A lot of brainless unicorns swaggering about and calling themselves educated just because they can push each other off a horse with a bit of stick! It makes me tired. Why, I believe Sir Ector would have been gladder to get a by-our-lady tilting blue for your tutor, that swings himself along on his knuckles like an anthropoid ape, rather than a magician of known probity and international reputation with first-class honours from every European university. The trouble with the Norman Aristocracy is that they are games-mad, that is what it is games-mad."

He broke off indignantly and deliberately made the sergeant's ears flap slowly twice, in unison.

"I was not thinking quite about that," said the Wart. "As a matter of fact, I was thinking how nice it would be to be a knight, like Kay."

"Well, you will be one soon enough, won't you?" asked the old man, impatiently.

Wart did not answer.

"Won't you?"

Merlyn turned round and looked closely at the boy through his spectacles.

"What is the matter now?" he enquired nastily. His inspection had shown him that his pupil was trying not to cry, and if he spoke in a kind voice he would break down and do it.

"I shall not be a knight," replied the Wart coldly. Merlyn's trick had worked and he no longer wanted to weep: he wanted to kick Merlyn. "I shall not be a knight because I am not a proper son of Sir Ector's. They will knight Kay, and I shall be his squire."

Merlyn's back was turned again, but his eyes were bright behind his spectacles. "Too bad," he said, without commiseration.

The Wart burst out with all his thoughts aloud. "Oh," he cried, "but I should have liked to be born with a proper father and mother, so that I could be a knight errant."

"What would you have done?"

"I should have had a splendid suit of armour and dozens of spears and a black horse standing eighteen hands, and I should have called myself The Black Knight. And I should have hoved at a well or a ford or something and made all true knights that came that way to joust with me for the honour of their ladies, and I should have spared them all after I had given them a great fall. And I should live out of doors all the year round in a pavilion, and never do anything but joust and go on quests and bear away the prize at tournaments, and I should not ever tell anybody my name."

"Your wife will scarcely enjoy the life."

"Oh, I am not going to have a wife. I think they are stupid.

"I shall have to have a lady-love, though," added the future knight uncomfortably, "so that I can wear her favour in my helm, and do deeds in her honour."

A humblebee came zooming between them, under the grandstand and out into the sunlight.

"Would you like to see some real knights errant?" asked the magician slowly. "Now, for the sake of your education?"

"Oh, I would! We have never even had a tournament since I was here."

"I suppose it could be managed."

"Oh, please do. You could take me to some like you did to the fish."

"I suppose it is educational, in a way."

"It is very educational," said the Wart. "I can't think of anything more educational than to see some real knights fighting. Oh, won't you please do it?''

"Do you prefer any particular knight?"

"King Pellinore," he said immediately. He had a weakness for this gentleman since their strange encounter in the Forest.

Merlyn said, "That will do very well. Put your hands to your sides and relax your muscles. *Cabricias arci thuram, catalamus, singulariter, nominativa, haec musa.* Shut your eyes and keep them shut. *Bonus, Bona, Bonum.* Here we go. *Deus Sanctus, est-ne oratio Latinas? Etiam, oui, quare? Pourquoi? Quai substantivo et adjectivum concordat in generi, numerum et casus.* Here we are.''

While this incantation was going on, the patient felt some queer sensations. First he could hear the sergeant calling out to Kay, "Nah, then, nah then, keep the 'eels dahn and swing the body from the 'ips.'' Then the words got smaller and smaller, as if he were looking at his feet through the wrong end of a telescope, and began to swirl round in a cone, as if they were at the pointed bottom end of a whirlpool which was sucking him into the air. Then there was nothing but a loud rotating roaring and hissing noise which rose to such a tornado that he felt that he could not stand it any more. Finally there was utter silence and Merlyn saying, "Here we are." All this happened in about the time that it would take a sixpenny rocket to start off with its fiery swish, bend down from its climax and disperse itself in thunder and coloured stars. He opened his eyes just at the moment when one would have heard the invisible stick hitting the ground.

They were lying under a beech tree in the Forest Sauvage.

"Here we are," said Merlyn. "Get up and dust your clothes.

"And there, I think," continued the magician, in a tone of satisfaction because his spells had worked for once without a hitch, "is your friend, King Pellinore, pricking toward us o'er the plain."

"Hallo, hallo," cried King Pellinore, popping his visor up and down. "It's the young boy with the feather bed, isn't it, I say, what?"

"Yes, it is," said the Wart. "And I am very glad to see you. Did you manage to catch the Beast?"

"No," said King Pellinore. "Didn't catch the beast. Oh, do come here, you brachet, and leave that bush alone. Tcha! Tcha! Naughty, naughty! She runs riot, you know, what. Very keen on rabbits. I tell you there's nothing in it, you beastly dog. Tcha! Tcha! Leave it, leave it! Oh, do come to heel, like I tell you.

"She never does come to heel," he added.

At this the dog put a cock pheasant out of the bush, which rocketed off with a tremendous clatter, and the dog became so excited that it ran round its master three or four times at the end of its rope, panting hoarsely as if it had asthma. King Pellinore's horse stood patiently while the rope was wound round its legs, and Merlyn and the Wart had to catch the brachet and unwind it before the conversation could go on.

"I say," said King Pellinore. "Thank you very much, I must say. Won't you introduce me to your friend, what?"

"This is my tutor Merlyn, a great magician."

"How-de-do," said the King. "Always like to meet magicians. In fact I always like to meet anybody. It passes the time away, what, on a quest."

"Hail," said Merlyn, in his most mysterious manner.

"Hail," replied the King, anxious to make a good impression.

They shook hands.

"Did you say Hail?" inquired the King, looking about him nervously. "I thought it was going to be fine, myself."

"He meant How-do-you-do," explained the Wart.

"Ah, yes, How-de-do?"

They shook hands again.

"Good afternoon," said King Pellinore. "What do you think the weather looks like now?"

"I think it looks like an anti-cyclone."

"Ah, yes," said the King. "An anti-cyclone. Well, I suppose I ought to be getting along."

At this the King trembled very much, opened and shut his visor several times, coughed, wove his reins into a knot, exclaimed, "I beg your pardon?" and showed signs of cantering away.

"He is a white magician," said the Wart. "You need not be afraid of him. He is my best friend, your majesty, and in any case he generally gets his spells muddled up."

"Ah, yes," said King Pellinore. "A white magician, what? How small the world is, is it not? How-de-do?"

"Hail," said Merlyn.

"Hail," said King Pellinore.

They shook hands for the third time.

"I should not go away," said the wizard, "if I were you. Sir Grummore Grummursum is on the way to challenge you to a joust."

"No, you don't say? Sir What-you-may-call-it coming here to challenge me to a joust?"

"Assuredly."

"Good handicap man?"

"I should think it would be an even match."

"Well, I must say," exclaimed the King, "it never hails but it pours."

"Hail," said Merlyn.

"Hail," said King Pellinore.

"Hail," said the Wart.

"Now I really won't shake hands with anybody else," announced the monarch. "We must assume that we have all met before."

"Is Sir Grummore really coming," inquired the Wart, hastily changing the subject, "to challenge King Pellinore to a battle?"

"Look yonder," said Merlyn, and both of them looked in the direction of his outstretched finger.

Sir Grummore Grummursum was cantering up the clearing in full panoply of war. Instead of his ordinary helmet with a visor he was wearing the proper tilting-helm, which looked like a large coal-scuttle, and as he cantered he clanged.

He was singing his old school song:

"We'll tilt together
Steady from crupper to poll,
And nothin' in life shall sever
Our love for the dear old coll.
Follow-up, follow-up, follow-up, follow-up, follow-up
Till the shield ring again and again
With the clanks of the clanky true men."

"Goodness," exclaimed King Pellinore. "It's about two months since I had a proper tilt, and last winter they put me up to eighteen. That was when they had the new handicaps."

Sir Grummore had arrived while he was speaking, and had recognized the Wart.

"Mornin'," said Sir Grummore. "You're Sir Ector's boy, ain't you? And who's that chap in the comic hat?"

"That is my tutor," said the Wart hurriedly. "Merlyn, the magician."

Sir Grummore looked at Merlyn—magicians were considered rather middle-class by the true jousting set in those days—and said distantly, "Ah, a magician. How-de-do?"

"And this is King Pellinore," said the Wart. "Sir Grummore Grummursum—King Pellinore."

"How-de-do?" inquired Sir Grummore.

"Hail," said King Pellinore. "No, I mean it won't hail, will it?"

"Nice day," said Sir Grummore.

"Yes, it is nice, isn't it, what?"

"Been questin' today?"

"Oh, yes, thank you. Always am questing, you know. After the Questing Beast."

"Interestin' job, that, very."

"Yes, it is interesting. Would you like to see some fewmets?"

"By Jove, yes. Like to see some fewmets."

"I have some better ones at home, but these are quite good, really."

"Bless my soul. So these are her fewmets."

"Yes, these are her fewmets."

"Interestin' fewmets."

"Yes, they are interesting, aren't they? Only you get tired of them," added King Pellinore.

"Well, well. It's a fine day, isn't it?"

"Yes, it is rather fine."

"Suppose we'd better have a joust, eh, what?"

"Yes, I suppose we had better," said King Pellinore, "really."

"What shall we have it for?"

"Oh, the usual thing, I suppose. Would one of you kindly help me on with my helm?"

They all three had to help him on eventually, for, what with the unscrewing of screws and the easing of nuts and bolts which the King had clumsily set on the wrong thread when getting up in a hurry that morning, it was quite a feat of engineering to get him out of his helmet and into his helm. The helm was an enormous thing like an oil drum, padded inside with two thicknesses of leather and three inches of straw.

As soon as they were ready, the two knights stationed themselves at each end of the clearing and then advanced to meet in the middle.

"Fair knight," said King Pellinore, "I pray thee tell me thy name."

"That me regards," replied Sir Grummore, using the proper formula.

"That is uncourteously said," said King Pellinore, "what? For no knight ne dreadeth for to speak his name openly, but for some reason of shame."

"Be that as it may, I choose that thou shalt not know my name as at this time, for no askin'."

"Then you must stay and joust with me, false knight."

"Haven't you got that wrong, Pellinore?" inquired Sir Grummore. "I believe it ought to be 'thou shalt.'"

"Oh, I'm sorry, Sir Grummore. Yes, so it should, of course. Then thou shalt stay and joust with me, false knight."

Without further words, the two gentlemen retreated to the opposite ends of the clearing, fewtered their spears, and prepared to hurtle together in the preliminary charge.

"I think we had better climb this tree," said Merlyn. "You never know what will happen in a joust like this."

They climbed up the big beech, which had easy branches sticking out in all directions, and the Wart stationed himself toward the end of a smooth bough about fifteen feet up, where he could get a good view. Nothing is so comfortable to sit in as a beech.

To be able to picture the terrible battle which now took place, there is one thing which ought to be known. A knight in his full armour of those days, or at any rate during the heaviest days of armour, was generally carrying as much or more than his own weight in metal. He often weighed no less than twenty-two stone, and sometimes as much as twenty-five. This meant that his horse had to be a slow and enormous weight-carrier, like the farm horse of today, and that his own movements were so hampered by his burden of iron and padding that they were toned down into slow motion, as on the cinema.

"They're off!" cried the Wart, holding his breath with excitement.

Slowly and majestically, the ponderous horses lumbered into a walk. The spears, which had been pointing in the air, bowed to a horizontal line and pointed at each other. King Pellinore and Sir Grummore could be seen to be thumping their horses' sides with their heels for all they were worth, and in a few minutes the splendid animals had shambled into an earth-shaking imitation of a trot. Clank, rumble, thump-thump went the horses, and now the two knights were flapping their elbows and legs in unison, showing a good deal of daylight at their seats. There was a change in tempo, and Sir Grummore's horse could be definitely seen to be cantering. In another minute King Pellinore's was doing so too. It was a terrible spectacle.

"Oh, dear!" exclaimed the Wart, feeling ashamed that his blood-thirstiness had been responsible for making these two knights joust before him. "Do you think they will kill each other?"

"Dangerous sport," said Merlyn, shaking his head.

"Now!" cried the Wart.

With a blood-curdling beat of iron hoofs the mighty equestrians came together. Their spears wavered for a moment within a few inches of each other's helms— each had chosen the difficult point-stroke—and then they were galloping off in opposite directions. Sir Grummore drove his spear deep into the beech tree where they were sitting, and stopped dead. King Pellinore, who had been run away with, vanished altogether behind his back.

"Is it safe to look?" inquired the Wart, who had shut his eyes at the critical moment.

"Quite safe," said Merlyn. "It will take them some time to get back in position."

"Whoa, whoa, I say!" cried King Pellinore in muffled and distant tones, far away among the gorse bushes.

"Hi, Pellinore, hi!" shouted Sir Grummore. "Come back, my dear fellah, I'm over here."

There was a long pause, while the complicated stations of the two knights readjusted themselves, and then King Pellinore was at the opposite end from that at which he had started, while Sir Grummore faced him from his original position.

"Traitor knight!" cried Sir Grummore.

"Yield, recreant, what?" cried King Pellinore.

They fewtered their spears again, and thundered into the charge.

"Oh," said the Wart, "I hope they don't hurt themselves."

But the two mounts were patiently blundering together, and the two knights had simultaneously decided on the sweeping stroke. Each held his spear at right angles toward the left, and, before the Wart could say anything further, there was a terrific yet melodious thump. Clang! went the armour, like a motor omnibus in collision with a smithy, and the jousters were sitting side by side on the green sward, while their horses cantered off in opposite directions.

"A splendid fall," said Merlyn.

The two horses pulled themselves up, their duty done, and began resignedly to eat the sward. King Pellinore and Sir Grummore sat looking straight before them, each with the other's spear clasped hopefully under his arm.

"Well!" said the Wart. "What a bump! They both seem to be all right, so far."

Sir Grummore and King Pellinore laboriously got up.

"Defend thee," cried King Pellinore.

"God save thee," cried Sir Grummore.

With this they drew their swords and rushed together with such ferocity that each, after dealing the other a dint on the helm, sat down suddenly backwards.

"Bah!" cried King Pellinore.

"Booh!" cried Sir Grummore, also sitting down.

"Mercy," exclaimed the Wart. "What a combat!"

The knights had now lost their tempers and the battle was joined in earnest. It did not matter much, however, for they were so encased in metal that they could not do each other much damage. It took them so long to get up, and the dealing of a blow when you weighed the eighth part of a ton was such a cumbrous business, that every stage of the contest could be marked and pondered.

In the first stage King Pellinore and Sir Grummore stood opposite each other for about half an hour, and walloped each other on the helm. There was only opportunity for one blow at a time, so they more or less took it in turns, King Pellinore striking while Sir Grummore was recovering, and vice versa. At first, if either of them dropped his sword or got it stuck in the ground, the other put in two or three extra blows while he was patiently fumbling for it or trying to tug it out. Later, they fell into the rhythm of the thing more perfectly, like the toy mechanical people who saw wood on Christmas trees. Eventually the exercise and the monotony restored their good humour and they began to get bored.

The second stage was introduced as a change, by common consent. Sir Grummore stumped off to one end of the clearing, while King Pellinore plodded off to the other. Then they turned round and swayed backward and forward once or twice, in order to get their weight on their toes. When they leaned forward they had to run forward, to keep up with their weight, and if they leaned too far backward they fell down. So even walking was complicated. When they had got their weight properly distributed in front of them, so that they were just off their balance, each broke into a trot to keep up with himself. They hurtled together as if it had been two boars.

They met in the middle, breast to breast, with a noise of shipwreck and great bells tolling, and both, bouncing off, fell breathless on their backs. They lay thus for a few minutes, panting. Then they slowly began to heave themselves to their feet, and it was obvious that they had lost their tempers once again.

King Pellinore had not only lost his temper but he seemed to have been a bit astonished by the impact. He got up facing the wrong way, and could not find Sir Grummore. There was some excuse for this, since he had only a slit to peep through—and that was three inches away from his eye owing to the padding of straw

—but he looked muddled as well. Perhaps he had broken his spectacles. Sir Grummore was quick to seize his advantage.

"Take that!" cried Sir Grummore, giving the unfortunate monarch a two-handed swipe on the nob as he was slowly turning his head from side to side, peering in the opposite direction.

King Pellinore turned round morosely, but his opponent had been too quick for him. He had ambled round so that he was still behind the King, and now gave him another terrific blow in the same place.

"Where are you?" asked King Pellinore.

"Here," cried Sir Grummore, giving him another.

The poor King turned himself round as nimbly as possible, but Sir Grummore had given him the slip again.

"Tally-ho back!" shouted Sir Grummore, with another wallop.

"I think you're a *cad,*" said the King.

"Wallop!" replied Sir Grummore, doing it.

What with the preliminary crash, the repeated blows on the back of his head, and the puzzling nature of his opponent, King Pellinore could now be seen to be visibly troubled in his brains. He swayed backward and forward under the hail of blows which were administered, and feebly wagged his arms.

"Poor King," said the Wart. "I wish he would not hit him so."

As if in answer to his wish, Sir Grummore paused in his labours.

"Do you want Pax?" asked Sir Grummore.

King Pellinore made no answer.

Sir Grummore favoured him with another whack and said, "If you don't say Pax, I shall cut your head off."

"I won't," said the King.

Whang! went the sword on the top of his head.

Whang! it went again.

Whang! for the third time.

"Pax," said King Pellinore, mumbling rather.

Then, just as Sir Grummore was relaxing with the fruits of victory, he swung round upon him, shouted "Non!" at the top of his voice, and gave him a good push in the middle of the chest.

Sir Grummore fell over backwards.

"Well!" exclaimed the Wart. "What a cheat! I would not have thought it of him."

King Pellinore hurriedly sat on his victim's chest, thus increasing the weight upon him to a quarter of a ton and making it quite impossible for him to move, and began to undo Sir Grummore's helm.

"You said Pax!"

"I said Pax Non under my breath."

"It's a swindle."

"It's not."

"You're a cad."

"No, I'm not."

"Yes, you are."

"No, I'm not."

"Yes, you are."

"I said Pax Non."

"You said Pax."

"No, I didn't."

"Yes, you did."

"No, I didn't."

"Yes, you did."

By this time Sir Grummore's helm was unlaced and they could see his bare head glaring at King Pellinore, quite purple in the face.

"Yield thee, recreant," said the King.

"Shan't," said Sir Grummore.

"You have got to yield, or I shall cut off your head."

"Cut it off then."

"Oh, come on," said the King. "You know you have to yield when your helm is off."

"Feign I," said Sir Grummore.

"Well, I shall just cut your head off."

"I don't care."

The King waved his sword menacingly in the air.

"Go on," said Sir Grummore. "I dare you to."

The King lowered his sword and said, "Oh, I say, do yield, please."

"You yield," said Sir Grummore.

"But I can't yield. I am on top of you after all, am I not, what?"

"Well, I have feigned yieldin'."

"Oh, come on, Grummore. I do think you are a cad not to yield. You know very well I can't cut your head off."

"I would not yield to a cheat who started fightin' after he said Pax."

"I am not a cheat."

"You are a cheat."

"No, I'm not."

"Yes, you are."

"No, I'm not."

"Yes, you are."

"Very well," said King Pellinore. "You can jolly well get up and put on your helm and we will have a fight. I won't be called a cheat for anybody."

"Cheat!" said Sir Grummore.

They stood up and fumbled together with the helm, hissing, "No, I'm not"—"Yes, you are," until it was safely on. Then they retreated to opposite ends of the clearing, got their weight upon their toes, and came rumbling and thundering together like two runaway trams.

Unfortunately they were now so cross that they had both ceased to be vigilant, and in the fury of the moment they missed each other altogether. The momentum of their armour was too great for them to stop till they had passed each other handsomely, and then they manoeuvred about in such a manner that neither happened to come within the other's range of vision. It was funny watching them, because King Pellinore, having already been caught from behind once, was continually spinning round to look behind him, and Sir Grummore, having used the stratagem himself, was doing the same thing. Thus they wandered for some five minutes, standing still, listening, clanking, crouching, creeping, peering, walking on tiptoe, and occasionally making a chance swipe behind their backs. Once they were standing within a few feet of each other, back to back, only to stalk off in opposite directions with infinite precaution, and once King Pellinore did hit Sir Grummore with one of his back strokes, but they both immediately spun round so often that they became giddy and mislaid each other afresh.

After five minutes Sir Grummore said, "All right, Pellinore. It is no use hidin'. I can see where you are."

"I am not hiding," exclaimed King Pellinore indignantly. "Where am I?"

They discovered each other and went up close together, face to face.

"Cad," said Sir Grummore.

"Yah," said King Pellinore.

They turned round and marched off to their corners, seething with indignation.

"Swindler," shouted Sir Grummore.

"Beastly bully," shouted King Pellinore.

With this they summoned all their energies together for one decisive encounter, leaned forward, lowered their heads like two billy-goats, and positively sprinted together for the final blow. Alas, their aim was poor. They missed each other by about five yards, passed at full steam doing at least eight knots, like ships that pass in the night but speak not to each other in passing, and hurtled onward to their doom. Both knights began waving their arms like windmills, anti-clockwise, in the vain effort to slow up. Both continued with undiminished speed. Then Sir Grummore rammed his head against the beech in which the Wart was sitting, and King Pellinore collided with a chestnut at the other side of the clearing. The trees shook, the forest rang. Blackbirds and squirrels cursed and wood-pigeons flew out of their leafy perches half a mile away. The two knights stood to attention while one could count three. Then, with a last unanimous melodious clang, they both fell prostrate on the fatal sward.

"Stunned," said Merlyn, "I should think."

"Oh, dear," said the Wart. "Ought we to get down and help them?"

"We could pour water on their heads," said Merlyn reflectively, "if there was any water. But I don't suppose they would thank us for making their armour rusty. They will be all right. Besides, it is time that we were home."

"But they might be dead!"

"They are not dead, I know. In a minute or two they will come round and go off home to dinner."

"Poor King Pellinore has not got a home."

"Then Sir Grummore will invite him to stay the night. They will be the best of friends when they come to. They always are."

"Do you think so?"

"My dear boy, I know so. Shut your eyes and we will be off."

The Wart gave in to Merlyn's superior knowledge. "Do you think," he asked with his eyes shut, "that Sir Grummore has a feather bed?"

"Probably."

"Good," said the Wart. "That will be nice for King Pellinore, even if he was stunned."

The Latin words were spoken and the secret passes made. The funnel of whistling noise and space received them. In two seconds they were lying under the grandstand, and the sergeant's voice was calling from the opposite side of the tilting ground, "Nah then, Master Art, nah then. You've been a-snoozing there long enough. Come aht into the sunlight 'ere with Master Kay, one-two, one-two, and see some real tilting."

chapter eight

It was a cold wet evening, such as may happen even toward the end of August, and the Wart did not know
how to bear himself indoors. He spent some time in
the kennels talking to Cavall, then wandered off to help
them turn the spit in the kitchen. But there it was too
hot. He was not forced to stay indoors because of the
rain, by his female supervisors, as happens too frequently to the unhappy children of our generation, but the
mere wetness and dreariness in the open discouraged
him from going out. He hated everybody.

"Confound the boy," said Sir Ector. "For goodness' sake stop mopin' by that window there, and go
and find your tutor. When I was a boy we always used
to study on wet days, yes, and eddicate our minds."

"Wart is stupid," said Kay.

"Ah, run along, my duck," said their old Nurse.
"I han't got time to attend to thy mopseys now, what
with all this sorbent washing."

"Now then, my young master," said Hob. "Let
thee run off to thy quarters, and stop confusing they
fowls."

"Nah, nah," said the sergeant. "You 'op orf art
of 'ere. I got enough to do a-polishing of this ber-lady
harmour."

Even the Dog Boy barked at him when he went back to the kennels.

Wart draggled off to the tower room, where Merlyn was busy knitting himself a woollen night-cap for the winter.

"I cast off two together at every other line," said the magician, "but for some reason it seems to end too sharply. Like an onion. It is the turning of the heel that does one, every time."

"I think I ought to have some eddication," said the Wart. "I can't think of anything to do."

"You think that education is something which ought to be done when all else fails?" inquired Merlyn nastily, for he was in a bad mood too.

"Well," said the Wart, "some sorts of education."

"Mine?" asked the magician with flashing eyes.

"Oh, Merlyn," exclaimed the Wart without answering, "please give me something to do, because I feel so miserable. Nobody wants me for anything today, and I just don't know how to be sensible. It rains so."

"You should learn to knit."

"Could I go out and be something, a fish or anything like that?"

"You have been a fish," said Merlyn. "Nobody with any go needs to do their education twice."

"Well, could I be a bird?"

"If you knew anything at all," said Merlyn, "which you do not, you would know that a bird does not like to fly in the rain because it wets its feathers and makes them stick together. They get bedraggled."

"I could be a hawk in Hob's mews," said the Wart stoutly. "Then I should be indoors and not get wet."

"That is pretty ambitious," said the old man, "to want to be a hawk."

"You know you will turn me into a hawk when you want to," shouted the Wart, "but you like to plague me because it is wet. I won't have it."

"Hoity-toity!"

"Please," said the Wart, "dear Merlyn, turn me into a hawk. If you don't do that I shall do something. I don't know what."

Merlyn put down his knitting and looked at his pupil over the top of his spectacles. "My boy," he said, "you shall be everything in the world, animal, vegetable, mineral, protista or virus, for all I care—before I have done with you—but you will have to trust to my superior backsight. The time is not yet ripe for you to be a hawk—for one thing Hob is still in the mews feeding them—so you may as well sit down for the moment and learn to be a human being."

"Very well," said the Wart, "if that's a go." And he sat down.

After several minutes he said, "Is one allowed to speak as a human being, or does the thing about being seen and not heard have to apply?"

"Everybody can speak."

"That's good, because I wanted to mention that you have been knitting your beard into the night-cap for three rows now."

"Well, I'll be. . . ."

"I should think the best thing would be to cut off the end of your beard. Shall I fetch some scissors?"

"Why didn't you tell me before?"

"I wanted to see what would happen."

"You run a grave risk, my boy," said the magician, "of being turned into a piece of bread, and toasted."

With this he slowly began to unpick his beard, muttering to himself meanwhile and taking the greatest precautions not to drop a stitch.

"Will it be as difficult to fly," asked the Wart when he thought his tutor had calmed down, "as it was to swim?"

"You will not need to fly. I don't mean to turn you into a loose hawk, but only to set you in the mews for the night, so that you can talk to the others. That is the way to learn, by listening to the experts."

"Will they talk?"

"They talk every night, deep into the darkness. They say about how they were taken, about what they can remember of their homes: about their lineage and the great deeds of their ancestors, about their training and what they have learned and will learn. It is military conversation really, like you might have in the mess of a crack cavalry regiment: tactics, small arms, maintenance, betting, famous hunts, wine, women and song.

"Another subject they have," he continued, "is food. It is a depressing thought, but of course they are mainly trained by hunger. They are a hungry lot, poor chaps, thinking of the best restaurants where they used to go, and how they had champagne and caviare and gypsy music. Of course, they all come of noble blood."

"What a shame that they should be kept prisoners and be hungry."

"Well, they do not really understand that they are prisoners, any more than the cavalry officers do. They look on themselves as being dedicated to their profession, like an order of knighthood or something of that sort. You see, the membership of the mews is, after all, restricted to the raptors—and that does help a lot. They know that none of the lower classes can get in. Their screen perches don't carry blackbirds or such trash as that. And then, as to the hungry part, they are far from starving or that kind of hunger. They are in

training, you know, and like everybody in strict training, they think about food.''

"How soon can I begin?''

"You can begin now, if you want to. My insight
tells me that Hob has this minute finished for the night.
But first of all you must choose what kind of hawk you
would prefer to be.''

"I should like to be a merlin,'' said the Wart
politely.

This answer flattered the magician. "A very good
choice,'' he said, "and if you please we will proceed
at once.''

The Wart got up from his stool and stood in front
of his tutor. Merlyn put down his knitting.

"First you go small,'' said he, pressing him on
the top of his head until he was a bit smaller than a
pigeon. "Then you stand on the ball of your toes, bend
at the knees, hold your elbows to your sides, lift your
hands to the level of your shoulders, and press your
first and second fingers together, as also your third and
fourth. Look, it is like this.''

With these words the ancient nigromant stood
upon tiptoe and did as he had explained.

The Wart copied him carefully and wondered
what would happen next. What did happen was that
Merlyn, who had been saying the final spells under his
breath, suddenly turned himself into a condor, leaving
the Wart standing on tiptoe unchanged. He stood there
as if he were drying himself in the sun, with a wingspread
of about eleven feet, a bright orange head and a magenta
carbuncle. He looked very surprised and rather funny.

"Come back,'' said the Wart. "You have changed
the wrong one.''

"It is this by-our-lady spring cleaning,'' exclaimed
Merlyn, turning back into himself. "Once you let a

woman into your study for half an hour, you do not know where to lay your hands on the right spell, not if it was ever so. Stand up and we will try again.''

This time the now tiny Wart felt his toes shooting out and scratching on the floor. He felt his heels rise and stick out behind and his knees draw into his stomach. His thighs became quite short. A web of skin grew from his wrists to his shoulders, while his primary feathers burst out in soft blue quills from the ends of his fingers and quickly grew. His secondaries sprouted along his forearms, and a charming little false primary sprang from the end of each thumb.

The dozen feathers of his tail, with the double deck-feathers in the middle, grew out in the twinkling of an eye, and all the covert feathers of his back and breast and shoulders slipped out of the skin to hide the roots of the more important plumes. Wart looked quickly at Merlyn, ducked his head between his legs and had a look through there, rattled his feathers into place, and began to scratch his chin with the sharp talon of one toe.

"Good," said Merlyn. "Now hop on my hand—ah, be careful and don't gripe—and listen to what I have to tell you. I shall take you into the mews now that Hob has locked up for the night, and I shall put you loose and unhooded beside Balin and Balan. Now pay attention. Don't go close to anybody without speaking first. You must remember that most of them are hooded and might be startled into doing something rash. You can trust Balin and Balan, also the kestrel and the spar-hawk. Don't go within reach of the falcon unless she invites you to. On no account must you stand beside Cully's special enclosure, for he is unhooded and will go for you through the mesh if he gets half a chance. He is not quite right in his brains, poor chap, and if he once grips you, you will never leave his grip alive. Remember that you are visiting a kind of Spartan military mess. These fellows are regulars. As the junior subaltern your only business is to keep your mouth shut, speak when you are spoken to, and not interrupt.''

"I bet I am more than a subaltern," said the Wart, "if I am a merlin."

"Well, as a matter of fact, you are. You will find that both the kestrel and the spar-hawk will be polite to you, but for all sake's sake don't interrupt the senior merlins or the falcon. She is the honorary colonel of the regiment. And as for Cully, well, he is a colonel too, even if he is infantry, so you must mind your p's and q's."

"I will be careful," said the Wart, who was beginning to feel rather scared.

"Good. I shall come for you in the morning, before Hob is up."

All the hawks were silent as Merlyn carried their new companion into the mews, and silent for some time afterward when they had been left in the dark. The rain had given place to a full August moonlight, so clear that you could see a woolly bear caterpillar fifteen yards away out of doors, as it climbed up and up the knobbly sandstone of the great keep, and it took the Wart only a few moments for his eyes to become accustomed to the diffused brightness inside the mews. The darkness became watered with light, with silver radiance, and then it was an eerie sight which dawned upon his vision. Each hawk or falcon stood in the silver upon one leg, the other tucked up inside the apron of its panel, and each was a motionless statue of a knight in armour. They stood gravely in their plumed helmets, spurred and armed. The canvas or sacking screens of their perches moved heavily in a breath of wind, like banners in a chapel, and the rapt nobility of the air kept their knight's vigil in knightly patience. In those days they used to hood everything they could, even the goshawk and the merlin, which are no longer hooded according to modern practice.

Wart drew his breath at the sight of all these stately figures, standing so still that they might have been cut of stone. He was overwhelmed by their magnificence, and felt no need of Merlyn's warning that he was to be humble and behave himself.

Presently there was a gentle ringing of a bell. The great peregrine falcon had bestirred herself and now said, in a high nasal voice which came from her aristocratic nose, "Gentlemen, you may converse."

There was dead silence.

Only, in the far corner of the room, which had been netted off for Cully—loose there, unhooded and deep in moult—they could hear a faint muttering from the choleric infantry colonel. "Damned niggers," he was mumbling. "Damned administration. Damned politicians. Damned bolsheviks. Is this a damned dagger that I see before me, the handle toward my hand? Damned spot. Now, Cully, hast thou but one brief hour to live, and then thou must be damned perpetually."

"Colonel," said the peregrine coldly, "not before the younger officers."

"I beg your pardon, Mam," said the poor colonel at once. "It is something that gets into my head, you know. Some deep damnation."

There was silence again, formal, terrible and calm.

"Who is the new officer?" inquired the first fierce and beautiful voice.

Nobody answered.

"Speak for yourself, sir," commanded the peregrine, looking straight before her as if she were talking in her sleep.

They could not see him through their hoods.

"Please," began the Wart, "I am a merlin. . . ."

And he stopped, scared in the stillness.

Balan, who was one of the real merlins standing beside him, leaned over and whispered quite kindly in his ear, "Don't be afraid. Call her Madam."

"I am a merlin, Madam, an it please you."

"A Merlin. That is good. And what branch of the Merlins do you stoop from?"

The Wart did not know in the least what branch he stooped from, but he dared not be found out now in his lie.

"Madam," he said, "I am one of the Merlins of the Forest Sauvage."

There was silence at this again, the silver silence which he had begun to fear.

"There are the Yorkshire Merlins," said the honorary colonel in her slow voice at last, "and the Welsh Merlins, and the McMerlins of the North. Then there are the Salisbury ones, and several from the neighbourhood of Exmoor, and the O'Merlins of Connaught. I do not think I have heard of any family in the Forest Sauvage."

"It would be a cadet branch, Madam," said Balan, "I dare say."

"Bless him," thought the Wart. "I shall catch him a special sparrow tomorrow and give it to him behind Hob's back."

"That will be the solution, Captain Balan, no doubt."

The silence fell again.

At last the peregrine rang her bell. She said, "We will proceed with the catechism, prior to swearing him in."

The Wart heard the spar-hawk on his left giving several nervous coughs at this, but the peregrine paid no attention.

"Merlin of the Forest Sauvage," said the peregrine, "what is a Beast of the Foot?"

"A Beast of the Foot," replied the Wart, blessing his stars that Sir Ector had chosen to give him a First Rate Eddication, "is a horse, or a hound, or a hawk."

"Why are these called beasts of the foot?"

"Because these beasts depend upon the powers of their feet, so that, by law, any damage to the feet of hawk, hound or horse, is reckoned as damage to its life. A lamed horse is a murdered horse."

"Good," said the peregrine. "What are your most important members?"

"My wings," said the Wart after a moment, guessing because he did not know.

At this there was a simultaneous tintinnabulation of all the bells, as each graven image lowered its raised foot in distress. They stood on both feet now, disturbed.

"Your what?" called the peregrine sharply.

"He said his damned wings," said Colonel Cully from his private enclosure. "And damned be he who first cries Hold, enough!"

"But even a thrush has wings!" cried the kestrel, speaking for the first time in his sharp-beaked alarm.

"Think!" whispered Balan, under his breath.

The Wart thought feverishly.

A thrush had wings, tail, eyes, legs—apparently everything.

"My talons!"

"It will do," said the peregrine kindly, after one of her dreadful pauses. "The answer ought to be Feet, just as it is to all the other questions, but Talons will do."

All the hawks, and of course we are using the term loosely, for some were hawks and some were falcons, raised their belled feet again and sat at ease.

"What is the first law of the foot?"

("Think," said friendly little Balan, behind his false primary.)

The Wart thought, and thought right.

"Never to let go," he said.

"Last question," said the peregrine. "How would you, as a Merlin, kill a pigeon bigger than yourself?"

Wart was lucky in this one, for he had heard Hob giving a description of how Balan did it one afternoon, and he answered warily, "I should strangle her with my foot."

"Good!" said the peregrine.

"Bravo!" cried the others, raising their feathers.

"Ninety per cent," said the spar-hawk after a quick sum. "That is, if you give him a half for the talons."

"The devil damn me black!"

"Colonel, please!"

Balan whispered to the Wart, "Colonel Cully is not quite right in his wits. It is his liver, we believe, but the kestrel says it is the constant strain of living up to her ladyship's standard. He says that her ladyship spoke to him from her full social station once, cavalry to infantry, you know, and that he just closed his eyes and got the vertigo. He has never been the same since.''

"Captain Balan," said the peregrine, "it is rude to whisper. We will proceed to swear the new officer in. Now, padre, if you please.''

The poor spar-hawk, who had been getting more and more nervous for some time, blushed deeply and began faltering out a complicated oath about varvels, jesses and hoods. "With this varvel," the Wart heard, "I thee endow . . . love, honour and obey . . . till jess us do part.''

But before the padre had got to the end of it, he broke down altogether and sobbed out, "Oh, please your ladyship. I beg your pardon, but I have forgotten to keep my tirings.''

("Tirings are bones and things," explained Balan, "and of course you have to swear on bones.'')

"Forgotten to keep any tirings? But it is your duty to keep tirings.''

"I—I know.''

"What have you done with them?''

The spar-hawk's voice broke at the enormity of his confession. "I—I ate 'em," wept the unfortunate priest.

Nobody said anything. The dereliction of duty was too terrible for words. All stood on two feet and turned their blind heads toward the culprit. Not a word of reproach was spoken. Only, during an utter silence of five minutes, they could hear the incontinent priest snivelling and hiccoughing to himself.

"Well," said the peregrine at last, "the initiation will have to be put off till tomorrow.''

"If you will excuse me, Madam," said Balin, "perhaps we could manage the ordeal tonight? I believe the candidate is loose, for I did not hear him being tied up.''

At the mention of an ordeal the Wart trembled within himself and privately determined that Balin should have not one feather of Balan's sparrow next day.

''Thank you, Captain Balin. I was reflecting upon that subject myself.''

Balin shut up.

''Are you loose, candidate?''

''Oh, Madam, yes, I am, if you please: but I do not think I want an ordeal.''

''The ordeal is customary.''

''Let me see,'' continued the honorary colonel reflectively. ''What was the last ordeal we had? Can you remember, Captain Balan?''

''My ordeal, Mam,'' said the friendly merlin, ''was to hang by my jesses during the third watch.''

''If he is loose he cannot do that.''

''You could strike him yourself, Mam,'' said the Kestrel, ''judiciously, you know.''

''Send him over to stand by Colonel Cully while we ring three times,'' said the other merlin.

''Oh, no!'' cried the crazy colonel in an agony out of his remoter darkness. ''Oh no, your ladyship. I beg of you not to do that. I am such a damned villain, your ladyship, that I do not answer for the consequences. Spare the poor boy, your ladyship, and lead us not into temptation.''

''Colonel, control yourself. That ordeal will do very well.''

''Oh, Madam, I was warned not to stand by Colonel Cully.''

''Warned? And by whom?''

The poor Wart realised that now he must choose between confessing himself a human, and learning no more of their secrets, or going through with this ordeal to earn his education. He did not want to be a coward.

"I will stand by the Colonel, Madam," he said, immediately noticing that his voice sounded insulting.

The peregrine falcon paid no attention to the tone.

"It is well," she said. "But first we must have the hymn. Now, padre, if you have not eaten your hymns as well as your tirings, will you be so kind as to lead us in Ancient but not Modern No. 23? The Ordeal Hymn.

"And you, Mr. Kee," she added to the kestrel, "you had better keep quiet, for you are always too high."

The hawks stood still in the moonlight, while the spar-hawk counted "One, Two, Three." Then all those curved or toothed beaks opened in their hoods to a brazen unison, and this is what they chanted:

> Life is blood, shed and offered.
> The eagle's eye can face this dree.
> To beasts of chase the lie is proffered:
> *Timor Mortis Conturbat Me.*

> The beast of foot sings Holdfast only,
> For flesh is bruckle and foot is slee.
> Strength to the strong and the lordly and lonely.
> *Timor Mortis Exultat Me.*

> Shame to the slothful and woe to the weak one.
> Death to the dreadful who turn to flee.
> Blood to the tearing, the talon'd, the beaked one.
> *Timor Mortis* are We.

"Very nice," said the peregrine. "Captain Balan, I think you were a little off on the top C. And now, candidate, you will go over and stand next to Colonel Cully's enclosure, while we ring our bells thrice. On the third ring you may move as quickly as you like."

"Very good, Madam," said the Wart, quite fearless with resentment. He flipped his wings and was sitting on the extreme end of the screen perch, next to Cully's enclosure of string netting.

"Boy!" cried the Colonel in an unearthly voice, "don't come near me, don't come near. Ah, tempt not the foul fiend to his damnation."

"I do not fear you, sir," said the Wart. "Do not vex yourself, for no harm will come to either of us."

"No harm, quotha! Ah, go, before it is too late. I feel eternal longings in me."

"Never fear, sir. They have only to ring three times."

At this the knights lowered their raised legs and gave them a solemn shake. The first sweet tinkling filled the room.

"Madam, Madam!" cried the Colonel in torture. "Have pity, have pity on a damned man of blood. Ring out the old, ring in the new. I can't hold off much longer."

"Be brave, sir," said the Wart softly.

"Be brave, sir! Why, but two nights since, one met the duke 'bout midnight in a lane behind Saint Mark's Church, with the leg of a man upon his shoulder: and he howled fearfully."

"It is nothing," said the Wart.

"Nothing! Said he was a wolf, only the difference was a wolf's skin was hairy on the outside, his on the inside. Rip up my flesh and try. Ah, for quietus, with a bare bodkin!"

The bells rang for the second time.

The Wart's heart was thumping, and now the Colonel was sidling toward him along the perch. Stamp, stamp, he went, striking the wood he trod on with a convulsive grip at every pace. His poor, mad, brooding eyes glared in the moonlight, shone against the persecuted darkness of his scowling brow. There was nothing cruel about him, no ignoble passion. He was terrified of the Wart, not triumphing, and he must slay.

"If it were done when 'tis done," whispered the Colonel, "then 'twere well it were done quickly. Who would have thought the young man had so much blood in him?"

"Colonel!" said the Wart, but held himself there.

"Boy!" cried the Colonel. "Speak, stop me, mercy!"

"There is a cat behind you," said the Wart calmly, "or a pinemarten. Look."

The Colonel turned, swift as a wasp's sting, and menaced into the gloom. There was nothing. He swung his wild eyes again upon the Wart, guessing the trick. Then, in the cold voice of an adder, "The bell invites me. Hear it not, Merlin, for it is a knell that summons thee to heaven or to hell."

The third bells were indeed ringing as he spoke, and honour was allowed to move. The ordeal was over and the Wart might fly. But as he moved, but as he flew, quicker than any movement or flight in the world, the terrible sickles had shot from the Colonel's plated legs—not flashed out, for they moved too quick for sight—and with a thump, with a clutch, with an apprehension, like being arrested by a big policeman, the great scimitars had fixed themselves in his retreating thumb.

They fixed themselves, and fixed irrevocably. Gripe, gripe, the enormous thigh muscles tautened in two convulsions. Then the Wart was two yards further down the screen, and Colonel Cully was standing on one foot with a few meshes of string netting and the Wart's false primary, with its covert-feathers, vice-fisted in the other. Two or three minor feathers drifted softly in a moonbeam toward the floor.

"Well stood!" cried Balan, delighted.

"A very gentlemanly exhibition," said the peregrine, not minding that Captain Balan had spoken before her.

"Amen!" said the spar-hawk.

"Brave heart!" said the kestrel.

"Might we give him the Triumph Song?" asked Balin, relenting.

"Certainly," said the peregrine.

And they all sang together, led by Colonel Cully at the top of his voice, all belling triumphantly in the terrible moonlight.

> The mountain birds are sweeter
> But the valley birds are fatter,
> And so we deemed it meeter
> To carry off the latter.
> We met a cowering coney
> And struck him through the vitals.
> The coney was like honey
> And squealed our requitals.
> Some struck the lark in feathers
> Whose puffing clouds were shed off.
> Some plucked the partridge's nethers,
> While others pulled his head off.
> But Wart the King of Merlins
> Struck foot most far before us.
> His birds and beasts
> Supply our feasts,
> And his feats our glorious chorus!

"Mark my words," cried the beautiful Balan, "we shall have a regular king in that young candidate. Now, boys, chorus altogether for the last time":

> But Wart the King of Merlins
> Struck foot most far before us.
> His birds and beasts
> Supply our feasts,
> And his feats our glorious chorus!

chapter nine

"Well!" said the Wart, as he woke up in his own bed next morning. "What a horrible, grand crew!"

Kay sat up in bed and began scolding like a squirrel. "Where were you last night?" he cried. "I believe you climbed out. I shall tell my father and get you tanned. You know we are not allowed out after curfew. What have you been doing? I looked for you everywhere. I know you climbed out."

The boys had a way of sliding down a rain-water pipe into the moat, which they could swim on secret occasions when it was necessary to be out at night—to wait for a badger, for instance, or to catch tench, which can only be taken just before dawn.

"Oh, shut up," said the Wart. "I'm sleepy."

Kay said, "Wake up, wake up, you beast. Where have you been?"

"I shan't tell you."

He was sure that Kay would not believe the story, but only call him a liar and get angrier than ever.

"If you don't tell me I shall kill you."

"You will not, then."

"I will."

The Wart turned over on his other side.

"Beast," said Kay. He took a fold of the Wart's arm between the nails of first finger and thumb, and pinched for all he was worth. Wart kicked like a salmon which has been suddenly hooked, and hit him wildly in the eye. In a trice they were out of bed, pale and indignant, looking rather like skinned rabbits—for in those days, nobody wore clothes in bed—and whirling their arms like windmills in the effort to do each other a mischief.

Kay was older and bigger than the Wart, so that he was bound to win in the end, but he was more nervous and imaginative. He could imagine the effect of each blow that was aimed at him, and this weakened his defence. Wart was only an infuriated hurricane.

"Leave me alone, can't you?" And all the while he did not leave Kay alone, but with head down and swinging arms made it impossible for Kay to do as he was bid. They punched entirely at each other's faces.

Kay had a longer reach and a heavier fist. He straightened his arm, more in self-defence than in anything else, and the Wart smacked his own eye upon the end of it. The sky became a noisy and shocking black, streaked outward with a blaze of meteors. The Wart began to sob and pant. He managed to get in a blow upon his opponent's nose, and this began to bleed. Kay lowered his defence, turned his back on the Wart, and said in a cold, snuffling, reproachful voice, "Now it's bleeding." The battle was over.

Kay lay on the stone floor, bubbling blood out of his nose, and the Wart, with a black eye, fetched the enormous key out of the door to put under Kay's back. Neither of them spoke.

Presently Kay turned over on his face and began to sob. He said, "Merlyn does everything for you, but he never does anything for me."

At this the Wart felt he had been a beast. He dressed himself in silence and hurried off to find the magician.

On the way he was caught by his nurse.

"Ah, you little helot," exclaimed she, shaking him by the arm, "you've been a-battling again with that there Master Kay. Look at your poor eye, I do declare. It's enough to baffle the college of sturgeons."

"It is all right," said the Wart.

"No, that it isn't, my poppet," cried his nurse, getting crosser and showing signs of slapping him. "Come now, how did you do it, before I have you whipped?"

"I knocked it on the bedpost," said the Wart sullenly.

The old nurse immediately folded him to her broad bosom, patted him on the back, and said, "There, there, my dowsabel. It's the same story Sir Ector told me when I caught him with a blue eye, gone forty years. Nothing like a good family for sticking to a good lie. There, my innocent, you come along of me to the kitchen and we'll slap a nice bit of steak across him in no time. But you hadn't ought to fight with people bigger than yourself."

"It is all right," said the Wart again, disgusted by the fuss, but fate was bent on punishing him, and the old lady was inexorable. It took him half an hour to escape, and then only at the price of carrying with him a juicy piece of raw beef which he was supposed to hold over his eye.

"Nothing like a mealy rump for drawing out the humours," his nurse had said, and the cook had answered:

"Us han't seen a sweeter bit of raw since Easter, no, nor a bloodier."

"I will keep the foul thing for Balan," thought the Wart, resuming his search for his tutor.

He found him without trouble in the tower room which he had chosen when he arrived. All philosophers prefer to live in towers, as may be seen by visiting the room which Erasmus chose in his college at Cambridge, but Merlyn's tower was even more beautiful than this. It was the highest room in the castle, directly below the look-out of the great keep, and from its window you could gaze across the open field—with its rights of war-ren—across the park, and the chase, until your eye finally wandered out over the distant blue tree-tops of the Forest Sauvage. This sea of leafy timber rolled away and away in knobs like the surface of porridge, until it was finally lost in remote mountains which no-body had ever visited, and the cloud-capped towers and gorgeous palaces of heaven.

Merlyn's comments upon the black eye were of a medical nature.

"The discoloration," he said, "is caused by hae-morrhage into the tissues (ecchymosis) and passes from dark purple through green to yellow before it disap-pears."

There seemed to be no sensible reply to this.

"I suppose you had it," continued Merlyn, "fight-ing with Kay?"

"Yes. How did you know?"

"Ah, well, there it is."

"I came to ask you about Kay."

"Speak. Demand. I'll answer."

"Well, Kay thinks it is unfair that you are always turning me into things and not him. I have not told him about it but I think he guesses. I think it is unfair too."

"It is unfair."

"So will you turn us both next time that we are turned?"

Merlyn had finished his breakfast, and was puffing at the meerschaum pipe which made his pupil believe that he breathed fire. Now he took a deep puff, looked at the Wart, opened his mouth to speak, changed his mind, blew out the smoke and drew another lungful.

"Sometimes," he said, "life does seem to be unfair. Do you know the story of Elijah and the Rabbi Jachanan?"

"No," said the Wart.

He sat down resignedly upon the most comfortable part of the floor, perceiving that he was in for something like the parable of the looking-glass.

"This rabbi," said Merlyn, "went on a journey with the prophet Elijah. They walked all day, and at nightfall they came to the humble cottage of a poor man, whose only treasure was a cow. The poor man ran out of his cottage, and his wife ran too, to welcome the strangers for the night and to offer them all the simple hospitality which they were able to give in straitened circumstances. Elijah and the Rabbi were entertained with plenty of the cow's milk, sustained by home-made bread and butter, and they were put to sleep in the best bed while their kindly hosts lay down before the kitchen fire. But in the morning the poor man's cow was dead."

"Go on."

"They walked all the next day, and came that evening to the house of a very wealthy merchant, whose hospitality they craved. The merchant was cold and proud and rich, and all that he would do for the prophet and his companion was to lodge them in a cowshed and feed them on bread and water. In the morning, however, Elijah thanked him very much for what he had done, and sent for a mason to repair one of his walls, which happened to be falling down, as a return for his kindness.

"The Rabbi Jachanan, unable to keep silence any longer, begged the holy man to explain the meaning of his dealings with human beings.

" 'In regard to the poor man who received us so hospitably,' replied the prophet, 'it was decreed that his wife was to die that night, but in reward for his goodness God took the cow instead of the wife. I repaired the wall of the rich miser because a chest of gold was concealed near the place, and if the miser had repaired the wall himself he would have discovered the treasure. Say not therefore to the Lord: What doest thou? But say in thy heart: Must not the Lord of all the earth do right?' "

"It is a nice sort of story," said the Wart, because it seemed to be over.

"I am sorry," said Merlyn, "that you should be the only one to get my extra tuition, but then, you see, I was only sent for that."

"I do not see that it would do any harm for Kay to come too."

"Nor do I. But the Rabbi Jachanan did not see why the the miser should have had his wall repaired."

"I understand that," said the Wart doubtfully, "but I still think it was a shame that the cow died. Could I not have Kay with me just once?"

Merlyn said gently, "Perhaps what is good for you might be bad for him. Besides, remember he has never asked to be turned into anything."

"He wants to be turned, for all that. I like Kay, you know, and I think people don't understand him. He has to be proud because he is frightened."

"You still do not follow what I mean. Suppose he had gone as a merlin last night, and failed in the ordeal, and lost his nerve?"

"How do you know about that ordeal?"

"Ah, well, there it is again."

"Very well," said the Wart obstinately. "But suppose he had not failed in the ordeal, and had not lost his nerve. I don't see why you should have to suppose that he would have."

"Oh, flout the boy!" cried the magician passionately. "You don't seem to see anything this morning. What is it that you want me to do?"

"Turn me and Kay into snakes or something."

Merlyn took off his spectacles, dashed them on the floor and jumped on them with both feet.

"Castor and Pollux blow me to Bermuda!" he exclaimed, and immediately vanished with a frightful roar.

The Wart was still staring at his tutor's chair in some perplexity, a few moments later, when Merlyn reappeared. He had lost his hat and his hair and beard were tangled up, as if by a hurricane. He sat down again, straightening his gown with trembling fingers.

"Why did you do that?" asked the Wart.

"I did not do it on purpose."

"Do you mean to say that Castor and Pollux did blow you to Bermuda?"

"Let this be a lesson to you," replied Merlyn, "not to swear. I think we had better change the subject."

"We were talking about Kay."

"Yes, and what I was going to say before my—ahem!—my visit to the still vexed Bermoothes, was this. I cannot change Kay into things. The power was not deputed to me when I was sent. Why this was so, neither you nor I am able to say, but such remains the fact. I have tried to hint at some of the reasons for the fact, but you will not take them, so you must just accept the fact in its naked reality. Now please stop talking until I have got my breath back, and my hat."

The Wart sat quiet while Merlyn closed his eyes and began to mutter to himself. Presently a curious black cylindrical hat appeared on his head. It was a topper.

Merlyn examined it with a look of disgust, said bitterly, "And they call this service!" and handed it back to the air. He closed his eyes and produced with growing indignation, in rapid succession,

    this   and this   and this.

Finally he stood up in a passion and exclaimed, "Come here!"

The Wart and Archimedes looked at each other, wondering which was meant—Archimedes had been sitting all the while on the window-sill and looking at the view, for, of course, he never left his master—but Merlyn did not pay them any attention.

"Now," said Merlyn furiously, apparently to nobody, "do you think you are being funny?

"Very well then, why do you do it?

"That is no excuse. Naturally I meant the one I was wearing.

"But wearing now, of course, you fool. I don't want a hat I was wearing in 1890. Have you no sense of time at all?"

Merlyn took off the sailor hat which had just appeared and held it out to the air for inspection.

"This is an anachronism," he said severely. "That is what it is, a beastly anachronism."

Archimedes seemed to be accustomed to these scenes, for he now said in a reasonable voice: "Why don't you ask for the hat by name, master? Say, 'I want my magician's hat,' not 'I want the hat I was wearing.' Perhaps the poor chap finds it as difficult to live backward as you do."

"I want my magician's hat," said Merlyn sulkily.

Instantly the long pointed cone was standing on his head.

The tension in the air relaxed. Wart sat down again on the floor, and Archimedes resumed his toilet, pulling his pinions and tail feathers through his beak to smooth the barbs together. Each barb had hundreds of little hooks or barbules on it, by means of which the barbs of the feather were held together. He was stroking them into place.

Merlyn said, "I beg your pardon. I am not having a very good day today, and there it is."

"About Kay," said the Wart. "Even if you can't change him into things, could you not give us both an adventure without changing?"

Merlyn made a visible effort to control his temper, and to consider this question dispassionately. He was sick of the subject altogether.

"I cannot do any magic for Kay," he said slowly, "except my own magic that I have anyway. Backsight and insight and all that. Do you mean anything I could do with that?"

"What does your backsight do?"

"It tells me what you would say is going to happen, and the insight sometimes says what is or was happening in other places."

"Is there anything happening just now, anything that Kay and I could go to see?"

Merlyn immediately struck himself on the brow and exclaimed excitedly, "Now I see it all. Yes, of course there is, and you are going to see it. Yes, you must take Kay and hurry up about it. You must go immediately after Mass. Have breakfast first and go immediately after Mass. Yes, that is it. Go straight to Hob's strip of barley in the open field and follow that line until you come to something. That will be splendid, yes, and I shall have a nap this afternoon instead of those filthy Summulae Logicals. Or have I had the nap?"

"You have not had it," said Archimedes. "That is still in the future, Master."

"Splendid, splendid. And mind, Wart, don't forget to take Kay with you so that I can have my nap."

"What shall we see?" asked the Wart.

"Ah, don't plague me about a little thing like that. You run along now, there's a good boy, and mind you don't forget to take Kay with you. Why ever didn't you mention it before? Don't forget to follow beyond the strip of barley. Well, well, well! This is the first half-holiday I have had since I started this confounded tutorship. First I think I shall have a little nap before luncheon, and then I think I shall have a little nap before tea. Then I shall have to think of something I can do before dinner. What shall I do before dinner, Archimedes?''

"Have a little nap, I expect,'' said the owl coldly, turning his back upon his master, because he, as well as the Wart, enjoyed to see life.

chapter ten

Wart knew that if he told the elder boy about this conversation with Merlyn, Kay would refuse to be condescended to, and would not come. So he said nothing. It was strange, but their battle had made them friends again, and each could look the other in the eye, with a kind of confused affection. They went together unanimously though shyly, without explanations, and found themselves standing at the end of Hob's barley strip after Mass. The Wart had no need to use ingenuity. When they were there it was easy.

"Come on," he said, "Merlyn told me to tell you that there was something along here that was specially for you."

"What sort of thing?" asked Kay.

"An adventure."

"How do we get to it?"

"We ought to follow along the line which this strip makes, and I suppose that would take us into the forest. We should have to keep the sun just there on our left, but allow for it moving."

"All right," said Kay. "What is the adventure?"

"I don't know."

They went along the strip, and followed its imaginary line over the park and over the chase, keeping their eyes skinned for some miraculous happening. They wondered whether half a dozen young pheasants they started had anything curious about them, and Kay was ready to swear that one of them was white. If it had been white, and if a black eagle had suddenly swooped down upon it from the sky, they would have known quite well that wonders were afoot, and that all they had to do was to follow the pheasant—or the eagle—until they reached the maiden in the enchanted castle. However, the pheasant was not white.

At the edge of the forest Kay said, "I suppose we shall have to go into this?"

"Merlyn said to follow the line."

"Well," said Kay, "I am not afraid. If the adventure was for me, it is bound to be a good one."

They went in, and were surprised to find that the going was not bad. It was about the same as a big wood might be nowadays, whereas the common forest of those times was like a jungle on the Amazon. There were no pheasant-shooting proprietors then, to see that the undergrowth was thinned, and not one thousandth part of the number of the present-day timber merchants who prune judiciously at the few remaining woods. The most of the Forest Sauvage was almost impenetrable, an enormous barrier of eternal trees, the dead ones fallen against the live and held to them by ivy, the living struggling up in competition with each other toward the sun which gave them life, the floor boggy through lack of drainage, or tindery from old wood so that you might suddenly tumble through a decayed tree trunk into an ants' nest, or laced with brambles and bindweed and honeysuckle and convolvulus and teazles and the stuff which country people call sweethearts, until you would be torn to pieces in three yards.

This part was good. Hob's line pointed down what seemed to be a succession of glades, shady and murmuring places in which the wild thyme was droning with bees. The insect season was past its peak, for it was really the time for wasps and fruit; but there were many fritillaries still, with tortoise-shells and red admirals on the flowering mint. Wart pulled a leaf of this, and munched it like chewing-gum as they walked.

"It is queer," he said, "but there have been people here. Look, there is a hoof-mark, and it was shod."

"You don't see much," said Kay, "for there is a man."

Sure enough, there was a man at the end of the next glade, sitting with a wood-axe by the side of a tree which he had felled. He was a queer-looking, tiny man, with a hunchback and a face like mahogany, and he was dressed in numerous pieces of old leather which he had secured about his brawny legs and arms with pieces of cord. He was eating a lump of bread and sheep's-milk cheese with a knife which years of sharpening had worn into a mere streak, leaning his back against one of the highest trees they had ever seen. The white flakes of wood lay all about him. The dressed stump of the felled tree looked very new. His eyes were bright like a fox's.

"I expect he will be the adventure," whispered Wart.

"Pooh," said Kay, "you have knights-in-armour, or dragons, or things like that in an adventure, not dirty old men cutting wood."

"Well, I am going to ask him what happens along here, anyway."

They went up to the small munching woodman, who did not seem to have seen them, and asked him where the glades were leading to. They asked two or three times before they discovered that the poor fellow was either deaf or mad, or both. He neither answered nor moved.

"Oh, come on," said Kay. "He is probably loopy like Wat, and does not know what he is at. Let's go on and leave the old fool."

They went on for nearly a mile, and still the going was good. There were no paths exactly, and the glades were not continuous. Anybody who came there by chance would have thought that there was just the one glade which he was in, a couple of hundred yards long, unless he went to the end of it and discovered another one, screened by a few trees. Now and then they found a stump with the marks of the axe on it, but mostly these had been carefully covered with brambles or altogether grubbed up. The Wart considered that the glades must have been made.

Kay caught the Wart by the arm, at the edge of a clearing, and pointed silently toward its further end. There was a grassy bank there, swelling gently to a gigantic sycamore, upward of ninety feet high, which stood upon its top. On the bank there was an equally gigantic man lying at his ease, with a dog beside him. This man was as notable as the sycamore, for he stood or lay seven feet without his shoes, and he was dressed in nothing but a kind of kilt made of Lincoln green worsted. He had a leather bracer on his left forearm. His enormous brown chest supported the dog's head—it had pricked its ears and was watching the boys, but had made no other movement—which the muscles gently lifted as they rose and fell. The man appeared to be asleep. There was a seven-foot bow beside him, with some arrows more than a clothyard long. He, like the woodman, was the colour of mahogany, and the curled hairs on his chest made a golden haze where the sun caught them.

"He is it," whispered Kay excitedly.

They went to the man cautiously, for fear of the dog. But the dog only followed them with its eyes, keeping its chin pressed firmly to the chest of its beloved master, and giving them the least suspicion of a wag from its tail. It moved its tail without lifting it, two inches sideways in the grass. The man opened his eyes —obviously he had not been asleep at all—smiled at the boys, and jerked his thumb in a direction which pointed further up the glade. Then he stopped smiling and shut his eyes.

"Excuse me," said Kay, "what happens up there?"

The man made no answer and kept his eyes closed, but he lifted his hand again and pointed onward with his thumb.

"He means us to go on," said Kay.

"It certainly is an adventure," said the Wart. "I wonder if that dumb woodman could have climbed up the big tree he was leaning against and sent a message to this tree that we were coming? He certainly seems to have been expecting us."

At this the naked giant opened one eye and looked at Wart in some surprise. Then he opened both eyes, laughed all over his big twinkling face, sat up, patted the dog, picked up his bow, and rose to his feet.

"Very well, then, young measters," he said, still laughing. "Us will come along of 'ee arter all. Young heads still meake the sharpest, they do say."

Kay looked at him in blank surprise. "Who are you?" he asked.

"Naylor," said the giant, "John Naylor in the wide world it were, till us come to be a man of the 'ood.

Then 'twere John Little for some time, in the 'ood like, but mostly folk does put it back'ard now, and calls us Little John.''

"Oh!'' cried the Wart in delight. "I have heard of you, often, when they tell Saxon stories in the evening, of you and Robin Hood.''

"Not Hood,'' said Little John reprovingly. "That bain't the way to name 'un, measter, not in the 'ood.''

"But it is Robin Hood in the stories,'' said Kay.

"Ah, them book-learning chaps. They don't know all. How'm ever, 'tis time us do be stepping along.''

They fell in on either side of the enormous man, and had to run one step in three to keep up with him; for, although he talked very slowly, he walked on his bare feet very fast. The dog trotted at heel.

"Please,'' asked the Wart, "where are you taking us?''

"Why, to Robin 'ood, seemingly. An't you sharp enough to guess that also, Measter Art?''

The giant gave him a sly peep out of the corner of his eye at this, for he knew that he had set the boys two problems at once—first, what was Robin's real name, and second, how did Little John come to know the Wart's?

The Wart fixed on the second question first.

"How did you know my name?''

"Ah,'' said Little John. "Us knowed.''

"Does Robin 'ood know we are coming?''

"Nay, my duck, a young scholard like thee should speak his name scholarly.''

"Well, what is his name?'' cried the boy, between exasperation and being out of breath from running to keep up. "You said 'ood.''

"So it is 'ood, my duck. Robin 'ood, like the 'oods you'm running through. And a grand fine name it is.''

"Robin Wood!"

"Aye, Robin 'ood. What else should un be, seeing as he rules 'em. They'm free pleaces, the 'oods, and fine pleaces. Let thee sleep in 'em, come summer, come winter, and hunt in 'em for thy commons lest thee starve; and smell to 'em as they brings forward their comely bright leaves, according to order, or loses of 'em by the same order back'ards: let thee stand in 'em that thou be'st not seen, and move in 'em that thou be'st not heard, and warm thee with 'em as thou fall'st on sleep—ah, they'm proper fine pleaces, the 'oods, for a free man of hands and heart."

Kay said, "But I thought all Robin Wood's men wore hose and jerkins of Lincoln green?"

"That us do in the winter like, when us needs 'em, or with leather leggings at 'ood 'ork: but here by summer 'tis more seasonable thus for the pickets, who have nought to do save watch."

"Were you a sentry then?"

"Aye, and so were wold Much, as you spoke to by the felled tree."

"And I think," exclaimed Kay triumphantly, "that this next big tree which we are coming to will be the stronghold of Robin Wood!"

They were coming to the monarch of the forest.

It was a lime tree as great as that which used to grow at Moor Park in Hertfordshire, no less than one hundred feet in height and seventeen feet in girth, a yard above the ground. Its beech-like trunk was embellished with a beard of twigs at the bottom, and where each of the great branches had sprung from the trunk the bark had split and was now discoloured with rain water or sap. The bees zoomed among its bright and sticky leaves, higher and higher toward heaven,

and a rope ladder disappeared among the foliage. Nobody could have climbed it without a ladder, even with
irons.

"You think well, Measter Kay," said Little John.
"And there be Measter Robin, atween her roots."

The boys, who had been more interested in the
look-out man perched in a crow's nest at the top of that
swaying and whispering pride of the earth, lowered
their eyes at once and clapped them on the great outlaw.

He was not, as they had expected, a romantic man
—or not at first—although he was nearly as tall as Little
John. These two, of course, were the only people in the
world who have ever shot an arrow the distance of a
mile, with the English long-bow. He was a sinewy fellow whose body did not carry fat. He was not half-
naked, like John, but dressed discreetly in faded green
with a silvery bugle at his side. He was clean-shaven,
sunburned, nervous, gnarled like the roots of the trees;
but gnarled and mature with weather and poetry rather
than with age, for he was scarcely thirty years old.
(Eventually he lived to be eighty-seven, and attributed
his long life to smelling the turpentine in the pines.)
At the moment he was lying on his back and looking
upward, but not into the sky.

Robin Wood lay happily with his head in Marian's
lap. She sat between the roots of the lime tree, clad in
a one-piece smock of green girded with a quiver of arrows, and her feet and arms were bare. She had let down
the brown shining waterfall of her hair, which was
usually kept braided in pigtails for convenience in hunting and cookery, and with the falling waves of this she
framed his head. She was singing a duet with him softly, and tickling the end of his nose with the fine hairs.

"Under the greenwood tree," sang Maid Marian,
"Who loves to lie with me,
    And tune his merry note
    Unto the sweet bird's throat."

"Come hither, come hither, come hither,"
hummed Robin.

"Here shall he see
No enemy
But winter and rough weather."

They laughed happily and began again, singing lines
alternately:

"Who doth ambition shun
And loves to lie in the sun,
Seeking the food he eats
And pleased with what he gets,"

then, both together:

"Come hither, come hither, come hither:
Here shall he see
No enemy
But winter and rough weather."

The song ended in laughter. Robin, who had been
twisting his brown fingers in the silk-fine threads which
fell about his face, gave them a shrewd tug and scrambled to his feet.

"Now, John," he said, seeing them at once.

"Now, Measter," said Little John.

"So you have brought the young squires?"

"They brought me."

"Welcome either way," said Robin. "I never
heard ill spoken of Sir Ector, nor reason why his

sounders should be pursued. How are you, Kay and Wart, and who put you into the forest at my glades, on this of all days?"

"Robin," interrupted the lady, "you can't take them!"

"Why not, sweet heart?"

"They are children."

"Exactly what we want."

"It is inhuman," she said in a vexed way, and began to do her hair.

The outlaw evidently thought it would be safer not to argue. He turned to the boys and asked them a question instead.

"Can you shoot?"

"Trust me," said the Wart.

"I can try," said Kay, more reserved, as they laughed at the Wart's assurance.

"Come, Marian, let them have one of your bows."

She handed him a bow and half a dozen arrows twenty-eight inches long.

"Shoot the popinjay," said Robin, giving them to the Wart.

He looked and saw a popinjay five-score paces away. He guessed that he had been a fool and said cheerfully, "I am sorry, Robin Wood, but I am afraid it is much too far for me."

"Never mind," said the outlaw. "Have a shot at it. I can tell by the way you shoot."

The Wart fitted his arrow as quickly and neatly as he was able, set his feet wide in the same line that he wished his arrow to go, squared his shoulders, drew the bow to his chin, sighted on the mark, raised his point through an angle of about twenty degrees, aimed two yards to the right because he always pulled to the left in his loose, and sped his arrow. It missed, but not so badly.

"Now, Kay," said Robin.

Kay went through the same motions and also made a good shot. Each of them had held the bow the right way up, had quickly found the cock feather and set it outward, each had taken hold of the string to draw the bow—most boys who have not been taught are inclined to catch hold of the nock of the arrow when they draw, between their finger and thumb, but a proper archer pulls back the string with his first two or three fingers and lets the arrow follow it—neither of them had allowed the point to fall away to the left as they drew, nor struck their left forearms with the bow-string—two common faults with people who do not know—and each had loosed evenly without a pluck.

"Good," said the outlaw. "No lute-players here."

"Robin," said Marian, sharply, "you can't take children into danger. Send them home to their father."

"That I won't," he said, "unless they wish to go. It is their quarrel as much as mine."

"What is the quarrel?" asked Kay.

The outlaw threw down his bow and sat cross-legged on the ground, drawing Maid Marian to sit beside him. His face was puzzled.

"It is Morgan le Fay," he said. "It is difficult to explain her."

"I should not try."

Robin turned on his mistress angrily. "Marian," he said. "Either we must have their help, or else we have to leave the other three without help. I don't want to ask the boys to go there, but it is either that or leaving Tuck to her."

The Wart thought it was time to ask a tactful question, so he made a polite cough and said: "Please, who is Morgan the Fay?"

All three answered at once.

"She'm a bad 'un," said Little John.

"She is a fairy," said Robin.

"No, she is not," said Marian. "She is an enchantress."

"The fact of the matter is," said Robin, "that nobody knows exactly what she is. In my opinion, she is a fairy.

"And that opinion," he added, staring at his wife, "I still hold."

Kay asked: "Do you mean she is one of those people with bluebells for hats, who spend the time sitting on toadstools?"

There was a shout of laughter.

"Certainly not. There are no such creatures. The Queen is a real one, and one of the worst of them."

"If the boys have got to be in it," said Marian, "you had better explain from the beginning."

The outlaw took a deep breath, uncrossed his legs, and the puzzled look came back to his face.

"Well," he said, "suppose that Morgan is the queen of the fairies, or at any rate has to do with them, and that fairies are not the kind of creatures your nurse has told you about. Some people say they are the Oldest Ones of All, who lived in England before the Romans came here—before us Saxons, before the Old Ones themselves—and that they have been driven underground. Some say they look like humans, like dwarfs, and others that they look ordinary, and others that they don't look like anything at all, but put on various shapes as the fancy takes them. Whatever they look like, they have the knowledge of the ancient Gaels. They know things down there in their burrows which the human race has forgotten about, and quite a lot of these things are not good to hear.''

''Whisper,'' said the golden lady, with a strange look, and the boys noticed that the little circle had drawn closer together.

''Well now,'' said Robin, lowering his voice, ''the thing about these creatures that I am speaking of, and if you will excuse me I won't name them again, is that they have no hearts. It is not so much that they wish to do evil, but that if you were to catch one and cut it open, you would find no heart inside. They are cold-blooded like fishes.''

''They are everywhere, even while people are talking.''

The boys looked about them.

''Be quiet,'' Robin said. ''I need not tell you any more. It is unlucky to talk about them. The point is that I believe this Morgan is the queen of the—well—of the Good Folk, and I know she sometimes lives in a castle to the north of our forest called the Castle Chariot. Marian says that the queen is not a fairy herself, but only a necromancer who is friendly with them. Other people say she is a daughter of the Earl of Cornwall. Never mind about that. The thing is that this morning, by her enchantments, the Oldest People of All have taken prisoner one of my servants and one of yours.''

''Not Tuck?'' cried Little John, who knew nothing of recent developments because he had been on sentry.

Robin nodded. ''The news came from the northern trees, before your message arrived about the boys.''

"Alas, poor Friar!"

"Tell how it happened," said Marian. "But perhaps you had better explain about the names."

"One of the few things we know," said Robin, "about the Blessed Ones, is that they go by the names of animals. For instance, they may be called Cow, or Goat, or Pig, and so forth. So, if you happen to be calling one of your own cows, you must always point to it when you call. Otherwise you may summon a fairy— a Little Person I ought to have said—who goes by the same name, and, once you have summoned it, it comes, and it can take you away."

"What seems to have happened," said Marian, taking up the story, "is that your Dog Boy from the castle took his hounds to the edge of the forest when they were going to scombre, and he happened to catch sight of Friar Tuck, who was chatting with an old man called Wat that lives hereabouts—"

"Excuse us," cried the two boys, "is that the old man who lived in our village before he lost his wits? He bit off the Dog Boy's nose, as a matter of fact, and now he lives in the forest, a sort of ogre?"

"It is the same person," replied Robin, "but— poor thing—he is not much of an ogre. He lives on grass and roots and acorns, and would not hurt a fly. I am afraid you have got your story muddled."

"Fancy Wat living on acorns!"

"What happened," said Marian patiently, "was this. The three of them came together to pass the time of day, and one of the hounds (I think it was the one called Cavall) began jumping up at poor Wat, to lick his face. This frightened the old man, and your Dog Boy called out, 'Come here, Dog!' to make him stop. He did not point with his finger. You see, he ought to have pointed."

"What happened?"

"Well, my man Scathelocke, or Scarlett, as they call him in the ballads, happened to be woodcutting a little way off, and he says that they vanished, just vanished, including the dog."

"My poor Cavall!"

"So the fairies have got them."

"You mean the People of Peace."

"I am sorry.

"But the point is, if Morgan is really the Queen of these creatures, and if we want to get them away before they are enchanted—one of their ancient Queens called Circe used to turn the ones she captured into hogs—we shall have to look for them in her castle."

"Then we must go there."

chapter eleven

Robin smiled at the elder boy and patted him on the back, while the Wart thought despairingly about his dog. Then the outlaw cleared his throat and began to speak again.

"You are right about going there," he said, "but I ought to tell you the unpleasant part. Nobody can get into the Castle Chariot, except a boy or girl."

"Do you mean you can't get in?"

"You could get in."

"I suppose," explained the Wart, when he had thought this over, "it is like the thing about unicorns."

"Right. A unicorn is a magic animal, and only a maiden can catch it. Fairies are magic too, and only innocent people can enter their castles. That is why they take away people's children out of cradles."

Kay and Wart sat in silence for a moment. Then Kay said: "Well, I am game. It is my adventure after all."

The Wart said: "I want to go too. I am fond of Cavall."

Robin looked at Marian.

"Very well," he said. "We won't make a fuss about it, but we will talk about plans. I think it is good of you two to go, without really knowing what you are in for, but it will not be so bad as you think.''

"We shall come with you," said Marian. "Our band will come with you to the castle. You will only have to do the going-in part at the end.''

"Yes, and the band will probably be attacked by that griffin of hers afterwards.''

"Is there a griffin?''

"Indeed there is. The Castle Chariot is guarded by a fierce one, like a watch dog. We shall have to get past it on the way there, or it will give the alarm and you won't be able to get in. It will be a terrific stalk.''

"We shall have to wait till night.''

The boys passed the morning pleasantly, getting accustomed to two of Maid Marian's bows. Robin had insisted on this. He said that no man could shoot with another's bow any more than he could cut with another's scythe. For their midday meal they had cold venison pattie, with mead, as did everybody else. The outlaws drifted in for the meal like a conjuring trick. At one moment there would be nobody at the edge of the clearing, at the next half a dozen right inside it—green or sunburned men who had silently appeared out of the bracken or the trees. In the end there were about a hundred of them, eating merrily and laughing. They were not outlaws because they were murderers, or for any reason like that. They were Saxons who had revolted against Uther Pendragon's conquest, and who refused to accept a foreign king. The fens and wild woods of England were alive with them. They were like soldiers of the resistance in later occupations. Their food was dished out from a leafy bower, where Marian and her attendants cooked.

The partisans usually posted a sentry to take the tree messages, and slept during the afternoon, partly because so much of their hunting had to be done in the times when most workmen sleep, and partly because the wild beasts take a nap in the afternoon and so should their hunters. This afternoon, however, Robin called the boys to a council.

"Look," he said, "you had better know what we are going to do. My band of a hundred will march with you toward Queen Morgan's castle, in four parties. You two will be in Marian's party. When we get to an oak which was struck by lightning in the year of the great storm, we shall be within a mile of the griffin guard. We shall meet at a rendezvous there, and afterward we shall have to move like shadows. We must get past the griffin without an alarm. If we do get past it and if all goes well, we shall halt at the castle at a distance of about four hundred yards. We can't come nearer, because of the iron in our arrow-heads, and from that moment you will have to go alone.

"Now, Kay and Wart, I must explain about iron. If our friends have really been captured by—by the Good People—and if Queen Morgan the Fay is really the queen of them, we have one advantage on our side. None of the Good People can bear the closeness of iron. The reason is that the Oldest Ones of All began in the days of flint, before iron was ever invented, and all their troubles have come from the new metal. The people who conquered them had steel swords (which is even better than iron) and that is how they succeeded in driving the Old Ones underground.

"This is the reason why we must keep away tonight, for fear of giving them the uncomfortable feeling. But you two, with an iron knife-blade hidden close in your hands, will be safe from the Queen, so long as you do not let go of it. A couple of small knives will not give them the feeling without being shown.

All you will have to do is to walk the last distance, keeping a good grip of your iron: enter the castle in safety: and make your way to the cell where the prisoners are. As soon as the prisoners are protected by your metal they will be able to walk out with you. Do you understand this, Kay and Wart?''

''Yes, please,'' they said. ''We understand this perfectly.''

''There is one more thing. The most important is to hold your iron, but the next most important is not to eat. Anybody who eats in a you-know-what stronghold has to stay there for ever, so, for all sake's sake, don't eat anything whatever inside the castle, however tempting it may look. Will you remember?''

''We will.''

After the staff lecture, Robin went to give his orders to the men. He made them a long speech, explaining about the griffin and the stalk and what the boys were going to do.

When he had finished his speech, which was listened to in perfect silence, an odd thing happened. He began it again at the beginning and spoke it from start to finish in the same words. On finishing it for the second time, he said, ''Now, captains,'' and the hundred men split into groups of twenty which went to different parts of the clearing and stood round Marian, Little John, Much, Scarlett and Robin. From each of these groups a humming noise rose to the sky.

''What on earth are they doing?''

''Listen,'' said the Wart.

They were repeating the speech, word for word. Probably none of them could read or write, but they had learned to listen and remember. This was the way in which Robin kept touch with his night raiders, by knowing that each man knew by heart all that the leader himself knew, and why he was able to trust them, when necessary, each man to move by himself.

When the men had repeated their instructions, and everyone was word perfect in the speech, there was an issue of war arrows, a dozen to each. These arrows had bigger heads, ground to razor sharpness, and they were heavily feathered in a square cut. There was a bow inspection, and two or three men were issued with new strings. Then all fell silent.

"Now then," cried Robin cheerfully.

He waved his arm, and the men, smiling, raised their bows in salute. Then there was a sigh, a rustle, a snap of one incautious twig, and the clearing of the giant lime tree was as empty as it had been before the days of man.

"Come with me," said Marian, touching the boys on the shoulder. Behind them the bees hummed in the leaves.

It was a long march. The artificial glades which led to the lime tree in the form of a cross were no longer of use after the first half-hour. After that they had to make their way through the virgin forest as best they might. It would not have been so bad if they had been able to kick and slash their way, but they were supposed to move in silence. Marian showed them how to go sideways, one side after the other; how to stop at once when a bramble caught them, and take it patiently out; how to put their feet down sensitively and roll their weight to that leg as soon as they were certain that no twig was under the foot; how to distinguish at a glance the places which gave most hope of an easy passage; and how a kind of rhythm in their movements would help them in spite of obstacles. Although there were a hundred invisible men on every side of them, moving toward the same goal, they heard no sounds but their own.

The boys had felt disgruntled at first, at being put in a woman's band. They would have preferred to have gone with Robin, and thought that being put under Marian was like being trusted to a governess. They soon found their mistake. She had objected to their coming, but, now that their coming was ordered, she accepted them as companions. It was not easy to be a companion of hers. In the first place, it was impossible to keep up with her unless she waited for them—for she could move on all fours or even wriggle like a snake almost as quickly as they could walk—and in the second place she was an accomplished soldier, which they were not. She was a true Weyve—except for her long hair, which most of the female outlaws of those days used to clip. One of the bits of advice which she gave them before talking had to be stopped was this: Aim high when you shoot in battle, rather than low. A low arrow strikes the ground, a high one may kill in the second rank.

"If I am made to get married," thought the Wart, who had doubts on the subject, "I will marry a girl like this: a kind of golden vixen."

As a matter of fact, though the boys did not know it, Marian could hoot like an owl by blowing into her fists, or whistle a shrill blast between tongue and teeth with the fingers in the corner of the mouth; could bring all the birds to her by imitating their calls, and understand much of their small language—such as when the tits exclaim that a hawk is coming; could hit the popinjay twice for three times of Robin's; and could turn cartwheels. But none of these accomplishments was necessary at the moment.

The twilight fell mistily—it was the first of the autumn mists—and in the dimity the undispersed families of the tawny owl called to each other, the young with keewick and the old with the proper hooroo, hooroo. The noise called Tu-Whit, Tu-Whoo, which is wished by poets on the owl, is really a family noise, made by separate birds. Proportionally as the brambles and obstacles became harder to see, so did they become easier to feel. It was odd, but in the deepening silence the Wart found himself able to move more silently, instead of less. Being reduced to touch and sound, he found himself in better sympathy with these, and could go quietly and quick.

It was about compline, or, as we should call it, at nine o'clock at night—and they had covered at least seven miles of the toilsome forest—when Marian touched Kay on the shoulder and pointed into the blue darkness. They could see in the dark now, as well as human beings can see in it and much better than townspeople will ever manage to, and there in front of them, struck through seven miles of trackless forest by Marian's woodcraft, was the smitten oak. They decided with one accord, without even a whisper, to creep up to it so silently that even the members of their own army, who might already be waiting there, would not know of their arrival.

But a motionless man has the advantage of a man in motion, and they had hardly reached the outskirts of the roots when friendly hands took told of them, patted their backs with pats as light as thistledown, and guided them to seats. The roots were crowded. It was like being a member of a band of starlings, or of roosting rooks. In the night mystery a hundred men breathed on every side of Wart, like the surge of our own blood which we can hear when we are writing or reading in the late and lonely hours. They were in the dark and stilly womb of night.

Presently the Wart noticed that the grasshoppers were creaking their shrill note, so tiny as to be almost extra-audible, like the creak of the bat. They creaked one after another. They creaked, when Marian had creaked three times to account for Kay and Wart as well as for herself, one hundred times. All the outlaws were present, and it was time to go.

There was a rustle, as if the wind had moved in the last few leaves of the nine-hundrèd-year-old oak. Then an owl hooted softly, a field mouse screamed, a rabbit thumped, a dog-fox barked his deep, single lion's cough, and a bat twittered above their heads. The leaves rustled again more lengthily while you could count a hundred, and then Maid Marian, who had done the rabbit's thump, was surrounded by her band of twenty plus two. The Wart felt a man on either side of him take his hand, as they stood in a circle, and then he noticed that the stridulation of the grasshoppers had begun again. It was going round in a circle, towards him, and, as the last grasshopper rubbed its legs together, the man on his right squeezed his hand. Wart stridulated. Instantly the man on his left did the same, and pressed his hand also. There were twenty-two grasshoppers before Maid Marian's band was ready for its last stalk through the silence.

The last stalk might have been a nightmare, but to the Wart it was heavenly. Suddenly he found himself filled with an exaltation of night, and felt that he was bodiless, silent, transported. He felt that he could have walked upon a feeding rabbit and caught her up by the ears, furry and kicking, before she knew of his presence. He felt that he could have run between the legs of the men on either side of him, or taken their bright daggers from their sheaths, while they still moved on undreaming. The passion of nocturnal secrecy was a wine in his blood. He really was small and young enough to move as secretly as the warriors. Their age and weight made them lumber, in spite of all their wood-craft, and his youth and lightness made him mobile, in spite of his lack of it.

It was an easy stalk, except for its danger. The bushes thinned and the sounding bracken grew rarely in the swampy earth, so that they could move three times as fast. They went in a dream, unguided by owl's hoot or bat's squeak, but only kept together by the necessary pace which the sleeping forest imposed upon them. Some of them were fearful, some revengeful for their comrade, some, as it were, disbodied in the sleep-walk of their stealth.

They had hardly crept for twenty minutes when Maid Marian paused in her tracks. She pointed to the left.

Neither of the boys had read the book of Sir John de Mandeville, so they did not know that a griffin was eight times larger than a lion. Now, looking to the left in the silent gloom of night, they saw cut out against the sky and against the stars something which they never would have believed possible. It was a young male griffin in its first plumage.

The front end, and down to the forelegs and shoul-ders, was like a huge falcon. The Persian beak, the long wings in which the first primary was the longest, and the mighty talons: all were the same, but, as Mande-ville observed, the whole eight times bigger than a lion. Behind the shoulders, a change began to take place. Where an ordinary falcon or eagle would content itself with the twelve feathers of its tail, Falco leonis serpen-tis began to grow the leonine body and the hind legs of the beast of Africa, and after that a snake's tail. The boys saw, twenty-four feet high in the mysterious night-light of the moon, and with its sleeping head bowed upon its breast so that the wicked beak lay on the breast feathers, an authentic griffin that was better worth seeing than a hundred condors. They drew their breath through their teeth and for the moment hurried secretly on, storing the majestic vision of terror in the chambers of remembrance.

They were close to the castle at last, and it was time for the outlaws to halt. Their captain touched hands silently with Kay and Wart, and the two went forward through the thinning forest, towards a faint glow which gleamed behind the trees.

They found themselves in a wide clearing or plain. They stood stock still with surprise at what they saw. It was a castle made entirely out of food, except that on the highest tower of all a carrion crow was sitting, with an arrow in its beak.

The Oldest Ones of All were gluttons. Probably it was because they seldom had enough to eat. You can read even nowadays a poem written by one of them, which is known as the Vision of Mac Conglinne. In this Vision there is a description of a castle made out of different kinds of food. The English for part of the poem goes like this:

> A lake of new milk I beheld
> In the midst of a fair plain.
> I saw a well-appointed house
> Thatched with butter.
>
> Its two soft door-posts of custard,
> Its dais of curds and butter,
> Beds of glorious lard,
> Many shields of thin pressed cheese.

Under the straps of those shields
Were men of soft sweet smooth cheese,
Men who knew not to wound a Gael,
Spears of old butter had each of them.

A huge cauldron full of meat
(Methought I'd try to tackle it),
Boiled, leafy kale, browny-white,
A brimming vessel full of milk.

A bacon house of two-score ribs,
A wattling of tripe—support of clans—
Of every food pleasant to man,
Meseemed the whole was gathered there.

Of chitterlings of pigs were made
Its beautiful rafters,
Splendid the beams and the pillars
Of marvellous pork.

The boys stood there in wonder and nausea, before just such a stronghold. It rose from its lake of milk in a mystic light of its own—in a greasy, buttery glow. It was the fairy aspect of Castle Chariot, which the Oldest Ones—sensing the hidden knife blades after all—had thought would be tempting to the children. It was to tempt them to eat.

The place smelt like a grocer's, a butcher's, a dairy and a fishmonger's, rolled into one. It was horrible beyond belief—sweet, sickly and pungent—so that they did not feel the least wish to swallow a particle of it. The real temptation was, to run away.

However, there were prisoners to rescue.

They plodded over the filthy drawbridge—a butter one, with cow hairs still in it—sinking to their ankles. They shuddered at the tripe and the chitterlings. They pointed their iron knives at the soldiers made of soft, sweet, smooth cheese, and the latter shrank away.

In the end they came to the inner chamber, where Morgan le Fay herself lay stretched upon her bed of glorious lard.

She was a fat, dowdy, middle-aged woman with black hair and a slight moustache, but she was made of human flesh. When she saw the knives, she kept her eyes shut—as if she were in a trance. Perhaps, when she was outside this very strange castle, or when she was not doing that kind of magic to tempt the appetite, she was able to assume more beautiful forms.

The prisoners were tied to pillars of marvellous pork.

"I am sorry if this iron is hurting you," said Kay, "but we have come to rescue our friends."

Queen Morgan shuddered.

"Will you tell your cheesy men to undo them?"

She would not.

"It is magic," said the Wart. "Do you think we ought to go up and kiss her, or something frightful like that?"

"Perhaps if we went and touched her with the iron?"

"You do it."

"No, you."

"We'll go together."

So they joined hands to approach the Queen. She began to writhe in her lard like a slug. She was in agony from the metal.

At last, and just before they reached her, there was a sloshing rumble or mumble—and the whole fairy appearance of Castle Chariot melted together in collapse, leaving the five humans and one dog standing together in the forest clearing—which still smelt faintly of dirty milk.

"Gor-blimey!" said Friar Tuck. "Gor blimey and coo! Dash my vig if I didn't think we was done for!"

"Master!" said Dog Boy.

Cavall contented himself with barking wildly, biting their toes, lying on his back, trying to wag his tail in that position, and generally behaving like an idiot. Old Wat touched his forelock.

"Now then," said Kay, "this is my adventure, and we must get home quick."

chapter twelve

But Morgan le Fay, although in her fairy shape she could not stand iron, still had the griffin. She had cast it loose from its golden chain, by a spell, the moment her castle disappeared.

The outlaws were pleased with their success, and less careful than they should have been. They decided to take a detour round the place where they had seen the monster tied up, and marched away through the darksome trees without a thought of danger.

There was a noise like a railway train letting off its whistle, and, answering to it—riding on it like the voice of the Arabian Bird—Robin Wood's horn of silver began to blow.

"Tone, ton, tavon, tontavon, tantontavon, tontantontavon," went the horn. "Moot, troot, trourourout, troutourourout. Troot, troot. Tran, tran, tran, tran."

Robin was blowing his hunting music and the ambushed archers swung round as the griffin charged. They set forward their left feet in the same movement and let fly such a shower of arrows as it had been snow.

The Wart saw the creature stagger in its tracks, a clothyard shaft sprouting from between the shoulder blades. He saw his own arrow fly wide, and eagerly bent to snatch another from his belt. He saw the rank of his companion archers sway as if by a preconcerted signal, when each man stooped for a second shaft. He heard the bowstrings twang again, the purr of the feathers in the air. He saw the phalanx of arrows gleam like an eyeflick in the moonlight. All his life up to then he had been shooting into straw targets which made a noise like Phutt! He had often longed to hear the noise that these clean and deadly missiles would make in solid flesh. He heard it.

But the griffin's plates were as thick as a crocodile's and all but the best placed arrows glanced off. It still came on. It squealed as it came. Men began to fall, swept to the left or right by the lashing tail.

The Wart was fitting an arrow to his bow. The cock feather would not go right. Everything was in slow motion.

He saw the huge body coming blackly through the moon-glare. He felt the claw which took him in the chest. He felt himself turning somersaults slowly, with a cruel weight on top of him. He saw Kay's face somewhere in the cartwheel of the universe, flushed with starlit excitement, and Maid Marian's on the other side with its mouth open, shouting. He thought, before he slid into blackness, that it was shouting at him.

They dragged him from under the dead griffin and found Kay's arrow sticking in its eye. It had died in its leap.

Then there was a time which made him feel sick— while Robin set his collar-bone and made him a sling from the green cloth of his hood—and after that the whole band lay down to sleep, dog-tired, beside the body. It was too late to return to Sir Ector's castle, or

even to get back to the outlaws' camp by the big tree.
The dangers of the expedition were over and all that
could be done that night was to make fires, post sentries, and sleep where they were.

Wart did not sleep much. He sat propped against
a tree, watching the red sentries passing to and fro in
the firelight, hearing their quiet passwords and thinking
about the excitements of the day. These went round
and round in his head, sometimes losing their proper
order and happening backwards or by bits. He saw the
leaping dragon, heard Marian shouting ''Good shot!'',
listened to the humming of the bees muddled up with
the stridulation of the grasshoppers, and shot and shot,
hundreds and thousands of times, at popinjays which
turned into griffins. Kay and the liberated Dog Boy slept
twitching beside him, looking alien and incomprehen-
sible as people do when they are asleep, and Cavall,
lying at his good shoulder, occasionally licked his hot
cheeks. The dawn came slowly, so slowly and pausing-
ly that it was impossible to determine when it really
had dawned, as it does during the summer months.

''Well,'' said Robin, when they had wakened and
eaten the breakfast of bread and cold venison which
they had brought with them, ''you will have to love us
and leave us, Kay. Otherwise I shall have Sir Ector
fitting out an expedition against me, to fetch you back.
Thank you for your help. Can I give you any little
present as a reward?''

''It has been lovely,'' said Kay. ''Absolutely lovely.
May I have the griffin I shot?''

''He will be too heavy to carry. Why not take
his head?''

''That would do,'' said Kay, ''if somebody would
not mind cutting it off. It was my griffin.''

"What are you going to do about old Wat?" asked the Wart.

"It depends on what he wants to do. Perhaps he will like to run off by himself and eat acorns, as he used to, or if he likes to join our band we shall be glad to have him. He ran away from your village in the first place, so I don't suppose he will care to go back there. What do you think?"

"If you are going to give me a present," said the Wart, slowly, "I would like to have him. Do you think that would be right?"

"As a matter of fact," said Robin, "I don't. I don't think you can very well give people as presents: they might not like it. That is what we Saxons feel, at any rate. What did you intend to do with him?"

"I don't want to keep him or anything like that. You see, we have a tutor who is a magician and I thought he might be able to restore him to his wits."

"Good boy," said Robin. "Have him by all means. I am sorry I made a mistake. At least, we will ask him if he would like to go."

When somebody had gone off to fetch Wat, Robin said, "You had better talk to him yourself."

They brought the poor old man, smiling, confused, hideous and very dirty, and stood him before Robin.

"Go on," said Robin.

The Wart did not know quite how to put it, but he said, "I say, Wat, would you like to come home with me, please, just for a little?"

"AhnaNanaWarraBaaBaa," said Wat, pulling his forelock, smiling, bowing and gently waving his arms in various directions.

"Come with me?"

"WanaNanaWanawana."

"Dinner?" asked the Wart in desperation.

"R!" cried the poor creature affirmatively, and his eyes glowed with pleasure at the prospect of being given something to eat.

"That way," said the Wart, pointing in the direction which he knew by the sun to be that of his guardian's castle. "Dinner. Come with. I take."

"Measter," said Wat, suddenly remembering one word, the word which he had always been accustomed to offer to the great people who made him a present of food, his only livelihood. It was decided.

"Well," said Robin, "it has been a good adventure and I am sorry you are going. I hope I shall see you again."

"Come any time," said Marian, "if you are feeling bored. You only have to follow the glades. And you, Wart, be careful of that collar-bone for a few days."

"I will send some men with you to the edge of the chase," said Robin. "After that you must go by yourselves. I expect the Dog Boy can carry the griffin's head."

"Good-bye," said Kay.

"Good-bye," said Robin.

"Good-bye," said Wart.

"Good-bye," said Marian, smiling.

"Good-bye," cried all the outlaws, waving their bows.

And Kay and the Wart and the Dog Boy and Wat and Cavall and their escort set off on the long track home.

They had an immense reception. The return on the previous day of all the hounds, except Cavall and the Dog Boy, and in the evening the failure to return of Kay and Wart, had set the household in an uproar. Their nurse had gone into hysterics—Hob had stayed out till midnight scouring the purlieus of the forest—the cooks had burnt the joint for dinner—and the sergeant-at-arms had polished all the armour twice and sharpened all the swords and axes to a razor blade in case of an invasion. At last somebody had thought of consulting Merlyn, whom they had found in the middle of his third nap. The magician, for the sake of peace and quietness to go on with his rest, had used his insight to tell Sir Ector exactly what the boys were doing, where they were, and when they might be expected back. He had prophesied their return to the minute.

So, when the small procession of returning warriors came within sight of the drawbridge, they were greeted by the whole household. Sir Ector was standing in the middle with a thick walking-stick with which he proposed to whack them for going out of bounds and causing so much trouble; the nurse had insisted on bringing out a banner which used to be put up when Sir Ector came home for the holidays, as a small boy, and this said Welcome Home; Hob had forgotten about his beloved hawks and was standing on one side, shading his eagle eyes to get the first view; the cooks and all the kitchen staff were banging pots and pans, singing "Will Ye No Come Back Again?" or some such music, out of tune; the kitchen cat was yowling; the hounds had escaped from the kennel because there was nobody to look after them, and were preparing to chase the kitchen cat; the sergeant-at-arms was blowing out his chest with pleasure so far that he looked as if he might burst at any moment, and was commanding everybody in an important voice to get ready to cheer when he said, "One, Two!"

"One, Two!" cried the sergeant.

"Huzza!" cried everybody obediently, including Sir Ector.

"Look what I have got," shouted Kay. "I have shot a griffin and the Wart has been wounded."

"Yow-yow-yow!" barked all the hounds, and poured over the Dog Boy, licking his face, scratching his chest, sniffing him all over to see what he had been up to, and looking hopefully at the griffin's head which the Dog Boy held high in the air so that they could not eat it.

"Bless my soul!" exclaimed Sir Ector.

"Alas, the poor Phillip Sparrow," cried the nurse, dropping her banner. "Pity his poor arm all to-brast in a green sling, God bless us!"

"It is all right," said the Wart. "Ah, don't catch hold of me. It hurts."

"May I have it stuffed?" asked Kay.

"Well, I be dommed," said Hob. "Be'nt thick wold chappie our Wat, that erst run lunatical?"

"My dear, dear boys," said Sir Ector. "I am so glad to see you back."

"Wold chuckle-head," exclaimed the nurse triumphantly. "Where be thy girt cudgel now?"

"Hem!" said Sir Ector. "How dare you go out of bounds and put us all to this anxiety?"

"It is a real griffin," said Kay, who knew there was nothing to be afraid of. "I shot dozens of them. Wart broke his collar-bone. We rescued the Dog Boy and Wat."

"That comes of teaching the young Hidea 'ow to shoot," said the sergeant proudly.

Sir Ector kissed both boys and commanded the griffin to be displayed before him.

"Well!" he exclaimed. "What a monster! We'll have him stuffed in the dinin'-hall. What did you say his measurements were?"

"Eighty-two inches from ear to ear. Robin said it might be a record."

"We shall have to get it chronicled."

"It is rather a good one, isn't it?" remarked Kay with studied calm.

"I shall have it set up by Sir Rowland Ward," Sir Ector went on in high delight, "with a little ivory card with KAY'S FIRST GRIFFIN on it in black letters, and the date."

"Arrah, leave thy childishness," exclaimed the nurse. "Now, Master Art, my innocent, be off with thee to thy bed upon the instant. And thou, Sir Ector, let thee think shame to be playing wi' monsters' heads like a godwit when the poor child stays upon the point of death. Now, sergeant, leave puffing of thy chest. Stir, man, and take horse to Cardoyle for the chirurgeon."

She waved her apron at the sergeant, who collapsed his chest and retreated like a shoo'd chicken.

"It is all right," said the Wart, "I tell you. It is only a broken collar-bone, and Robin set it for me last night. It does not hurt a bit."

"Leave the boy, nurse," commanded Sir Ector, taking sides with the men against the women, anxious to re-establish his superiority after the matter of the cudgel. "Merlyn will see to him if he needs it, no doubt. Who is this Robin?"

"Robin Wood," cried the boys together.

"Never heard of him."

"You call him Robin Hood," exclaimed Kay in a superior tone. "But it is Wood really, like the Wood that he is the spirit of."

"Well, well, well, so you've been foragin' with that rascal! Come in to breakfast, boys, and tell me all about him."

"We have had breakfast," said the Wart, "hours ago. May I please take Wat with me to see Merlyn?"

"Why, it's the old man who went wild and started rootin' in the forest. Wherever did you get hold of him?"

"The Good People had captured him with the Dog Boy and Cavall."

"But we shot the griffin," Kay put in. "I shot it myself."

"So now I want to see if Merlyn can restore him to his wits."

"Master Art," said the nurse sternly. She had been breathless up to now on account of Sir Ector's rebuke. "Master Art, thy room and thy bed is where thou art tending to, and that this instant. Wold fools may be wold fools, whether by yea or by nay, but I ha'nt served the Family for fifty year without a-learning of my duty. A flibberty-gibbeting about wi' a lot of want-wits, when thy own arm may be dropping to the floor!

"Yes, thou wold turkey-cock," she added, turning fiercely upon Sir Ector, "and thou canst keep thy magician away from the poor mite's room till he be rested, that thou canst!

"A-wantoning wi' monsters and lunaticals," continued the victor as she led her helpless captive from the stricken field. "I never heard the like."

"Please someone to tell Merlyn to look after Wat," cried the victim over his shoulder, in diminishing tones.

He woke up in his cool bed, feeling better. The old fire-eater who looked after him had covered the windows with a curtain, so that the room was dark and comfortable, but he could tell by the one ray of golden sunlight which shot across the floor that it was late afternoon. He not only felt better. He felt very well, so well that it was not possible to stay in bed. He moved quickly to throw back the sheet, but stopped with a hiss at the creak or scratch of his shoulder, which he had forgotten in his sleep. Then he got out more carefully by sliding down the bed and pushing himself upright with one hand, shoved his bare feet into a pair of slippers, and managed to wrap a dressing-gown round him more or less. He padded off through the stone passages up the worn circular stairs to find Merlyn.

When he reached the schoolroom, he found that Kay was continuing his First Rate Eddication. He was doing dictation, for as Wart opened the door he heard Merlyn pronouncing in measured tones the famous mediaeval mnemonic: "Barabara Celarent Darii Ferioque Prioris," and Kay saying, "Wait a bit. My pen has gone all squee-gee."

"You will catch it," remarked Kay, when they saw him. "You are supposed to be in bed, dying of gangrene or something."

"Merlyn," said the Wart. "What have you done with Wat?"

"You should try to speak without assonances," said the wizard. "For instance, 'The beer is never clear near here, dear,' is unfortunate, even as an assonance. And then again, your sentence is ambiguous to say the least of it. 'What what?' I might reply, taking it to be a conundrum, or if I were King Pellinore, 'What what, what?' Nobody can be too careful about their habits of speech."

Kay had evidently been doing his dictation well and the old gentleman was in a good humour.

"You know what I mean," said the Wart. "What have you done with the old man with no nose?"

"He has cured him," said Kay.

"Well," said Merlyn, "you might call it that, and then again you might not. Of course, when one has lived in the world as long as I have, and backwards at that, one does learn to know a thing or two about pathology. The wonders of analytical psychology and plastic surgery are, I am afraid, to this generation but a closed book."

"What did you do to him?"

"Oh, I just psycho-analysed him," replied the magician grandly. "That, and of course I sewed on a new nose on both of them."

"What kind of nose?" asked the Wart.

"It is too funny," said Kay. "He wanted to have the griffin's nose for one, but I would not let him. So then he took the noses off the young pigs which we are going to have for supper, and used those. Personally I think they will grunt."

"A ticklish operation," said Merlyn, "but a successful one."

"Well," said the Wart, doubtfully. "I hope it will be all right. What did they do then?"

"They went off to the kennels. Old Wat is very sorry for what he did to the Dog Boy, but he says he can't remember having done it. He says that suddenly everything went black, when they were throwing stones once, and he can't remember anything since. The Dog Boy forgave him and said he did not mind a bit. They are going to work together in the kennels in future, and not think of what is past any more. The Dog Boy says that the old man was good to him while they were prisoners of the Fairy Queen, and that he knows he ought not to have thrown stones at him in the first place. He says he often thought about that when other boys were throwing stones at him.''

''Well,'' said the Wart, ''I am glad it has all turned out for the best. Do you think I could go and visit them?''

''For heaven's sake, don't do anything to annoy your nurse,'' exclaimed Merlyn, looking about him anxiously. ''That old woman hit me with a broom when I came to see you this forenoon, and broke my spectacles. Could you not wait until tomorrow?''

On the morrow Wat and the Dog Boy were the firmest of friends. Their common experiences of being stoned by the mob and then tied to columns of pork by Morgan le Fay served as a bond and a topic of reminiscence, as they lay among the dogs at night, for the rest of their lives. Also, by the morning, they had both pulled off the noses which Merlyn had kindly given them. They explained that they had got used to having no noses, now, and anyway they preferred to live with the dogs.

chapter thirteen

In spite of his protests, the unhappy invalid was confined to his chamber for three mortal days. He was
alone except at bedtime, when Kay came, and Merlyn
was reduced to shouting his eddication through the key-
hole, at times when the nurse was known to be busy
with her washing.

The boy's only amusement was the ant-nests—the
ones between glass plates which had been brought when
he first came from Merlyn's cottage in the forest.

"Can't you," he howled miserably under the
door, "turn me into something while I'm locked up
like this?"

"I can't get the spells through the key-hole."

"Through the what?"

"The KEY-HOLE."

"Oh!"

"Are you there?"

"Yes."

"What?"

"What?"

"Confusion take this shouting!" exclaimed the
magician, stamping on his hat. "May Castor and Pollux.
. . . No, not again. God bless my blood pressure. . . ."

"Could you turn me into an ant?"

"A what?"

"An ANT! It would be a small spell for ants, wouldn't it? It would go through the key-hole?"

"I don't think we ought to."

"Why?"

"They are dangerous."

"You could watch with your insight, and turn me back again if it got too bad. Please turn me into something, or I shall go weak in the head."

"The ants are not our Norman ones, dear boy. They come from the Afric shore. They are belligerent."

"I don't know what belligerent is."

There was a long silence behind the door.

"Well," said Merlyn eventually. "It is far too soon in your education. But you would have had to do it sometime. Let me see. Are there two nests in that contraption?"

"There are two pairs of plates."

"Take a rush from the floor and lean it between the two nests, like a bridge. Have you done that?"

"Yes."

The place where he was seemed like a great field of boulders, with a flattened fortress at one end of it—between the glass plates. The fortress was entered by tunnels in the rock, and, over the entrance to each tunnel, there was a notice which said:

EVERYTHING NOT FORBIDDEN IS COMPULSORY

He read the notice with dislike, though he did not understand its meaning. He thought to himself: I will explore a little, before going in. For some reason the notice gave him a reluctance to go, making the rough tunnel look sinister.

He waved his antennae carefully, considering the notice, assuring himself of his new senses, planting his feet squarely in the insect world as if to brace himself in it. He cleaned his antennae with his forefeet, frisking and smoothing them so that he looked like a Victorian villain twirling his moustachios. He yawned—for ants do yawn—and stretch themselves too, like human beings. Then he became conscious of something which had been waiting to be noticed—that there was a noise in his head which was articulate. It was either a noise or a complicated smell, and the easiest way to explain it is to say that it was like a wireless broadcast. It came through his antennae.

The music had a monotonous rhythm like a pulse, and the words which went with it were about June—moon—noon—spoon, or Mammy—mammy—mammy—mammy, or Ever—never, or Blue—true—you. He liked them at first, especially the ones about Love—dove—above, until he found that they did not vary. As soon as they had been finished once, they were begun again. After an hour or two, they began to make him feel sick inside.

There was a voice in his head also, during the pauses of the music, which seemed to be giving directions. "All two-day-olds will be moved to the West Aisle" it would say, or "Number 210397/WD will report to the soup squad, in replacement for 333105/WD who has fallen off the nest." It was a fruity voice, but it seemed to be somehow impersonal—as if its charm were an accomplishment that had been practised, like a circus trick. It was dead.

The boy, or perhaps we ought to say the ant, walked away from the fortress as soon as he was prepared to walk about. He began exploring the desert of boulders uneasily, reluctant to visit the place from which the orders were coming, yet bored with the narrow view. He found small pathways among the boulders, wandering tracks both aimless and purposeful, which led toward the grain store, and also in various other directions which he could not understand. One of these paths ended at a clod with a natural hollow underneath it. In the hollow—again with the strange appearance of aimless purpose—he found two dead ants. They were laid there tidily but yet untidily, as if a very tidy person had taken them to the place, but had forgotten the reason when he got there. They were curled up, and did not seem to be either glad or sorry to be dead. They were there, like a couple of chairs.

While he was looking at the corpses, a live ant came down the pathway carrying a third one.

It said: "Hail, Barbarus!"

The boy said Hail, politely.

In one respect, of which he knew nothing, he was lucky. Merlyn had remembered to give him the proper smell for the nest—for, if he had smelled of any other nest, they would have killed him at once. If Miss Edith Cavell had been an ant, they would have had to write on her statue: SMELL IS NOT ENOUGH.

The new ant put down the cadaver vaguely and began dragging the other two in various directions. It did not seem to know where to put them. Or rather, it knew that a certain arrangement had to be made, but it could not figure how to make it. It was like a man with a tea-cup in one hand and a sandwich in the other, who wants to light a cigarette with a match. But, where the man would invent the idea of putting down the cup and sandwich—before picking up the cigarette and the match—this ant would have put down the sandwich and picked up the match, then it would have been down with the match and up with the cigarette, then down with the cigarette and up with the sandwich, then down with the cup and up with the cigarette, until finally it had put down the sandwich and picked up the match. It was inclined to rely on a series of accidents to achieve its object. It was patient, and did not think. When it had pulled the three dead ants into several positions, they would fall into line under the clod eventually, and that was its duty.

Wart watched the arrangements with a surprise which turned into vexation and then into dislike. He felt like asking why it did not think things out in advance—the annoyed feeling which people have on seeing a job being badly done. Later he began to wish that he could put several other questions, such as "Do you like being a sexton?" or "Are you a slave?" or even "Are you happy?"

The extraordinary thing was that he could not ask these questions. In order to ask them, he would have had to put them into ant language through his antennae—and he now discovered, with a helpless feeling, that there were no words for the things he wanted to say. There were no words for happiness, for freedom, for liking, nor were there any words for their opposites. He felt like a dumb man trying to shout "Fire!" The nearest he could get to Right or Wrong, even, was to say Done or Not Done.

The ant finished fiddling with its corpses and turned back down the pathway, leaving them in the haphazard order. It found that the Wart was in its way, so it stopped, waving its wireless aerials at him as if it were a tank. With its mute, menacing helmet of a face, and its hairiness, and the things like spurs on the front leg-joint, perhaps it was more like a knight-in-armour on an armoured horse: or like a combination of the two, a hairy centaur-in-armour.

It said "Hail, Barbarus!" again.

"Hail!"

"What are you doing?"

The boy answered truthfully: "I am not doing anything."

It was baffled by this for several seconds, as you would be if Einstein had told you his latest ideas about space. Then it extended the twelve joints of its aerial and spoke past him into the blue.

It said: "105978/UDC reporting from square five. There is an insane ant on square five. Over to you."

The word it used for insane was Not-Done. Later on, the Wart discovered that there were only two qualifications in the language, Done and Not-Done—which applied to all questions of value. If the seeds which the collectors found were sweet, they were Done seeds. If somebody had doctored them with corrosive sublimate, they would have been Not-Done seeds, and that was that. Even the moons, mammies, doves, etc., in the broadcasts were completely described when they were stated to be done ones.

The broadcast stopped for a moment, and the fruity voice said: "G.H.Q. replying to 105978/UDC. What is its number? Over."

The ant asked: "What is your number?"

"I don't know."

When this news had been exchanged with headquarters, a message came back to ask whether he could give an account of himself. The ant asked him. It used the same words as the broadcaster had used, and in the same voice. This made him feel uncomfortable and angry, two emotions which he disliked.

"Yes," he said sarcastically, for it was obvious that the creature could not detect sarcasm, "I have fallen on my head and can't remember anything about it."

"105978/UDC reporting. Not-Done ant has a black-out from falling off the nest. Over."

"G.H.Q. replying to 105978/UDC. Not-Done ant is number 42436/WD, who fell off the nest this morning while working with mash squad. If it is competent to continue its duties——" Competent-to-continue-its-duties was easier in the ant speech, for it was simply Done, like everything else that was not Not Done. But enough of the language question. "If it is competent to continue its duties, instruct 42436/WD to rejoin mash squad, relieving 210021/WD, who was sent to replace it. Over."

The creature repeated the message.

It seemed that he could not have made a better explanation than this one about falling on his head, even if he had meant to—for the ants did occasionally tumble off. They were a species of ant called Messor barbarus.

"Very well."

The sexton paid no further attention to him, but crawled off down the path for another body, or for anything else that needed to be scavenged.

The Wart took himself away in the opposite direction, to join the mash squad. He memorized his own number and the number of the unit who had to be relieved.

The mash squad were standing in one of the outer chambers of the fortress like a circle of worshippers. He joined the circle, announcing that 210021/WD was to return to the main nest. Then he began filling himself with the sweet mash like the others. They made it by scraping the seeds which others had collected, chewing up the scrapings till they made a kind of paste or soup, and then swallowing it into their own crops. At first it was delicious to him, so that he ate greedily, but in a few seconds it began to be unsatisfactory. He could not understand why. He chewed and swallowed busily, copying the rest of the squad, but it was like eating a banquet of nothing, or like a dinner-party on the stage. In a way it was like a nightmare, in which you might continue to consume huge masses of putty without being able to stop.

There was a coming and going round the pile of seeds. The ants who had filled their crops to the brim were walking back to the inner fortress, to be replaced by a procession of empty ants who were coming from the same direction. There were never any new ants in the procession, only this same dozen going backward and forward, as they would do during all their lives.

He realized suddenly that what he was eating was not going into his stomach. A small proportion of it had penetrated to his private self at the beginning, and now the main mass was being stored in a kind of upper stomach or crop, from which it could be removed. It dawned on him at the same time that when he joined the westward stream he would have to disgorge the store, into a larder or something of that sort.

The mash squad conversed with each other while they worked. He thought this was a good sign at first, and listened, to pick up what he could.

"Oh Ark!" one of them would say. "Ear comes that Mammy-mammy—mammy—mammy song again. I dew think that Mammy—mammy—mammy—mammy song is loverly (done). It is so high-class (done)."

Another would remark, "I dew think our beloved Leader is wonderful, don't yew? They sigh she was stung three hundred times in the last war, and was awarded the Ant Cross for Valour."

"How lucky we are to be born in the 'A' nest, don't yew think, and wouldn't it be hawful to be one of those orrid 'B's."

"Wasn't it hawful about 310099/WD! Of course e was hexecuted at once, by special order of ar beloved Leader."

"Oh Ark! Ear comes that Mammy—mammy—mammy—mammy song again. I dew think . . ."

He walked away to the nest with a full gorge, leaving them to do the round again. They had no news, no scandal, nothing to talk about. Novelties did not happen to them. Even the remarks about the executions were in a formula, and only varied as to the registration number of the criminal. When they had finished with the mammy—mammy—mammy—mammy, they had to go on to the beloved Leader, and then to the filthy Barbarus B and to the latest execution. It went round in a circle. Even the beloveds, wonderfuls, luckies and so on were all Dones, and the awfuls were Not-Dones.

The boy found himself in the hall of the fortress, where hundreds and hundreds of ants were licking or feeding in the nurseries, carrying grubs to various aisles to get an even temperature, and opening or closing the ventilation passages. In the middle, the Leader sat complacently, laying eggs, attending to the broadcasts, issuing directions or commanding executions, surrounded by a sea of adulation. (He learned from Merlyn later that the method of succession among these Leaders was variable according to the different kind of ant. In Bothriomyrmex, for instance, the ambitious founder of a

New Order would invade a nest of Tapinoma and jump on the back of the older tyrant. There, concealed by the smell of her host, she would slowly saw off the latter's head, until she herself had achieved the right of leadership.)

There was no larder for his store of mash, after all. When anybody wanted a meal, they stopped him, got him to open his mouth, and fed from it. They did not treat him as a person, and indeed, they were impersonal themselves. He was a dumb-waiter from which dumb-diners fed. Even his stomach was not his own.

But we need not go on about the ants in too much detail—they are not a pleasant subject. It is enough to say that the boy went on living among them, conforming to their habits, watching them so as to understand as much as he could, but unable to ask questions. It was not only that their language had not got the words in which humans are interested—so that it would have been *impossible* to ask them whether they believed in Life, Liberty and the Pursuit of Happiness—but also that it was dangerous to ask questions at all. A question was a sign of insanity to them. Their life was not questionable: it was dictated. He crawled from nest to seeds and back again, exclaimed that the Mammy song was loverly, opened his jaws to regurgitate, and tried to understand as well as he could.

Later in the afternoon a scouting ant wandered across the rush bridge which Merlyn had commanded him to make. It was an ant of exactly the same species, but it came from the other nest. It was met by one of the scavenging ants and murdered.

The broadcasts changed after this news had been reported—or rather, they changed as soon as it had been discovered by spies that the other nest had a good store of seeds.

Mammy—mammy—mammy gave place to *Antland, Antland Over All,* and the stream of orders were discontinued in favour of lectures about war, patriotism or the economic situation. The fruity voice said that their beloved country was being encircled by a horde of filthy Other-nesters—at which the wireless chorus sang:

> When Other blood spurts from the knife,
> Then everything is fine.

It also explained that Ant the Father had ordained in his wisdom that Othernest pismires should always be the slaves of Thisnest ones. Their beloved country had only one feeding tray at present—a disgraceful state of affairs which would have to be remedied if the dear race were not to perish. A third statement was that the national property of Thisnest was being threatened. Their boundaries were to be violated, their domestic animals, the beetles, were to be kidnapped, and their communal stomach would be starved. The Wart listened to two of these broadcasts carefully, so that he would be able to remember them afterwards.

The first one was arranged as follows:

A. We are so numerous that we are starving.
B. Therefore we must encourage still larger families so as to become yet more numerous and starving.
C. When we are so numerous and starving as all that, obviously we shall have a right to take other people's stores of seed. Besides, we shall by then have a numerous and starving army.

It was only after this logical train of thought had been put into practice, and the output of the nurseries trebled—both nests meanwhile getting ample mash for all their needs from Merlyn—for it has to be admitted that starving nations never seem to be quite so starving that they cannot afford to have far more expensive armaments than anybody else—it was only then that the second type of lecture was begun.

This is how the second kind went:

A. We are more numerous than they are, therefore we have a right to their mash.
B. They are more numerous than we are, therefore they are wickedly trying to steal our mash.
C. We are a mighty race and have a natural right to subjugate their puny one.
D. They are a mighty race and are unnaturally trying to subjugate our inoffensive one.
E. We must attack them in self-defence.
F. They are attacking us by defending themselves.
G. If we do not attack them today, they will attack us tomorrow.
H. In any case we are not attacking them at all. We are offering them incalculable benefits.

After the second kind of address, the religious services began. These dated—the Wart discovered later—from a fabulous past so ancient that one could scarcely find a date for it—a past in which the emmets had not yet settled down to communism. They came from a time when ants were still like men, and very impressive some of the services were.

A psalm at one of them—beginning, if we allow for the difference of language, with the well-known words, "The earth is the Sword's and all that therein is, the compass of the bomber and they that bomb therefrom"—ended with the terrific conclusion: "Blow up your heads, O ye Gates, and be ye blown up, ye Everlasting Doors, that the King of Glory may come in. Who is the King of Glory? Even the Lord of Ghosts, He is the King of Glory.''

A strange feature was that the ordinary ants were not excited by the songs, nor interested by the lectures. They accepted them as matters of course. They were rituals to them, like the Mammy songs or the conversations about their Beloved Leader. They did not look at these things as good or bad, exciting, rational or terrible. They did not look at them at all, but accepted them as Done.

The time for the war came soon enough. The preparations were in order, the soldiers were drilled to the last ounce, the walls of the nest had patriotic slogans written on them, such as *"Stings or Mash?"* or *"I Vow to Thee, my Smell,"* and the Wart was past hoping. The repeating voices in his head, which he could not shut off—the lack of privacy, under which others ate from his stomach while others again sang in his brain—the dreary blank which replaced feeling—the dearth of all but two values—the total monotony more than the wickedness: these had begun to kill the joy of life which belonged to his boyhood.

The horrible armies were on the point of joining battle, to dispute the imaginary boundary between their glass trays when Merlyn came to his rescue. He magicked the sickened explorer of animals back to bed, and glad enough he was to be there.

chapter fourteen

In the autumn everybody was preparing for the winter. At night they spent the time rescuing Daddy-long-legs from their candles and rushlights. In the daytime the cows were turned into the high stubble and weeds which had been left by the harvest sickles. The pigs were driven into the purlieus of the forest, where boys beat the trees to supply them with acorns. Everybody was at a different job. From the granary there proceeded an invariable thumping of flails; in the strip fields the slow and enormously heavy wooden ploughs sailed up and down for the rye and the wheat, while the sowers swung rhythmically along, with their hoffers round their necks, casting right hand for left foot and vice versa. Foraging parties came lumbering in with their spike-wheeled carts full of bracken, remarking wisely that they must:

> Get whome with ee breakes ere all summer be gone
> For tethered up cattle to sit down upon,

while others dragged in timber for the castle fires. The forest rang in the sharp air with the sound of beetle and wedge.

Everybody was happy. The Saxons were slaves to their Norman masters if you chose to look at it in one way—but, if you chose to look at it in another, they were the same farm labourers who get along on too few shillings a week today. Only neither the villein nor the farm labourer starved, when the master was a man like Sir Ector. It has never been an economic proposition for an owner of cattle to starve his cows, so why should an owner of slaves starve them? The truth is that even nowadays the farm labourer accepts so little money because he does not have to throw his soul in with the bargain—as he would have to do in a town— and the same freedom of spirit has obtained in the country since the earliest times. The villeins were labourers. They lived in the same one-roomed hut with their families, few chickens, litter of pigs, or with a cow possibly called Crumbocke—most dreadful and insanitary! But they liked it. They were healthy, free of an air with no factory smoke in it, and, which was most of all to them, their heart's interest was bound up with their skill in labour. They knew that Sir Ector was proud of them. They were more valuable to him than his cattle even, and, as he valued his cattle more than anything else except his children, this was saying a good deal. He walked and worked among his villagers, thought of their welfare, and could tell the good workman from the bad. He was the eternal farmer, in fact —one of those people who seem to be employing labour at so many shillings a week, but who are actually paying half as much again in voluntary overtime, providing a cottage free, and possibly making an extra present of milk and eggs and home-brewed beer into the bargain.

In other parts of Gramarye, of course, there did exist wicked and despotic masters—feudal gangsters whom it was to be King Arthur's destiny to chasten—

but the evil was in the bad people who abused it, not in the feudal system.

Sir Ector was moving through these activities with a brow of thunder. When an old lady who was sitting in a hedge by one of the strips of wheat, to scare away the rooks and pigeons, suddenly rose up beside him with an unearthly screech, he jumped nearly a foot in the air. He was in a nervous condition.

"Dang it," said Sir Ector. Then, considering the subject more attentively, he added in a loud, indignant voice, "Splendour of God!" He took the letter out of his pocket and read it again.

The Overlord of The Castle of Forest Sauvage was more than a farmer. He was a military captain, who was ready to organize and lead the defence of his estate against the gangsters, and he was a sportsman who sometimes took a day's joustin' when he could spare the time. But he was not only these. Sir Ector was an M.F.H.—or rather a Master of stag and other hounds —and he hunted his own pack himself. Clumsy, Trowneer, Phoebe, Colle, Gerland, Talbot, Luath, Luffra, Apollon, Orthros, Bran, Gelert, Bounce, Boy, Lion, Bungey, Toby, Diamond and Cavall were not pet dogs. They were the Forest Sauvage Hounds, no subscription, two days a week, huntsman the Master.

This is what the letter said, if we translate it from Latin:

The King to Sir Ector, etc.
We send you William Twyti, our huntsman, and his fellows to hunt in the Forest Sauvage with our boar-hounds (canibus nostris porkericis) in order that they may capture two or three boars. You are to cause the flesh they capture to be salted and kept in good condition, but the skins you are to cause to be bleached which they give you, as the said William shall tell you. And we

command you to provide necessaries for them as long as they shall be with you by our command, and the cost, etc., shall be accounted, etc.

Witnessed at the Tower of London, 20 November, in the twelfth year of our reign.

UTHER PENDRAGON
12 Uther.

Now the forest belonged to the King, and he had every right to send his hounds to hunt in it. Also he maintained a number of hungry mouths—what with his court and his army—so that it was natural that he should want as many dead boars, bucks, roes, etc., to be salted down as possible.

He was in the right. This did not take away the fact that Sir Ector regarded the forest as *his* forest, and resented the intrusion of the royal hounds—as if his own would not do just as well! The King had only to send for a couple of boars and he would have been delighted to supply them himself. He feared that his coverts would be disturbed by a lot of wild royal retainers—never know what these city chaps will be up to next—and that the King's huntsman, this fellow Twyti, would sneer at his humble hunting establishment, unsettle the hunt servants and perhaps even try to interfere with his own kennel management. In fact, Sir Ector was shy. Then there was another thing. Where the devil were the royal hounds to be kept? Was he, Sir Ector, to turn his own hounds into the street, so as to put the King's hounds in his kennels? "Splendour of God!" repeated the unhappy master. It was as bad as paying tithes.

Sir Ector put the accursed letter in his pocket and stumped off the ploughing. The villeins, seeing him go, remarked cheerfully, "Our wold measter be on the gad again seemingly."

It was a confounded piece of tyranny, that was what it was. It happened every year, but it was still that. He always solved the kennel problem in the same way, but it still worried him. He would have to invite his neighbours to the meet specially, to look as impressive as possible under the royal huntsman's eye, and this would mean sendin' messengers through the forest to Sir Grummore, etc. Then he would have to show sport. The King had written early, so that evidently he intended to send the fellow at the very beginnin' of the season. The season did not begin till the 25th of December. Probably the chap would insist on one of these damned Boxin' Day meets—all show-off and no business—with hundreds of foot people all hollerin' and headin' the boar and trampin' down the seeds and spoil-in' sport generally. How the devil was he to know in November where the best boars would be on Boxin' Day? What with sounders and gorgeaunts and hogsteers, you never knew where you were. And another thing. A hound that was going to be used next summer for the proper Hart huntin' was always entered at Christ-mas to the boar. It was the very beginnin' of his eddi-cation—which led up through hares and what-nots to its real quarry—and this meant that the fellow Twyti would be bringin' down a lot of raw puppies which would be nothin' but a plague to everybody. "Dang it!" said Sir Ector, and stamped upon a piece of mud.

He stood gloomily for a moment, watching his two boys trying to catch the last leaves in the chase. They had not gone out with that intention, and did not really, even in those distant days, believe that every leaf you caught would mean a happy month next year. Only, as the west wind tore the golden rags away, they looked fascinating and difficult to catch. For the mere sport of catching them, of shouting and laughing and

feeling giddy as they looked up, and of darting about
to trap the creatures, which were certainly alive in the
cunning with which they slipped away, the two boys
were prancing about like young fauns in the ruin of the
year. Wart's shoulder was well again.

The only chap, reflected Sir Ector, who could be
really useful in showin' the King's huntsman proper
sport was that fellow Robin Hood. Robin Wood, they
seemed to be callin' him now—some new-fangled idea,
no doubt. But Wood or Hood, he was the chap to know
where a fine tush was to be found. Been feastin' on the
creatures for months now, he would not be surprised,
even if they were out of season.

But you could hardly ask a fellow to hunt up a few
beasts of venery for you, and then not invite him to the
meet. While, if you did invite him to the meet, what
would the King's huntsman and the neighbours say at
havin' a partisan for a fellow guest? Not that this Robin
Wood was not a good fellow: he was a good chap, and
a good neighbour too. He had often tipped Sir Ector
the wink when a raiding party was on its way from the
Marches, and he never molested the knight or his farm-
ing in any way. What did it matter if he did chase himself a bit of venison now and then? There was four hundred square miles of forest, so they said, and enough
for all. Leave well alone, that was Sir Ector's motto.
But that did not alter the neighbours.

Another thing was the riot. It was all very well
for the crack hunts in practically artificial forests like
those at Windsor, where the King hunted, but it was a
different thing in the Forest Sauvage. Suppose His Majesty's famous hounds were to go runnin' riot after a
unicorn or something? Everybody knew that you could
never catch a unicorn without a young virgin for bait
(in which case the unicorn meekly laid its white head

and mother-of-pearl horn in her lap) and so the puppies would go chargin' off into the forest for leagues and leagues, and never catch it, and get lost, and then what would Sir Ector say to his sovereign? It was not only unicorns. There was the Beast Glatisant that everybody had heard so much about. If you had the head of a serpent, the body of a leopard, the haunches of a lion, and were footed like a hart, and especially if you made a noise like thirty couple of hounds questin', it stood to reason that you would account for an excessive number of royal puppies before they pulled you down. Serve them right too. And what would King Pellinore say if Master William Twyti did succeed in killing his beast? Then there were the small dragons which lived under stones and hissed like kettles—dangerous varmints, very. Or suppose they were to come across one of the really big dragons? Suppose they was to run into a griffin?

Sir Ector considered the prospect moodily for some time, then began to feel better. It would be a jolly good thing, he concluded, if Master Twyti and his beastly dogs did meet the Questing Beast, yes, and get eaten up by it too, every one.

Cheered by this vision, he turned round at the edge of the ploughing and stumped off home. At the hedge where the old lady lay waiting to scare rooks he was lucky enough to spot some approaching pigeons before she was aware of him or them, which gave him a chance to let out such a screech that he felt amply repaid for his own jump by seeing hers. It was going to be a good evening after all. "Good night to you," said Sir Ector affably, when the old lady recovered herself enough to drop him a curtsey.

He felt so much restored by this that he called on the parish priest, half-way up the village street, and invited him to dinner. Then he climbed to the solar, which was his special chamber, and sat down heavily to write a submissive message to King Uther in the two or three hours which remained to him before the meal. It would take him quite that time, what with sharpening pens, using too much sand to blot with, going to the top of the stairs to ask the butler how to spell things, and starting again if he had made a mess.

Sir Ector sat in the solar, while the wintering sunlight threw broad orange beams across his bald head. He scratched and pluttered away, and laboriously bit the end of his pen, and the castle room darkened about him. It was a room as big as the main hall over which it stood, and it could afford to have large southern windows because it was on the second story. There were two fireplaces, in which the ashy logs of wood turned from grey to red as the sunlight retreated. Round these, some favourite hounds lay snuffling in their dreams, or scratching themselves for fleas, or gnawing mutton bones which they had scrounged from the kitchens. The peregrine falcon stood hooded on a perch in the corner, a motionless idol dreaming of other skies.

If you were to go now to view the solar of Castle Sauvage, you would find it empty of furniture. But the sun would still stream in at those stone windows two feet thick, and, as it barred the mullions, it would catch a warmth of sandstone from them—the amber light of age. If you went to the nearest curiosity shop you might find some clever copies of the furniture which it was supposed to contain. These would be oak chests and cupboards with Gothic panelling and strange faces of men or angels—or devils—carved darkly upon them, black, bees-waxed, worm-eaten and shiny—gloomy testimonies to the old life in their coffin-like solidity. But the furniture in the solar was not like that. The devil's heads were there and the linen-fold panelling, but the wood was six or seven or eight centuries younger. So, in the warm-looking light of sunset, it was not only the mullions which had an amber glow. All the spare, strong chests in the room (they were converted for sitting by laying bright carpets on them) were the young, the golden oak, and the cheeks of the devils and cherubim shone as if they had been given a good soaping.

chapter fifteen

God Speed pe plough

It was Christmas night, the eve of the Boxing Day
Meet. You must remember that this was in the old
Merry England of Gramarye, when the rosy barons ate
with their fingers, and had peacocks served before them
with all their tail feathers streaming, or boars' heads
with the tusks stuck in again—when there was no un-
employment because there were too few people to be
unemployed—when the forests rang with knights wal-
loping each other on the helm, and the unicorns in the
wintry moonlight stamped with their silver feet and
snorted their noble breaths of blue upon the frozen air.
Such marvels were great and comfortable ones. But in
the Old England there was a greater marvel still. The
weather behaved itself.

In the spring, the little flowers came out obediently in the meads, and the dew sparkled, and the birds
sang. In the summer it was beautifully hot for no less
than four months, and, if it did rain just enough for
agricultural purposes, they managed to arrange it so that
it rained while you were in bed. In the autumn the
leaves flamed and rattled before the west winds, tem-
pering their sad adieu with glory. And in the winter,
which was confined by statute to two months, the snow
lay evenly, three feet thick, but never turned into slush.

It was Christmas night in the Castle of the Forest Sauvage, and all around the castle the snow lay as it ought to lie. It hung heavily on the battlements, like thick icing on a very good cake, and in a few convenient places it modestly turned itself into the clearest icicles of the greatest possible length. It hung on the boughs of the forest trees in rounded lumps, even better than apple-blossom, and occasionally slid off the roofs of the village when it saw the chance of falling on some amusing character and giving pleasure to all. The boys made snowballs with it, but never put stones in them to hurt each other, and the dogs, when they were taken out to scombre, bit it and rolled in it, and looked surprised but delighted when they vanished into the bigger drifts. There was skating on the moat, which roared with the gliding bones which they used for skates, while hot chestnuts and spiced mead were served on the bank to all and sundry. The owls hooted. The cooks put out plenty of crumbs for the small birds. The villagers brought out their red mufflers. Sir Ector's face shone redder even than these. And reddest of all shone the cottage fires down the main street of an evening, while the winds howled outside and the old English wolves wandered about slavering in an appropriate manner, or sometimes peeping in at the key-holes with their blood-red eyes.

It was Christmas night and the proper things had been done. The whole village had come to dinner in hall. There had been boar's head and venison and pork and beef and mutton and capons—but no turkey, because this bird had not yet been invented. There had been plum pudding and snap-dragon, with blue fire on the tips of one's fingers, and as much mead as anybody could drink. Sir Ector's health had been drunk with "Best respects, Measter," or "Best compliments of

the Season, my lords and ladies, and many of them.''
There had been mummers to play an exciting dramatic
presentation of a story in which St. George and a Saracen and a funny Doctor did surprising things, also
carol-singers who rendered ''Adeste Fideles'' and ''I
Sing of a Maiden,'' in high, clear, tenor voices. After
that, those children who had not been sick from their
dinner played Hoodman Blind and other appropriate
games, while the young men and maidens danced morris
dances in the middle, the tables having been cleared
away. The old folks sat round the walls holding glasses
of mead in their hands and feeling thankful that they
were past such capers, hoppings and skippings, while
those children who had been sick sat with them, and
soon went to sleep, the small heads leaning against
their shoulders. At the high table Sir Ector sat with his
knightly guests, who had come for the morrow's hunting, smiling and nodding and drinking burgundy or
sherries sack or malmsey wine.

After a bit, silence was prayed for Sir Grummore.
He stood up and sang his old school song, amid great
applause—but forgot most of it and had to make a humming noise in his moustache. Then King Pellinore was
nudged to his feet and sang bashfully:

> Oh, I was born a Pellinore in famous Lincolnshire.
> Full well I chased the Questing Beast for more than
>   seventeen year.
> Till I took up with Sir Grummore here
> In the season of the year.
> (Since when) 'tis my delight
> On a feather-bed night
> To sleep at home, my dear.

''You see,'' explained King Pellinore blushing, as
he sat down with everybody whacking him on the

back, "old Grummore invited me home, what, after
we had been having a pleasant joust together, and since
then I've been letting my beastly Beast go and hang itself on the wall, what?"

"Well done," they told him. "You live your own
life while you've got it."

William Twyti was called for, who had arrived on
the previous evening, and the famous huntsman stood
up with a perfectly straight face, and his crooked eye
fixed upon Sir Ector, to sing:

> D'ye ken William Twyti
>   With his jerkin so dagged?
> D'ye ken William Twyti
>   Who never yet lagged?
> Yes, I ken William Twyti,
>   And he ought to be gagged
> With his hounds and his horn in the morning.

"Bravo!" cried Sir Ector. "Did you hear that,
eh? Said he ought to be gagged, my dear feller. Blest
if I didn't think he was going to boast when he began.
Splendid chaps, these huntsmen, eh? Pass Master Twyti
the malmsey, with my compliments."

The boys lay curled up under the benches near the
fire, Wart with Cavall in his arms. Cavall did not like
the heat and the shouting and the smell of mead, and
wanted to go away, but Wart held him tightly because
he needed something to hug, and Cavall had to stay
with him perforce, panting over a long pink tongue.

"Now Ralph Passelewe." "Good wold Ralph."
"Who killed the cow, Ralph?" "Pray silence for
Master Passelewe that couldn't help it."

At this the most lovely old man got up at the
furthest and humblest end of the hall, as he had got up
on all similar occasions for the past half-century. He

was no less than eighty-five years of age, almost blind, almost deaf, but still able and willing and happy to quaver out the same song which he had sung for the pleasure of the Forest Sauvage since before Sir Ector was bound up in a kind of tight linen puttee in his cradle. They could not hear him at the high table—he was too far away in Time to be able to reach across the room—but everybody knew what the cracked voice was singing, and everybody loved it. This is what he sang:

Whe-an / Wold King-Cole / was a / wakkin doon-t'street,
H-e / saw a-lovely laid-y a / steppin-in-a-puddle. /
She-a / lifted hup-er-skeat /
For to /
   Hop acrorst ter middle, /
An ee / saw her / an-kel.
Wasn't that a fuddle? /
Ee could'ernt elp it, / ee Ad to.

There were about twenty verses of this song, in which Wold King Cole helplessly saw more and more things that he ought not to have seen, and everybody cheered at the end of each verse until, at the conclusion, old Ralph was overwhelmed with congratulations and sat down smiling dimly to a replenished mug of mead.

It was now Sir Ector's turn to wind up the proceedings. He stood up importantly and delivered the following speech:

"Friends, tenants and otherwise. Unaccustomed as I am to public speakin'—"

There was a faint cheer at this, for everybody recognized the speech which Sir Ector had made for the last twenty years, and welcomed it like a brother.

"—unaccustomed as I am to public speakin', it is my pleasant duty—I might say my *very* pleasant duty—to welcome all and sundry to this our homely feast. It has been a good year, and I say it without fear of contradiction, in pasture and plow. We all know how Crumbocke of Forest Sauvage won the first prize at Cardoyle Cattle Show for the second time, and one more year will win the cup outright. More power to the Forest Sauvage. As we sit down tonight, I notice some faces now gone from among us and some which have added to the family circle. Such matters are in the hands of an almighty Providence, to which we all feel thankful. We ourselves have been first created and then spared to enjoy the rejoicin's of this pleasant evening. I think we are all grateful for the blessin's which have been showered upon us. Tonight we welcome in our midst the famous King Pellinore, whose labours in riddin' our forest of the redoubtable Questin' Beast are known to all. God bless King Pellinore. (Hear, hear!) Also Sir Grummore Grummursum, a sportsman, though I say it to his face, who will stick to his mount as long as his Quest will stand up in front of him. (Hooray!) Finally, last but not least, we are honoured by a visit from His Majesty's most famous huntsman, Master William Twyti, who will, I feel sure, show us such sport tomorrow that we will rub our eyes and wish that a royal pack of hounds could always be huntin' in the Forest which we all love so well. (View-halloo and several recheats blown in imitation.) Thank you, my dear friends, for your spontaneous welcome to these gentlemen. They will, I know, accept it in the true and warmhearted spirit in which it is offered. And now it is time that I should bring my brief remarks to a close. Another year has almost sped and it is time that we should be lookin' forward to the challengin' future. What about the Cattle Show next year? Friends, I can only wish you a very Merry Christmas, and, after Father Sidebottom has said our Grace for us, we shall conclude with a singin' of the National Anthem.''

The cheers which broke out at the end of Sir Ector's speech were only just prevented, by several hushes, from drowning the last part of the vicar's Grace in Latin, and then everybody stood up loyally in the firelight and sang:

> God save King Pendragon,
> May his reign long drag on,
> God save the King.
> Send him most gorious,
> Great and uproarious,
> Horrible and Hoarious,
> God save our King.

The last notes died away, the hall emptied of its rejoicing humanity. Lanterns flickered outside, in the village street, as everybody went home in bands for fear of the moonlit wolves, and The Castle of the Forest Sauvage slept peacefully and lightless, in the strange silence of the holy snow.

chapter sixteen

The Wart got up early next morning. He made a determined effort the moment he woke, threw off the great bearskin rug under which he slept, and plunged his body into the biting air. He dressed furiously, trembling, skipping about to keep warm, and hissing blue breaths to himself as if he were grooming a horse. He broke the ice in a basin and dipped his face in it with a grimace like eating something sour, said A-a-ah, and rubbed his stinging cheeks vigorously with a towel. Then he felt quite warm again and scampered off to the emergency kennels, to watch the King's huntsman making his last arrangements.

Master William Twyti turned out in daylight to be a shrivelled, harassed-looking man, with an expression of melancholy on his face. All his life he had been forced to pursue various animals for the royal table, and, when he had caught them, to cut them up into proper joints. He was more than half a butcher. He had to know what parts the hounds should eat, and what parts should be given to his assistants. He had to cut everything up handsomely, leaving two vertebrae on the tail to make the chine look attractive, and almost ever since he could remember he had been either pursuing a hart or cutting it up into helpings.

He was not particularly fond of doing this. The harts and hinds in their herds, the boars in their singulars, the skulks of foxes, the richesses of martens, the bevies of roes, the cetes of badgers and the routs of wolves—all came to him more or less as something which you either skinned or flayed and then took home to cook. You could talk to him about os and argos, suet and grease, croteys, fewmets and fiants, but he only looked polite. He knew that you were showing off your knowledge of these words, which were to him a business. You could talk about a mighty boar which had nearly slashed you last winter, but he only stared at you with his distant eyes. He had been slashed sixteen times by mighty boars, and his legs had white weals of shiny flesh that stretched right up to his ribs. While you talked, he got on with whatever part of his profession he had in hand. There was only one thing which could move Master William Twyti. Summer or winter, snow or shine, he was running or galloping after boars and harts, and all the time his soul was somewhere else. Mention a *hare* to Master Twyti and, although he would still go on galloping after the wretched hart which seemed to be his destiny, he would gallop with one eye over his shoulder yearning for puss. It was the only thing he ever talked about. He was always being sent to one castle or another, all over England, and when he was there the local servants would fête him and keep his glass filled and ask him about his greatest hunts. He would answer distractedly in monosyllables. But if anybody mentioned a huske of hares he was all attention, and then he would thump his glass upon the table and discourse upon the marvels of this astonishing beast, declaring that you could never blow a menee for it, because the same hare could at one time be male and another time female, while it carried grease and croteyed and gnawed, which things no beast in the earth did except it.

Wart watched the great man in silence for some time, then went indoors to see if there was any hope of breakfast. He found that there was, for the whole castle was suffering from the same sort of nervous excitement which had got him out of bed so early, and even Merlyn had dressed himself in a pair of breeches which had been fashionable some centuries later with the University Beagles.

Boar-hunting was fun. It was nothing like badger-digging or covert-shooting or fox-hunting today. Perhaps the nearest thing to it would be ferreting for rabbits—except that you used dogs instead of ferrets, had a boar that easily might kill you, instead of a rabbit, and carried a boar-spear upon which your life depended instead of a gun. They did not usually hunt the boar on horseback. Perhaps the reason for this was that the boar season happened in the two winter months, when the old English snow would be liable to ball in your horse's hoofs and render galloping too dangerous. The result was that you were yourself on foot, armed only with steel, against an adversary who weighed a good deal more than you did and who could unseam you from the nave to the chaps, and set your head upon his battlements. There was only one rule in boar-hunting. It was: Hold on. If the boar charged, you had to drop on one knee and present your boar-spear in his direction. You held the butt of it with your right hand on the ground to take the shock, while you stretched your left arm to its fullest extent and kept the point toward the charging boar. The spear was as sharp as a razor, and it had a cross-piece about eighteen inches away from the point. This cross-piece or horizontal bar prevented the spear from going more than eighteen inches into his chest.

Without the cross-piece, a charging boar would have been capable of rushing right up the spear, even if it did go through him, and getting at the hunter like that. But with the cross-piece he was held away from you at a spear's length, with eighteen inches of steel inside him. It was in this situation that you had to hold on.

He weighed between ten and twenty score, and his one object in life was to heave and weave and side-step, until he could get at his assailant and champ him into chops, while the assailant's one object was not to let go of the spear, clasped tight under his arm, until somebody had come to finish him off. If he could keep hold of his end of the weapon, while the other end was stuck in the boar, he knew that there was at least a spear's length between them, however much the boar ran him round the forest. You may be able to understand, if you think this over, why all the sportsmen of the castle got up early for the Boxing Day Meet, and ate their breakfast with a certain amount of suppressed feeling.

"Ah," said Sir Grummore, gnawing a pork chop which he held in his fingers, "down in time for breakfast, hey?"

"Yes, I am," said the Wart.

"Fine huntin' mornin'," said Sir Grummore. "Got your spear sharp, hey?"

"Yes, I have, thank you," said the Wart. He went over to the sideboard to get a chop for himself.

"Come on, Pellinore," said Sir Ector. "Have a few of these chickens. You're eatin' nothin' this mornin'."

King Pellinore said, "I don't think I will, thank you all the same. I don't think I feel quite the thing, this morning, what?"

Sir Grummore took his nose out of his chop and inquired sharply, "Nerves?"

"Oh, no," cried King Pellinore. "Oh, no, really not that, what? I think I must have taken something last night that disagreed with me."

"Nonsense, my dear fellah," said Sir Ector, "here you are, just you have a few chickens to keep your strength up."

He helped the unfortunate King to two or three capons, and the latter sat down miserably at the end of the table, trying to swallow a few bits of them.

"Need them," said Sir Grummore meaningly, "by the end of the day, I dare say."

"Do you think so?"

"Know so," said Sir Grummore, and winked at his host.

The Wart noticed that Sir Ector and Sir Grummore were eating with rather exaggerated gusto. He did not feel that he could manage more than one chop himself, and, as for Kay, he had stayed away from the breakfast-room altogether.

When breakfast was over, and Master Twyti had been consulted, the Boxing Day cavalcade moved off to the Meet. Perhaps the hounds would have seemed rather a mixed pack to a master of hounds today. There were half a dozen black and white alaunts, which looked like greyhounds with the heads of bull-terriers or worse. These, which were the proper hounds for boars, wore muzzles because of their ferocity. The gaze-hounds, of which there were two taken just in case, were in reality nothing but greyhounds according to modern language, while the lymers were a sort of mixture between the bloodhound and the red setter of today. The latter had collars on, and were led with straps. The braches were like beagles, and trotted along with the master in the way that beagles always have trotted, and a charming way it is.

With the hounds went the foot-people. Merlyn, in his running breeches, looked rather like Lord Baden-Powell, except, of course, that the latter did not wear a beard. Sir Ector was dressed in "sensible" leather clothes—it was not considered sporting to hunt in armour—and he walked beside Master Twyti with that bothered and important expression which has always been worn by masters of hounds. Sir Grummore, just behind, was puffing and asking everybody whether they had sharpened their spears. King Pellinore had dropped back among the villagers, feeling that there was safety in numbers. All the villagers were there, every male soul on the estate from Hob the austringer down to old Wat with no nose, every man carrying a spear or a pitchfork or a worn scythe blade on a stout pole. Even some of the young women who were courting had come out, with baskets of provisions for the men. It was a regular Boxing Day Meet.

At the edge of the forest the last follower joined up. He was a tall, distinguished-looking person dressed in green, and he carried a seven-foot bow.

"Good morning, Master," he said pleasantly to Sir Ector.

"Ah, yes," said Sir Ector. "Yes, yes, good mornin', eh? Yes, good mornin'."

He led the gentleman in green aside and said in a loud whisper that could be heard by everybody, "For heaven's sake, my dear fellow, do be careful. This is the King's own huntsman, and those two other chaps are King Pellinore and Sir Grummore. Now do be a good chap, my dear fellow, and don't say anything controversial, will you, old boy, there's a good chap?"

"Certainly I won't," said the green man reassuringly, "but I think you had better introduce me to them."

Sir Ector blushed deeply and called out: "Ah, Grummore, come over here a minute, will you? I want to introduce a friend of mine, old chap, a chap called Wood, old chap—Wood with a W, you know, not an H. Yes, and this is King Pellinore. Master Wood —King Pellinore."

"Hail," said King Pellinore, who had not quite got out of the habit when nervous.

"How do?" said Sir Grummore. "No relation to Robin Hood I suppose?"

"Oh, not in the least," interrupted Sir Ector hastily. "Double you, double owe, dee, you know, like the stuff they make furniture out of—furniture, you know, and spears, and—well—spears, you know, and furniture."

"How do you do?" said Robin.

"Hail," said King Pellinore.

"Well," said Sir Grummore, "it is funny you should both wear green."

"Yes, it is funny, isn't it?" said Sir Ector anxiously. "He wears it in mournin' for an aunt of his, who died by fallin' out of a tree."

"Beg pardon, I'm sure," said Sir Grummore, grieved at having touched upon this tender subject— and all was well.

"Now, then, Mr. Wood," said Sir Ector when he had recovered. "Where shall we go for our first draw?"

As soon as this question had been put, Master Twyti was fetched into the conversation, and a brief confabulation followed in which all sorts of technical terms like "lesses" were bandied about. Then there was a long walk in the wintry forest, and the fun began.

Wart had lost the panicky feeling which had taken hold of his stomach when he was breaking his fast. The exercise and the snow-wind had breathed him, so that his eyes sparkled almost as brilliantly as the frost crystals in the white winter sunlight, and his blood raced with the excitement of the chase. He watched the lymerer who held the two bloodhound dogs on their leashes, and saw the dogs straining more and more as the boar's lair was approached. He saw how, one by one and ending with the gaze-hounds—who did not hunt by scent—the various hounds became uneasy and began to whimper with desire. He noticed Robin pause and pick up some lesses, which he handed to Master Twyti, and then the whole cavalcade came to a halt. They had reached the dangerous spot.

Boar-hunting was like cub-hunting to this extent, that the boar was attempted to be held up. The object of the hunt was to kill him as quickly as possible. Wart took up his position in the circle round the monster's lair, and knelt down on one knee in the snow, with the handle of his spear couched on the ground, ready for emergencies. He felt the hush which fell upon the company, and saw Master Twyti wave silently to the lymerer to uncouple his hounds. The two lymers plunged immediately into the covert which the hunters surrounded. They ran mute.

There were five long minutes during which nothing happened. The hearts beat thunderously in the circle, and a small vein on the side of each neck throbbed in harmony with each heart. The heads turned quickly from side to side, as each man assured himself of his neighbours, and the breath of life steamed away on the north wind sweetly, as each realized how beautiful life was, which a reeking tusk might, in a few seconds, rape away from one or another of them if things went wrong.

The boar did not express his fury with his voice. There was no uproar in the covert or yelping from the lymers. Only, about a hundred yards away from the Wart, there was suddenly a black creature standing on the edge of the clearing. It did not seem to be a boar particularly, not in the first seconds that it stood there. It had come too quickly to seem to be anything. It was charging Sir Grummore before the Wart had recognized what it was.

The black thing rushed over the white snow, throwing up little puffs of it. Sir Grummore—also looking black against the snow—turned a quick somersault in a larger puff. A kind of grunt, but no noise of falling, came clearly on the north wind, and then the boar was gone. When it was gone, but not before, the Wart knew certain things about it—things which he had not had time to notice while the boar was there. He remembered the rank mane of bristles standing upright on its razor back, one flash of a sour tush, the staring ribs, the head held low, and the red flame from a piggy eye.

Sir Grummore got up, dusting snow out of himself unhurt, blaming his spear. A few drops of blood were to be seen frothing on the white earth. Master Twyti put his horn to his lips. The alaunts were uncoupled as the exciting notes of the menee began to ring through the forest, and then the whole scene began to move. The lymers which had reared the boar—the proper word for dislodging—were allowed to pursue him to make them keen on their work. The braches gave musical tongue. The alaunts galloped baying through the drifts. Everybody began to shout and run.

"Avoy, avoy!" cried the foot-people. "Shahou, shahou! Avaunt, sire, avaunt!"

"Swef, swef!" cried Master Twyti anxiously. "Now, now, gentlemen, give the hounds room, if you please."

"I say, I say!" cried King Pellinore. "Did anybody see which way he went? What an exciting day, what? Sa sa cy avaunt, cy sa avaunt, sa cy avaunt!"

"Hold hard, Pellinore!" cried Sir Ector. "'Ware, hounds, man, 'ware hounds. Can't catch him yourself, you know. Il est hault. Il est hault!"

And "Til est ho," echoed the foot-people. "Tilly-ho," sang the trees. "Tally-ho," murmured the distant snow-drifts as the heavy branches, disturbed by the vibrations, slid noiseless puffs of sparkling powder to the muffled earth.

The Wart found himself running with Master Twyti.

It was like beagling in a way, except that it was beagling in a forest where it was sometimes difficult even to move. Everything depended on the music of the hounds and the various notes which the huntsman could blow to tell where he was and what he was doing. Without these the whole field would have been lost in two minutes—and even with them about half of it was lost in three.

Wart stuck to Twyti like a burr. He could move as quickly as the huntsman because, although the latter had the experience of a life-time, he himself was smaller to get through obstacles and had, moreover, been taught by Maid Marian. He noticed that Robin kept up too, but soon the grunting of Sir Ector and the baa-ing of King Pellinore were left behind. Sir Grummore had given in early, having had most of the breath knocked out of him by the boar, and stood far in the rear declaring that his spear could no longer be quite sharp. Kay had stayed with him, so that he should not get lost. The foot-people had been early mislaid because they did not understand the notes of the horn. Merlyn had torn his breeches and stopped to mend them up by magic.

The sergeant had thrown out his chest so far in crying Tally-ho and telling everybody which way they ought to run that he had lost all sense of place, and was leading a disconsolate party of villagers, in Indian file, at the double, with knees up, in the wrong direction. Hob was still in the running.

"Swef, swef," panted the huntsman, addressing the Wart as if he had been a hound. "Not so fast, master, they are going off the line."

Even as he spoke, Wart noticed that the hound music was weaker and more querulous.

"Stop," said Robin, "or we may tumble over him."

The music died away.

"Swef, swef!" shouted Master Twyti at the top of his voice. "Sto arere, so howe, so howe!" He swung his baldrick in front of him, and, lifting the horn to his lips, began to blow a recheat.

There was a single note from one of the lymers.

"Hoo arere," cried the huntsman.

The lymer's note grew in confidence, faltered, then rose to the full bay.

"Hoo arere! Here how, amy. Hark to Beaumont the valiant! Ho moy, ho moy, hole, hole, hole, hole."

The lymer was taken up by the tenor bells of the braches. The noises grew to a crescendo of excitement as the blood-thirsty thunder of the alaunts pealed through the lesser notes.

"They have him," said Twyti briefly, and the three humans began to run again, while the huntsman blew encouragement with Trou-rou-root.

In a small bushment the grimly boar stood at bay. He had got his hindquarters into the nook of a tree blown down by a gale, in an impregnable position. He stood on the defensive with his upper lip writhed back in a snarl. The blood of Sir Grummore's gash welled fatly among the bristles of his shoulder and down his leg, while the foam of his chops dropped on the blushing snow and melted it. His small eyes darted in every direction. The hounds stood round, yelling at his mask, and Beaumont, with his back broken, writhed at his feet. He paid no further attention to the living hound, which could do him no harm. He was black, flaming and bloody.

"So-ho," said the huntsman.

He advanced with his spear held in front of him, and the hounds, encouraged by their master, stepped forward with him pace by pace.

The scene changed as suddenly as a house of cards falling down. The boar was not at bay any more, but charging Master Twyti. As it charged, the alaunts closed in, seizing it fiercely by the shoulder or throat or leg, so that what surged down on the huntsman was not one boar but a bundle of animals. He dared not use his spear for fear of hurting the dogs. The bundle rolled forward unchecked, as if the hounds did not impede it at all. Twyti began to reverse his spear, to keep the charge off with its butt end, but even as he reversed it the tussle was upon him. He sprang back, tripped over a root, and the battle closed on top. The Wart pranced round the edge, waving his own spear in an agony, but there was nowhere where he dared to thrust it in. Robin dropped his spear, drew his falchion in the same movement, stepped into the huddle of snarls, and calmly picked an alaunt up by the leg. The dog did not let go, but there was space where its body had been. Into this space the falchion went slowly, once, twice, thrice. The whole superstructure stumbled, recovered itself, stumbled again, and sank down ponderously on its left side. The hunt was over.

Master Twyti drew one leg slowly from under the boar, stood up, took hold of his knee with his right hand, moved it inquiringly in various directions, nodded to himself and stretched his back straight. Then he picked up his spear without saying anything and limped over to Beaumont. He knelt down beside him and took his head on his lap. He stroked Beaumont's head and said, "Hark to Beaumont. Softly, Beaumont, mon amy. Oyez à Beaumont the valiant. Swef, le douce Beaumont, swef, swef." Beaumont licked his hand but could not wag his tail. The huntsman nodded to Robin, who was standing behind, and held the hound's eyes with his own. He said, "Good dog, Beaumont the valiant, sleep now, old friend Beaumont, good old dog." Then Robin's falchion let Beaumont out of this world, to run free with Orion and roll among the stars.

The Wart did not like to watch Master Twyti for a moment. The strange, leathery man stood up without saying anything and whipped the hounds off the corpse of the boar as he was accustomed to do. He put his horn to his lips and blew the four long notes of the mort without a quaver. But he was blowing the notes for a different reason, and he startled the Wart because he seemed to be crying.

The mort brought most of the stragglers up in due time. Hob was there already and Sir Ector came next, whacking the brambles aside with his boar-spear, puffing importantly and shouting, "Well done, Twyti. Splendid hunt, very. That's the way to chase a beast of venery, I will say. What does he weigh?" The others dribbled in by batches, King Pellinore bounding along and crying out, "Tally-ho! Tally-ho! Tally-ho!" in ignorance that the hunt was done. When informed of this, he stopped and said "Tally-ho, what?" in a feeble voice, then relapsed into silence. Even the sergeant's Indian file arrived in the end, still doubling with knees up, and were halted in the clearing while the sergeant explained to them with great satisfaction that if it had not been for him, all would have been lost. Merlyn appeared holding up his running shorts, having failed in his magic. Sir Grummore came stumping along with Kay, saying that it had been one of the finest points he had ever seen run, although he had not seen it, and then the butcher's business of the "undoing" was proceeded with apace.

Over this there was a bit of excitement. King Pellinore, who had really been scarcely himself all day, made the fatal mistake of asking when the hounds were going to be given their quarry. Now, as everybody knows, a quarry is a reward of entrails, etc., which is given to the hounds on the hide of the dead beast (sur le quir), and, as everybody else knows, a slain boar is not skinned. It is disembowelled without the hide being taken off, and, since there can be no hide, there can be no quarry. We all know that the hounds are rewarded with a fouail, or mixture of bowels and bread cooked over a fire, and, of course, poor King Pellinore had used the wrong word.

So King Pellinore was bent over the dead beast amid loud huzzas, and the protesting monarch was given a hearty smack with a sword blade by Sir Ector. The King then said, "I think you are all a lot of beastly cads," and wandered off mumbling into the forest.

The boar was undone, the hounds rewarded, and the foot-people, standing about in chattering groups because they would have got wet if they had sat down in the snow, ate the provisions which the young women had brought in baskets. A small barrel of wine which had been thoughtfully provided by Sir Ector was broached, and a good drink was had by all. The boar's feet were tied together, a pole was slipped between his legs, and two men hoisted it upon their shoulders. William Twyti stood back, and courteously blew the prise.

It was at this moment that King Pellinore reappeared. Even before he came into view they could hear him crashing in the undergrowth and calling out, "I say, I say! Come here at once! A most dreadful thing has happened!" He appeared dramatically upon the edge of the clearing, just as a disturbed branch, whose burden was too heavy, emptied a couple of hundred-weight of snow on his head. King Pellinore paid no attention. He climbed out of the snow heap as if he had not noticed it, still calling out, "I say. I say!"

"What is it, Pellinore?" shouted Sir Ector.

"Oh, come quick!" cried the King, and, turning round distracted, he vanished again into the forest.

"Is he all right," inquired Sir Ector, "do you suppose?"

"Excitable character," said Sir Grummore. "Very."

"Better follow up and see what he's doin'."

The procession moved off sedately in King Pellinore's direction, following his erratic course by the fresh tracks in the snow.

The spectacle which they came across was one for which they were not prepared. In the middle of a dead gorse bush King Pellinore was sitting, with the tears streaming down his face. In his lap there was an enormous snake's head, which he was patting. At the other end of the snake's head there was a long, lean, yellow body with spots on it. At the end of the body there were some lion's legs which ended in the slots of a hart.

"There, there," the King was saying. "I did not mean to leave you altogether. It was only because I wanted to sleep in a feather bed, just for a bit. I was coming back, honestly I was. Oh, please don't die, Beast, and leave me without any fewmets!"

When he saw Sir Ector, the King took command of the situation. Desperation had given him authority.

"Now, then, Ector," he exclaimed. "Don't stand there like a ninny. Fetch that barrel of wine along at once."

They brought the barrel and poured out a generous tot for the Questing Beast.

"Poor creature," said King Pellinore indignantly. "It has pined away, positively pined away, just because there was nobody to take an interest in it. How I could have stayed all that while with Sir Grummore and never given my old Beast a thought I really don't know. Look at its ribs, I ask you. Like the hoops of a barrel. And lying out in the snow all by itself, almost without the will to live. Come on, Beast, you see if you can't get down another gulp of this. It will do you good.

"Mollocking about in a feather bed," added the remorseful monarch, glaring at Sir Grummore, "like a—like a kidney!"

"But how did you—how did you find it?" faltered Sir Grummore.

"I happened on it. And small thanks to you. Running about like a lot of nincompoops and smacking each other with swords. I happened on it in this gorse bush here, with snow all over its poor back and tears in its eyes and nobody to care for it in the wide world. It's what comes of not leading a regular life. Before, it was all right. We got up at the same time, and quested for regular hours, and went to bed at half past ten. Now look at it. It has gone to pieces altogether, and it will be your fault if it dies. You and your bed."

"But, Pellinore!" said Sir Grummore. . . .

"Shut your mouth," replied the King at once. "Don't stand there bleating like a fool, man. Do something. Fetch another pole so that we can carry old Glatisant home. Now, then, Ector, haven't you got any sense? We must just carry him home and put him in front of the kitchen fire. Send somebody on to make some bread and milk. And you, Twyti, or whatever you choose to call yourself, stop fiddling with that trumpet of yours and run ahead to get some blankets warmed.

"When we get home," concluded King Pellinore, "the first thing will be to give it a nourishing meal, and then, if it is all right in the morning, I will give it a couple of hours' start and then hey-ho for the old life once again. What about that, Glatisant, hey? You'll tak' the high road and I'll tak' the low road, what? Come along, Robin Hood, or whoever you are—you may think I don't know, but I do—stop leaning on your bow with that look of negligent woodcraft. Pull yourself together, man, and get that muscle-bound sergeant to help you carry her. Now then, lift her easy. Come along, you chuckle-heads, and mind you don't trip. Feather beds and quarry, indeed; a lot of childish nonsense. Go on, advance, proceed, step forward, march! Feather brains, I call it, that's what I do.

"And as for you, Grummore," added the King, even after he had concluded, "you can just roll yourself up in your bed and stifle in it."

chapter seventeen

"I think it must be time," said Merlyn, looking at him over the top of his spectacles one afternoon, "that you had another dose of education. That is, as Time goes."

It was an afternoon in early spring and everything outside the window looked beautiful. The winter mantle had gone, taking with it Sir Grummore, Master Twyti, King Pellinore and the Questing Beast—the latter having revived under the influence of kindliness and bread and milk. It had bounded off into the snow with every sign of gratitude, to be followed two hours later by the excited King, and the watchers from the battlements had observed it confusing its snowy footprints most ingeniously, as it reached the edge of the chase. It was running backward, bounding twenty foot sideways, rubbing out its marks with its tail, climbing along horizontal branches, and performing many other tricks with evident enjoyment. They had also seen King Pellinore—who had dutifully kept his eyes shut and counted ten thousand while this was going on—becoming quite confused when he arrived at the difficult spot, and finally galloping off in the wrong direction with his brachet trailing behind him.

It was a lovely afternoon. Outside the schoolroom window the larches of the distant forest had already taken on the fullness of their dazzling green, the earth twinkled and swelled with a million drops, and every bird in the world had come home to court and sing. The village folk were forth in their gardens every evening, planting garden beans, and it seemed that, what with these emergencies and those of the slugs (coincidentally with the beans), the buds, the lambs, and the birds, every living thing had conspired to come out.

"What would you like to be?" asked Merlyn.

Wart looked out of the window, listening to the thrush's twice-done song of dew.

He said, "I have been a bird once, but it was only in the mews at night, and I never got a chance to fly. Even if one ought not to do one's education twice, do you think I could be a bird so as to learn about that?"

He had been bitten with the craze for birds which bites all sensible people in the spring, and which sometimes even leads to excesses like birds' nesting.

"I can see no reason why you should not," said the magician. "Why not try it at night?"

"But they will be asleep at night."

"All the better chance of seeing them, without their flying away. You could go with Archimedes this evening, and he would tell you about them."

"Would you do that, Archimedes?"

"I should love to," said the owl. "I was feeling like a little saunter myself."

"Do you know," asked the Wart, thinking of the thrush, "why birds sing, or how? Is it a language?"

"Of course it is a language. It is not a big language like human speech, but it is large."

"Gilbert White," said Merlyn, "remarks, or will remark, however you like to put it, that 'the language of birds is very ancient, and, like other ancient modes of speech, little is said, but much is intended.' He also says somewhere that 'the rooks, in the breeding season, attempt sometimes, in the gaiety of their hearts, to sing—but with no great success.'"

"I love rooks," said the Wart. "It is funny, but I think they are my favourite bird."

"Why?" asked Archimedes.

"Well, I like them. I like their sauce."

"Neglectful parents," quoted Merlyn, who was in a scholarly mood, "and saucy, perverse children."

"It is true," said Archimedes reflectively, "that all the corvidae have a distorted sense of humour."

Wart explained.

"I love the way they enjoy flying. They don't just fly, like other birds, but they fly for fun. It is lovely when they hoist home to bed in a flock at night, all cheering and making rude remarks and pouncing on each other in a vulgar way. They turn over on their backs sometimes and tumble out of the air, just to be ridiculous, or else because they have forgotten they are flying and have coarsely begun to scratch themselves for fleas, without thinking about it."

"They are intelligent birds," said Archimedes, "in spite of their low humour. They are one of the birds that have parliaments, you know, and a social system."

"Do you mean they have laws?"

"Certainly they have laws. They meet in the autumn, in a field, to talk them over."

"What sort of laws?"

"Oh, well, laws about the defence of the rookery, and marriage, and so forth. You are not allowed to marry outside the rookery, and, if you do become quite lost to all sense of decency, and bring back a sable virgin from a neighbouring settlement, then every-body pulls your nest to pieces as fast as you can build it up. They make you go into the suburbs, you know, and that is why every rookery has out-lying nests all round it, several trees away.''

"Another thing I like about them," said the Wart, "is their Go. They may be thieves and practical jokers, and they do quarrel and bully each other in a squawky way, but they have got the courage to mob their ene-mies. I should think it takes some courage to mob a hawk, even if there is a pack of you. And even while they are doing it they clown.''

"They are mobs," said Archimedes, loftily. "You have said the word."

"Well, they are larky mobs, anyway," said the Wart, "and I like them."

"What is your favourite bird?" asked Merlyn po-litely, to keep the peace.

Archimedes thought this over for some time, and then said, "Well, it is a large question. It is rather like asking you what is your favourite book. On the whole, however, I think that I must prefer the pigeon.''

"To eat?"

"I was leaving that side of it out," said the owl in civilized tones. "Actually the pigeon is the favourite dish of all raptors, if they are big enough to take her, but I was thinking of nothing but domestic habits.''

"Describe them."

"The pigeon," said Archimedes, "is a kind of Quaker. She dresses in grey. A dutiful child, a constant lover, and a wise parent, she knows, like all philoso-phers, that the hand of every man is against her. She has learned throughout the centuries to specialize in es-cape. No pigeon has ever committed an act of aggres-sion nor turned upon her persecutors: but no bird, likewise, is so skilful in eluding them. She has learned to drop out of a tree on the opposite side to man, and to fly low so that there is a hedge between them. No other bird can estimate a range so well. Vigilant, powdery, odorous and loose-feathered—so that dogs object to take them in their mouths—armoured against pellets by the padding of these feathers, the pigeons coo to one another with true love, nourish their cunningly hidden children with true solicitude, and flee from the aggressor with true philosophy—a race of peace lovers continually caravaning away from the destructive Indian in covered wagons. They are loving individualists surviving against the forces of massacre only by wisdom in escape.

"Did you know," added Archimedes, "that a pair of pigeons always roosts head to tail, so that they can keep a look-out in both directions?"

"I know our tame pigeons do," said the Wart. "I suppose the reason why people are always trying to kill them is because they are so greedy. What I like about wood-pigeons is the clap of their wings, and how they soar up and close their wings and sink, during their courting flights, so that they fly rather like woodpeckers."

"It is not very like woodpeckers," said Merlyn.

"No, it is not," admitted the Wart.

"And what is your favourite bird?" asked Archimedes, feeling that his master ought to be allowed a say.

Merlyn put his fingers together like Sherlock Holmes and replied immediately, "I prefer the chaffinch. My friend Linnaeus calls him coelebs or bachelor bird. The flocks have the sense to separate during the winter, so that all the males are in one flock and all the females in the other. For the winter months, at any rate, there is perfect peace."

"The conversation," observed Archimedes, "arose out of whether birds could talk."

"Another friend of mine," said Merlyn immediately, in his most learned voice, "maintains, or will maintain, that the question of the language of birds arises out of imitation. Aristotle, you know, also attributes tragedy to imitation."

Archimedes sighed heavily, and remarked in prophetic tones, "You had better get it off your chest."

"It is like this," said Merlyn. "The kestrel drops upon a mouse, and the poor mouse, transfixed with those needle talons, cries out in agony his one squeal of K-e-e-e! Next time the kestrel sees a mouse, his own soul cries out Kee in imitation. Another kestrel, perhaps his mate, comes to that cry, and after a few million years all the kestrels are calling each other with their individual note of Kee-kee-kee."

"You can't make the whole story out of one bird," said the Wart.

"I don't want to. The hawks scream like their prey. The mallards croak like the frogs they eat, the shrikes also, like these creatures in distress. The blackbirds and thrushes click like the snail shells they hammer to pieces. The various finches make the noise of cracking seeds, and the woodpecker imitates the tapping on wood which he makes to get the insects that he eats."

"But all birds don't give a single note!"

"No, of course not. The call note arises out of imitation and then the various bird songs are developed by repeating the call note and descanting upon it."

"I see," said Archimedes coldly. "And what about me?"

"Well, you know quite well," said Merlyn, "that the shrewmouse you pounce upon squeals out Kweek!

That is why the young of your species call Kee-wick.''

"And the old?'' inquired Archimedes sarcastically.

"Hooroo, Hooroo,'' cried Merlyn, refusing to be damped. "It is obvious, my dear fellow. After their first winter, that is the wind in the hollow trees where they prefer to sleep.''

"I see,'' said Archimedes, more coolly than ever. "This time, we note, it is not a question of prey at all.''

"Oh, come along,'' replied Merlyn. "There are other things besides the things you eat. Even a bird drinks sometimes, for instance, or bathes itself in water. It is the liquid notes of a river that we hear in a robin's song.''

"It seems now,'' said Archimedes, "that it is no longer a question of what we eat, but also what we drink or hear.''

"And why not?''

The owl said resignedly, "Oh, well.''

"I think it is an interesting idea,'' said the Wart, to encourage his tutor. "But how does a language come out of these imitations?''

"They repeat them at first,'' said Merlyn, "and then they vary them. You don't seem to realize what a lot of meaning there resides in the tone and the speed of voice. Suppose I were to say 'What a nice day,' just like that. You would answer, 'Yes, so it is.' But if I were to say, 'What a *nice* day,' in caressing tones, you might think I was a nice person. But then again, if I were to say, 'What a nice day,' quite breathless, you might look about you to see what had put me in a fright. It is like this that the birds have developed their language.''

"Would you mind telling us,'' said Archimedes, "since you know so much about it, how many various things we birds are able to express by altering the tempo and emphasis of the elaborations of our call-notes?''

"But a large number of things. You can cry Kee-wick in tender accents, if you are in love, or Kee-wick angrily in challenge or in hate: you can cry it on a rising scale as a call-note, if you do not know where your partner is, or to attract their attention away if strangers are straying near your nest: if you go near the old nest in the winter-time you may cry Kee-wick lovingly, a conditioned reflex from the pleasures which you once enjoyed within it, and if I come near to you in a startling way you may cry out Keewick-keewick-keewick, in loud alarm.''

"When we come to conditioned reflexes,'' remarked Archimedes sourly, "I prefer to look for a mouse.''

"So you may. And when you find it I dare say you will make another sound characteristic of owls, though not often mentioned in books of ornithology. I refer to the sound 'Tock' or 'Tck' which human beings call a smacking of the lips.''

"And what sound is that supposed to imitate?''

"Obviously, the breaking of mousy bones.''

"You are a cunning master,'' said Archimedes, "and as far as a poor owl is concerned you will just have to get away with it. All I can tell you from my personal experience is that it is not like that at all. A tit can tell you not only that it is in danger, but what kind of danger it is in. It can say, 'Look out for the cat,' or 'Look out for the hawk,' or 'Look out for the tawny owl,' as plainly as A.B.C.''

"I don't deny it,'' said Merlyn. "I am only telling you the beginnings of the language. Suppose you try to tell me the song of any single bird which I can't attribute originally to imitation?''

"The night-jar," said the Wart.

"The buzzing of the wings of beetles," replied his tutor at once.

"The nightingale," cried Archimedes desperately.

"Ah," said Merlyn, leaning back in his comfortable chair. "Now we are to imitate the soul-song of our beloved Proserpine, as she stirs to wake in all her liquid self."

"Tereu," said the Wart softly.

"Pieu," added the owl quietly.

"Music!" concluded the necromancer in ecstasy, unable to make the smallest beginnings of an imitation.

"Hallo," said Kay, opening the door of the afternoon school room. "I'm sorry I am late for the geography lesson. I was trying to get a few small birds with my cross-bow. Look, I have killed a thrush."

chapter eighteen

The Wart lay awake as he had been told to do. He was
to wait until Kay was asleep, and then Archimedes
would come for him with Merlyn's magic. He lay under the great bearskin and stared out of the window
at the stars of spring, no longer frosty and metallic, but
as if they had been new washed and had swollen with
the moisture. It was a lovely evening, without rain or
cloud. The sky between the stars was of the deepest
and fullest velvet. Framed in the thick western window, Aldebaran and Betelgeuse were racing Sirius over
the horizon, the hunting dog-star looking back to his
master Orion, who had not yet heaved himself above
the rim. In at the window came also the unfolding
scent of benighted flowers, for the currants, the wild
cherries, the plums and the hawthorn were already in
bloom, and no less than five nightingales within earshot were holding a contest of beauty among the bow-
ery, the looming trees.

Wart lay on his back with his bearskin half off him
and his hands clasped behind his head. It was too beautiful to sleep, too temperate for the rug. He watched
out at the stars in a kind of trance. Soon it would be
the summer again, when he could sleep on the battlements and watch these stars hovering as close as moths

above his face—and, in the Milky Way at least, with something of the mothy pollen. They would be at the same time so distant that unutterable thoughts of space and eternity would baffle themselves in his sighing breast, and he would imagine to himself how he was falling upward higher and higher among them, never reaching, never ending, leaving and losing everything in the tranquil speed of space.

He was fast asleep when Archimedes came for him.

"Eat this," said the owl, and handed him a dead mouse.

The Wart felt so strange that he took the furry atomy without protest, and popped it into his mouth without any feelings that it was going to be nasty. So he was not surprised when it turned out to be excellent, with a fruity taste like eating a peach with the skin on, though naturally the skin was not so nice as the mouse.

"Now, we had better fly," said the owl. "Just flip to the window-sill here, to get accustomed to yourself before we take off."

Wart jumped for the sill and automatically gave himself an extra kick with his wings, just as a high jumper swings his arms. He landed on the sill with a thump, as owls are apt to do, did not stop himself in time, and toppled straight out of the window. "This," he thought to himself, cheerfully, "is where I break my neck." It was curious, but he was not taking life seriously. He felt the castle walls streaking past him, and the ground and the moat swimming up. He kicked with his wings, and the ground sank again, like water in a leaking well. In a second that kick of his wings had lost its effect, and the ground was welling up. He kicked again. It was strange, going forward with the earth ebbing and flowing beneath him, in the utter silence of his down-fringed feathers.

"For heaven's sake," panted Archimedes, bobbing in the dark air beside him, "stop flying like a woodpecker. Anybody would take you for a Little Owl, if the creatures had been imported. What you are doing is to give yourself flying speed with one flick of your wings. You then rise on that flick until you have lost flying speed and begin to stall. Then you give another just as you are beginning to drop out of the air, and do a switch-back. It is confusing to keep up with you."

"Well," said the Wart recklessly, "if I stop doing this I shall go bump altogether."

"Idiot," said the owl. "Waver your wings all the time, like me, instead of doing these jumps with them."

The Wart did what he was told, and was surprised to find that the earth became stable and moved underneath him without tilting, in a regular pour. He did not feel himself to be moving at all.

"That's better."

"How curious everything looks," observed the boy with some wonder, now that he had time to look about him.

And, indeed, the world did look curious. In some ways the best description of it would be to say that it looked like a photographer's negative, for he was seeing one ray beyond the spectrum which is visible to human beings. An infra-red camera will take photographs in the dark, when we cannot see, and it will also take photographs in daylight. The owls are the same, for it is untrue that they can only see at night. They see in the day just as well, only they happen to possess the advantage of seeing pretty well at night also. So naturally they prefer to do their hunting then, when other creatures are more at their mercy. To the Wart the green trees would have looked whitish in the daytime, as if they were covered with apple blossom, and now, at night, everything had the same kind of different look. It was like flying in a twilight which had reduced everything to shades of the same colour, and, as in the twilight, there was a considerable amount of gloom.

"Do you like it?" asked the owl.

"I like it very much. Do you know, when I was a fish there were parts of the water which were colder or warmer than the other parts, and now it is the same in the air."

"The temperature," said Archimedes, "depends on the vegetation of the bottom. Woods or weeds, they make it warm above them."

"Well," said the Wart, "I can see why the reptiles who had given up being fishes decided to become birds. It certainly is fun."

"You are beginning to fit things together," remarked Archimedes. "Do you mind if we sit down?"

"How does one?"

"You must stall. That means you must drive yourself up until you lose flying speed, and then, just as you feel yourself beginning to tumble—why, you sit down. Have you never noticed how birds fly upward to perch? They don't come straight down on the branch, but dive below it and then rise. At the top of their rise they stall and sit down."

"But birds land on the ground too. And what about mallards on the water? They can't rise to sit on that."

"Well, it is perfectly possible to land on flat things, but more difficult. You have to glide in at stalling speed all the way, and then increase your wind resistance by cupping your wings, dropping your feet, tail, etc. You may have noticed that few birds do it gracefully. Look how a crow thumps down and how the mallard splashes. The spoon-winged birds like heron and plover seem to do it best. As a matter of fact, we owls are not so bad at it ourselves."

"And the long-winged birds like swifts, I suppose they are the worst, for they can't rise from a flat surface at all?"

"The reasons are different," said Archimedes, "yet the fact is true. But need we talk on the wing? I am getting tired."

"So am I."

"Owls usually prefer to sit down every hundred yards."

The Wart copied Archimedes in zooming up toward the branch which they had chosen. He began to fall just as they were above it, clutched it with his furry feet at the last moment, swayed backward and forward twice, and found that he had landed successfully. He folded up his wings.

While the Wart sat still and admired the view, his friend proceeded to give him a lecture about flight in birds. He told how, although the swift was so fine a flyer that he could sleep on the wing all night, and although the Wart himself had claimed to admire the way in which rooks enjoyed their flights, the real aeronaut of the lower strata—which cut out the swift— was the plover. He explained how plovers indulged in aerobatics, and would actually do such stunts as spins, stall turns and even rolls for the mere grace of the thing. They were the only birds which made a practice of slipping off height to land—except occasionally the oldest, gayest and most beautiful of all the conscious aeronauts, the raven. Wart paid little or no attention to the lecture, but got his eyes accustomed to the strange tones of light instead, and watched Archimedes from the corner of one of them. For Archimedes, while he was talking, was absent-mindedly spying for his dinner. This spying was an odd performance.

A spinning top which is beginning to lose its spin slowly describes circles with its highest point before falling down. The leg of the top remains in the same place, but the apex makes circles which get bigger and bigger toward the end. This is what Archimedes was absent-mindedly doing. His feet remained stationary, but he moved the upper part of his body round and round, like somebody trying to see from behind a fat lady at a cinema, and uncertain which side of her gave the best view. As he could also turn his head almost completely round on his shoulders, you may imagine that his antics were worth watching.

"What are you doing?" asked the Wart.

Even as he asked, Archimedes was gone. First there had been an owl talking about plover, and then there was no owl. Only, far below the Wart, there was a thump and a rattle of leaves, as the aerial torpedo went smack into the middle of a bush, regardless of obstructions.

In a minute the owl was sitting beside him again on the branch, thoughtfully breaking up a dead sparrow.

"May I do that?" asked the Wart, inclined to be blood-thirsty.

"As a matter of fact," said Archimedes, after waiting to crop his mouthful, "you may not. The magic mouse which turned you into an owl will be enough for you—after all, you have been eating as a human all day—and no owl kills for pleasure. Besides, I am supposed to be taking you for education, and, as soon as I have finished my snack here, that is what we shall have to do.''

''Where are you going to take me?''

Archimedes finished his sparrow, wiped his beak politely on the bough, and turned his eyes full on the Wart. These great, round eyes had, as a famous writer has expressed it, a bloom of light upon them like the purple bloom of powder on a grape.

''Now that you have learned to fly,'' he said, ''Merlyn wants you to try the Wild Geese.''

The place in which he found himself was absolutely flat. In the human world we seldom see flatness, for the trees and houses and hedges give a serrated edge to the landscape. Even the grass sticks up with its myriad blades. But here, in the belly of the night, the illimitable, flat, wet mud was as featureless as a dark junket. If it had been wet sand, even, it would have had those little wave marks, like the palate of your mouth.

In this enormous flatness, there lived one element —the wind. For it was an element. It was a dimension, a power of darkness. In the human world, the wind comes from somewhere, and goes somewhere, and, as it goes, it passes through somewhere—through trees or streets or hedgerows. This wind came from nowhere. It was going through the flatness of nowhere, to no place. Horizontal, soundless except for a peculiar boom, tangible, infinite, the astounding dimensional weight of it streamed across the mud. You could have ruled it with a straight-edge. The titanic grey line of it was unwavering and solid. You could have hooked the crook of your umbrella over it, and it would have hung there.

The Wart, facing into this wind, felt that he was uncreated. Except for the wet solidity under his webbed feet, he was living in nothing—a solid nothing, like chaos. His were the feelings of a point in geometry, existing mysteriously on the shortest distance between two points: or of a line, drawn on a plane surface which had length, breadth but no magnitude. No magnitude! It was the very self of magnitude. It was power, current, force, direction, a pulseless world-stream steady in limbo.

Bounds had been set to this unhallowed purgatory. Far away to the east, perhaps a mile distant, there was an unbroken wall of sound. It surged a little, seeming to expand and contract, but it was solid. It was menacing, being desirous for victims—for it was the huge, remorseless sea.

Two miles to the west, there were three spots of light in a triangle. They were the weak wicks from fishermen's cottages, who had risen early to catch a tide in the complicated creeks of the salt marsh. Its waters sometimes ran contrary to the ocean. These were the total features of his world—the sea sound and the three small lights: darkness, flatness, vastness, wetness: and, in the gulf of night, the gulf-stream of the wind.

When daylight began to come, by premonition, the boy found that he was standing among a crowd of people like himself. They were seated on the mud, which now began to be disturbed by the angry, thin, returning sea, or else were already riding on the water, wakened by it, outside the annoyance of the surf. The seated ones were large teapots, their spouts tucked under their wings. The swimming ones sometimes ducked their heads and shook them. Some, waking on the mud, stood up and wagged their wings vigorously. Their profound silence became broken by a conversational gabble. There were about four hundred of them in the grey vicinity—very beautiful creatures, the wild White-fronted Geese, whom, once he has seen them close, no man ever forgets.

Long before the sun came, they were making ready for flight. Family parties of the previous year's breeding were coming together in batches, and these batches were themselves inclined to join with others, possibly under the command of a grandfather, or else of a great-grandfather, or else of some noted leader in the host. When the drafts were complete, there came a faint tone of excitement into their speech. They began moving their heads from side to side in jerks. And then, turning into the wind, suddenly they would all be in the air together, fourteen or forty at a time, with wide wings scooping the blackness and a cry of triumph in their throats. They would wheel round, climbing rapidly, and be gone from sight. Twenty yards up, they were invisible in the dark. The earlier departures were not vocal. They were inclined to be taciturn before the sun came, only making occasional remarks, or crying their single warning-note if danger threatened. Then, at the warning, they would all rise vertically to the sky.

The Wart began to feel an uneasiness in himself. The dim squadrons about him, setting out minute by minute, infected him with a tendency. He became restless to embrace their example, but he was shy. Perhaps their family groups, he thought, would resent his intrusion. Yet he wanted not to be lonely. He wanted to join in, and to enjoy the exercise of morning flight, which was so evidently a pleasure. They had a comradeship, free discipline and *joie de vivre*.

When the goose next to the boy spread her wings and leaped, he did so automatically. Some eight of those

nearby had been jerking their bills, which he had imi-
tated as if the act were catching, and now, with these
same eight, he found himself on pinion in the horizontal air. The moment he had left the earth, the wind had
vanished. Its restlessness and brutality had dropped away
as if cut off by a knife. He was in it, and at peace.

The eight geese spread out in line astern, evenly
spaced, with him behind. They made for the east, where
the poor lights had been, and now, before them, the
bold sun began to rise. A crack of orange-vermilion
broke the black cloud-bank far beyond the land. The
glory spread, the salt marsh growing visible below. He
saw it like a featureless moor or bogland, which had
become maritime by accident—its heather, still looking like heather, having mated with the seaweed until
it was a salt wet heather, with slippery fronds. The
burns which should have run through the moorland
were of sea-water on blueish mud. There were long
nets here and there, erected on poles, into which un-
wary geese might fly. These, he now guessed, had been
the occasions for those warning-notes. Two or three
widgeon hung in one of them, and, far away to the
eastward, a fly-like man was plodding over the slob in
tiny persistence, to collect his bag.

The sun, as it rose, tinged the quick-silver of the
creeks and the gleaming slime itself with flame. The
curlew, who had been piping their mournful plaints
since long before the light, flew now from weed-bank
to weed-bank. The widgeon, who had slept on water,
came whistling their double notes, like whistles from
a Christmas cracker. The mallard toiled from land,
against the wind. The redshanks scuttled and prodded
like mice. A cloud of tiny dunlin, more compact than
starlings, turned in the air with the noise of a train.

The black-guard of crows rose from the pine trees on the dunes with merry cheers. Shore birds of every sort populated the tide line, filling it with business and beauty.

The dawn, the sea-dawn and the mastery of ordered flight, were of such intense beauty that the boy was moved to sing. He wanted to cry a chorus to life, and, since a thousand geese were on the wing about him, he had not long to wait. The lines of these creatures, wavering like smoke upon the sky as they breasted the sunrise, were all at once in music and in laughter. Each squadron of them was in different voice, some larking, some triumphant, some in sentiment or glee. The vault of daybreak filled itself with heralds, and this is what they sang:

> You turning world, pouring beneath our pinions,
> Hoist the hoar sun to welcome morning's minions.
>
> See, on each breast the scarlet and vermilion,
> Hear, from each throat the clarion and carillion.
>
> Hark, the wild wandering lines in black battalions,
> Heaven's horns and hunters, dawn-bright hounds and
>   stallions.
>
> Free, free: far, far: and fair on wavering wings
> Comes Anser albifrons, and sounds, and sings.

He was in a coarse field, in daylight. His companions of the flight were grazing round him, plucking the grass with sideways wrenches of their soft small bills, bending their necks into abrupt loops, unlike the graceful curves of the swan. Always, as they fed, one of their number was on guard, its head erect and snakelike. They had mated during the winter months, or else in previous winters, so that they tended to feed in pairs within the family and squadron. The young female, his neighbour of the mud-flats, was in her first year. She kept an intelligent eye upon him.

The boy, watching her cautiously, noted her plump compacted frame and a set of neat furrows on her neck. These furrows, he saw out of the corner of his eye, were caused by a difference in the feathering. The feathers were concave, which separated them from one another, making a texture of ridges which he considered graceful.

Presently the young goose gave him a shove with her bill. She had been acting sentry.

"You next," she said.

She lowered her head without waiting for an answer, and began to graze in the same movement. Her feeding took her from his side.

He stood sentry. He did not know what he was watching for, nor could he see any enemy, except the tussocks and his nibbling mates. But he was not sorry to be a trusted sentinel for them.

"What are you doing?" she asked, passing him after half an hour.

"I was on guard."

"Go on with you," she said with a giggle, or should it be a gaggle? "You are a silly!"

"Why?"

"You know."

"Honestly," he said, "I don't. Am I doing it wrong? I don't understand."

"Peck the next one. You have been on for twice your time, at least."

He did as she told him, at which the grazer next to them took over, and then he walked along to feed beside her. They nibbled, noting one another out of beady eyes.

"You think I am stupid," he said shyly, confessing the secret of his real species for the first time to an animal, "but it is because I am not a goose. I was born as a human. This is my first flight really."

She was mildly surprised.

"It is unusual," she said. "The humans generally try the swans. The last lot we had were the Children of Lir. However, I suppose we're all anseriformes together."

"I have heard of the Children of Lir."

"They didn't enjoy it. They were hopelessly nationalistic and religious, always hanging about round one of the chapels in Ireland. You could say that they hardly noticed the other swans at all."

"I am enjoying it."

"I thought you were. What were you sent for?"

"To learn my education."

They grazed in silence, until his own words reminded him of something he had wanted to ask.

"The sentries," he asked. "Are we at war?"

She did not understand the word.

"War?"

"Are we fighting people?"

"Fighting?" she asked doubtfully. "The men fight sometimes, about their wives and that. Of course there is no bloodshed—only scuffling, to find the better man. Is that what you mean?"

"No. I meant fighting against armies—against other geese, for instance."

She was amused.

"How ridiculous! You mean a lot of geese all scuffling at the same time. It would be fun to watch."

Her tone surprised him, for his heart was still a kind one, being a boy's.

"Fun to watch them kill each other?"

"To kill each other? An army of geese to kill each other?"

She began to understand this idea slowly and doubtfully, an expression of distaste coming over her face. When it had sank in, she left him. She went away to another part of the field in silence. He followed, but she turned her back. Moving round to get a glimpse of her eyes, he was startled by their dislike—a look as if he had made some obscene suggestion.

He said lamely: "I am sorry. I don't understand."

"Leave talking about it."

"I am sorry."

Later he added, with annoyance, "A person can ask, I suppose. It seems a natural question, with the sentries."

But she was thoroughly angry.

"Will you stop about it at once! What a horrible mind you must have! You have no right to say such things. And of course there are sentries. There are the jer-falcons and the peregrines, aren't there: the foxes and the ermines and the humans with their nets? These are natural enemies. But what creature could be so low as to go about in bands, to murder others of its own blood?"

"Ants do," he said obstinately. "And I was only trying to learn."

She relented with an effort to be good-natured. She wanted to be broad-minded if she could, for she was rather a blue-stocking.

"My name is Lyo-lyok. You had better call yourself Kee-kwa, and then the rest will think you came from Hungary."

"Do you all come here from different places?"

"Well, in parties, of course. There are some here from Siberia, some from Lapland and I can see one or two from Iceland."

"But don't they fight each other for the pasture?"

"Dear me, you are a silly," she said. "There are no boundaries among the geese."

"What are boundaries, please?"

"Imaginary lines on the earth, I suppose. How can you have boundaries if you fly? Those ants of yours —and the humans too—would have to stop fighting in the end, if they took to the air."

"I like fighting," said the Wart. "It is knightly."

"Because you're a baby."

chapter nineteen

There was something magical about the time and space commanded by Merlyn, for the Wart seemed to be passing many days and nights among the grey people, during the one spring night when he had left his body asleep under the bearskin.

He grew to be fond of Lyo-lyok, in spite of her being a girl. He was always asking her questions about the geese. She taught him what she knew with gentle kindness, and the more he learned, the more he came to love her brave, noble, quiet and intelligent relations. She told him how every White-front was an individual—not governed by laws or leaders, except when they came about spontaneously. They had no Kings like Uther, no laws like the bitter Norman ones. They did not own things in common. Any goose who found something nice to eat considered it his own, and would peck any other one who tried to thieve it. At the same time, no goose claimed any exclusive territorial right in any part of the world—except its nest, and that was private property. She told him a great deal about migration.

"The first goose," she said, "I suppose, who made the flight from Siberia to Lincolnshire and back again must have brought up a family in Siberia. Then, when the winter came and it was necessary to find new food, he must have groped his way over the same route, being the only one who knew it. He will have been followed by his growing family, year after year, their pilot and their admiral. When the time came for him to die, obviously the next best pilots would have been his eldest sons, who would have covered the route more often than the others. Naturally the younger sons and fledglings would have been uncertain about it, and therefore would have been glad to follow somebody who knew. Perhaps, among the eldest sons, there would have been some who were famous for being muddle-headed, and the family would hardly care to trust to them.

"This," she said, "is how an admiral is elected. Perhaps Wink-wink will come to our family in the autumn, and he will say: 'Excuse me, but have you by any chance got a reliable pilot in your lot? Poor old grand-dad died at cloud-berry time, and Uncle Onk is inefficient. We were looking for somebody to follow.' Then we will say: 'Great-uncle will be delighted if you care to hitch up with us; but mind, we cannot take responsibility if things go wrong.' 'Thank you very much,' he will say. 'I am sure your great-uncle can be relied on. Do you mind if I mention this matter to the Honks, who are, I happen to know, in the same dificulty?' 'Not at all.'

"And that," she explained, "is how Great-uncle became an admiral."

"It is a good way."

"Look at his bars," she said respectfully, and they both glanced at the portly patriarch, whose breast was indeed barred with black stripes, like the gold rings on an admiral's sleeve.

There was a growing excitement among the host. The young geese flirted outrageously, or collected in parties to discuss their pilots. They played games, too, like children excited at the prospect of a party. One of these games was to stand in a circle, while the junior ganders, one after another, walked into the middle of it with their heads stretched out, pretending to hiss. When they were half-way across the circle they would run the last part, flapping their wings. This was to show how brave they were, and what excellent admirals they would make, when they grew up. Also the strange habit of shaking their bills sideways, which was usual before flight, began to grow upon them. The elders and sages, who knew the migration routes, became uneasy also. They kept a wise eye on the cloud formations, summing up the wind, and the strength of it, and what airt it was coming from. The admirals, heavy with responsibility, paced their quarter-decks with ponderous tread.

"Why am I restless?" he asked. "Why do I have this feeling in my blood?"

"Wait and see," she said mysteriously. "Tomorrow, perhaps, or the day after. . . ."

When the day came, there was a difference about the salt marsh and the slob. The ant-like man, who had walked out so patiently every sunrise to his long nets, with the tides fixed firmly in his head—because to make a mistake in them was certain death—heard a far bugle in the sky. He saw no thousands on the mud flats, and there were none in the pastures from which he had come. He was a nice man in his way—for he stood still solemnly, and took off his leather hat. He did this every spring religiously, when the wild geese left him, and every autumn, when he saw the first returning gaggle.

In a steamer it takes two or three days to cross the North Sea—so many hours of slobbering through the viscous water. But for the geese, for the sailors of the air, for the angled wedges tearing clouds to tatters, for the singers of the sky with the gale behind them—seventy miles an hour behind another seventy—for those mysterious geographers—three miles up, they say—with cumulus for their floor instead of water—for them it was a different matter.

The songs they sang were full of it. Some were vulgar, some were sagas, some were light-hearted to a degree. One silly one which amused the Wart was as follows:

> We wander the sky with many a Cronk
> And land in the pasture fields with a Plonk.
> Hank-hank, Hink-hink, Honk-honk.
>
> Then we bend our necks with a curious kink
> Like the bend which the plumber puts under the sink.
> Honk-honk, Hank-hank, Hink-hink.
>
> And we feed away in a sociable rank
> Tearing the grass with a sideways yank.
> Hink-hink, Honk-honk, Hank-hank.
>
> But Hink or Honk we relish the Plonk,
> And Honk or Hank we relish the Rank,
> And Hank or Hink we think it a jink
> To Honk or Hank or Hink!

A sentimental one was:

> Wild and free, wild and free,
> Bring back my gander to me, to me.

And once, while they were passing over a rocky island populated by barnacle geese, who looked like spinsters in black leather gloves, grey toques and jet beads, the entire squadron burst out derisively with:

> Branta bernicla sits a-slumming in the slob,
> Branta bernicla sits a-slumming in the slob,
> Branta bernicla sits a-slumming in the slob,
>   While we go sauntering along.
> Glory, glory, here we go, dear.
> Glory, glory, here we go, dear.
> Glory, glory, here we go, dear.
>   To the North Pole sauntering along.

One of the more Scandinavian songs was called "The Boon of Life":

> Ky-yow replied: The boon of life is health.
> Paddle-foot, Feather-straight, Supple-neck, Button-eye:
> These have the world's wealth.
>
> Aged Ank answered: Honour is our all.
> Path-finder, People-feeder, Plan-provider, Sage-commander:
> These hear the call.
>
> Lyo-lyok the lightsome said: Love I had liefer.
> Douce-down, Tender-tread, Warm-nest and Walk-in-line:
> These live for ever.
>
> Aahng-ung was for Appetite. Ah, he said, Eating!
> Gander-gobble, Tear-grass, Stubble-stalk, Stuff-crop:
> These take some beating.
>
> Wink-wink praised Comrades, the fair free fraternity.
> Line-astern, Echelon, Arrow-head, Over-cloud:
> These learn Eternity.
>
> But I, Lyow, choose Lay-making, of loud lilts which linger.
> Horn-music, Laughter song, Epic-heart, Ape-the-world:
> These Lyow, the singer.

Sometimes, when they came down from the cirrus levels to catch a better wind, they would find themselves among the flocks of cumulus—huge towers of modelled vapour, looking as white as Monday's washing and as solid as meringues. Perhaps one of these piled-up blossoms of the sky, these snow-white droppings of a gigantic Pegasus, would lie before them several miles away. They would set their course toward it, seeing it grow bigger silently and imperceptibly, a motionless growth—and then, when they were at it, when they were about to bang their noses with a shock against its seeming solid mass, the sun would dim. Wraiths of mist suddenly moving like serpents of the air would coil about them for a second. Grey damp would be around them, and the sun, a copper penny, would fade away. The wings next to their own wings would shade into vacancy, until each bird was a lonely sound in cold annihilation, a presence after uncreation. And there they would hang in chartless nothing, seemingly without speed or left or right or top or bottom, until as suddenly as ever the copper penny glowed and the serpents writhed. Then, in a moment of time, they would be in the jewelled world once more—a sea under them like turquoise and all the gorgeous palaces of heaven new created, with the dew of Eden not yet dry.

One of the peaks of the migration came when they passed a rock-cliff of the ocean. There were other peaks, when, for instance, their line of flight was crossed by an Indian file of Bewick Swans who were off to Abisko, making a noise as they went like little dogs barking through handkerchiefs, or when they overtook a horned owl plodding manfully along—among the warm feathers of whose back, *so they said,* a tiny wren was taking her free ride. But the lonely island was the best.

It was a town of birds. They were all hatching, all quarrelling, all friendly nevertheless. On top of the cliff, where the short turf was, there were myriads of puffins busy with their burrows. Below them, in Razor-bill Street, the birds were packed so close, and on such narrow ledges, that they had to stand with their backs to the sea, holding tight with long toes. In Guillemot Street, below that, the guillemots held their sharp, toy-like faces upward, as thrushes do when hatching. Lowest of all, there were the Kittiwake Slums. And all the birds—who, like humans, only laid one egg each—were jammed so tight that their heads were interlaced—had so little of this famous living-space of ours that, when a new bird insisted on landing at a ledge which was already full, one of the other birds had to tumble off. Yet they were in good humour, so cheerful and cockneyfied and teasing one another. They were like an innumerable crowd of fish-wives on the largest grandstand in the world, breaking out into private disputes, eating out of paper bags, chipping the referee, singing comic songs, admonishing their children and complaining of their husbands. "Move over a bit, Auntie," they said, or "Shove along, Grandma"; "There's that Flossie gone and sat on the shrimps"; "Put the toffee in your pocket, dearie, and blow your nose"; "Lawks, if it isn't Uncle Albert with the beer"; "Any room for a little 'un?"; "There goes Aunt Emma, fallen off the ledge"; "Is me hat on straight?"; "Crikey, this isn't arf a do!"

They kept more or less to their own kind, but they were not mean about it. Here and there, in Guillemot Street, there would be an obstinate Kittiwake sitting on a projection and determined to have her rights. Perhaps there were ten thousand of them, and the noise they made was deafening.

Then there were the fiords and islands of Norway. It was about one of these islands, by the way, that the great W. H. Hudson related a true goose-story which ought to make people think. There was a coastal farmer, he tells us, whose islands suffered under a nuisance of foxes—so he set up a fox-trap on one of them. When he visited the trap next day, he found that an old wild goose had been caught in it, obviously a Grand Admiral, because of his toughness and his heavy bars. This farmer took the goose home alive, pinioned it, bound up its leg, and turned it out with his own ducks and poultry in the farmyard. Now one of the effects of the fox plague was that the farmer had to lock his henhouse at night. He used to go round in the evening to drive them in, and then he would lock the door. After a time, he began to notice a curious circumstance, which was that the hens, instead of having to be collected, would be found waiting for him in the hut. He watched the process one evening, and discovered that the captive potentate had taken on himself the responsibility, which he had with his own intelligence observed. Every night at locking-up time, the sagacious old admiral would round up his domestic comrades, whose leadership he had assumed, and would prudently assemble them in the proper place by his own efforts, as if he had fully understood the situation. Nor did the free wild geese, his sometime followers, ever again settle on the other island—previously a haunt of theirs—from which their captain had been spirited away.

Last of all, beyond the islands, there was the landing at their first day's destination. Oh, the whiffling of delight and self-congratulation! They tumbled out of the sky, side-slipping, stunting, even doing spinning nosedives. They were proud of themselves and of their pilot, agog for the family pleasures which were in store.

They planed for the last part on down-curved wings. At the last moment they scooped the wind with them, flapping them vigorously. Next—bump—they were on the ground. They held their wings above their heads for a moment, then folded them with a quick and pretty neatness. They had crossed the North Sea.

"Well, Wart," said Kay in an exasperated voice, "do you want all the rug? And why do you heave and mutter so? You were snoring, too."

"I don't snore," replied the Wart indignantly.

"You do."

"I don't."

"You do. You honk like a goose."

"I don't."

"You do."

"I don't. And you snore worse."

"No, I don't."

"Yes, you do."

"How can I snore worse if you don't snore at all?"

By the time they had thrashed this out, they were late for breakfast. They dressed hurriedly and ran out into the spring.

chapter twenty

It was hay-making again, and Merlyn had been with them a year. The wind had visited them, and the snow, and the rain, and the sun once more. The boys looked longer in the leg, but otherwise everything was the same.

Six other years passed by.

Sometimes Sir Grummore came on a visit. Sometimes King Pellinore could be descried galloping over the purlieus after the Beast, or with the Beast after him if they happened to have got muddled up. Cully lost the vertical stripes of his first year's plumage and became greyer, grimmer, madder, and distinguished by smart horizontal bars where the long stripes had been. The merlins were released every winter and new ones caught again next year. Hob's hair went white. The sergeant-at-arms developed a pot-belly and nearly died of shame, but continued to cry out One-Two, in a huskier voice, on every possible occasion. Nobody else seemed to change at all, except the boys.

These grew longer. They ran like wild colts as before, and went to see Robin when they had a mind to, and had innumerable adventures too lengthy to be recorded.

Merlyn's extra tuition went on just the same—for in those days even the grown-up people were so childish that they saw nothing uninteresting in being turned into owls. The Wart was changed into countless different animals. The only difference was that now, in their fencing lessons, Kay and his companion were an easy match for the pot-bellied sergeant, and paid him back accidentally for many of the buffets which he had once given them. They had more and more proper weapons as presents, when they had reached their 'teens, until in the end they had full suits of armour and bows nearly six feet long, which would shoot the cloth-yard shaft. You were not supposed to use a bow longer than your own height, for it was considered that by doing so you were expending unnecessary energy, rather like using an elephant-gun to shoot an *ovis ammon* with. At any rate, modest men were careful not to over-bow themselves. It was a form of boasting.

As the years went by, Kay became more difficult. He always used a bow too big for him, and did not shoot very accurately with it either. He lost his temper and challenged nearly everybody to have a fight, and in those few cases where he did actually have the fight he was invariably beaten. Also he became sarcastic. He made the sergeant miserable by nagging about his stomach, and went on at the Wart about his father and mother when Sir Ector was not about. He did not seem to want to do this. It was as if he disliked it, but could not help it.

The Wart continued to be stupid, fond of Kay, and interested in birds.

Merlyn looked younger every year—which was only natural, because he was.

Archimedes was married, and brought up several handsome families of quilly youngsters in the tower room.

Sir Ector got sciatica. Three trees were struck by lightning. Master Twyti came every Christmas without altering a hair. Master Passelewe remembered a new verse about King Cole.

The years passed regularly and the Old English snow lay as it was expected to lie—sometimes with a Robin Redbreast in one corner of the picture, a church bell or lighted window in the other—and in the end it was nearly time for Kay's initiation as a full-blown knight. Proportionately as the day became nearer, the two boys drifted apart—for Kay did not care to associate with the Wart any longer on the same terms, because he would need to be more dignified as a knight, and could not afford to have his squire on intimate terms with him. The Wart, who would have to be the squire, followed him about disconsolately as long as he was allowed to do so, and then went off full miserably to amuse himself alone, as best he might.

He went to the kitchen.

"Well, I am a Cinderella now," he said to himself. "Even if I have had the best of it for some mysterious reason, up to the present time—in our education—now I must pay for my past pleasures and for seeing all those delightful dragons, witches, fishes, cameleopards, pismires, wild geese and such like, by being a second-rate squire and holding Kay's extra spears for him, while he hoves by some well or other and jousts with all comers. Never mind, I have had a good time while it lasted, and it is not such bad fun being a Cinderella, when you can do it in a kitchen which has a fireplace big enough to roast an ox."

And the Wart looked round the busy kitchen, which was coloured by the flames till it looked like hell, with sorrowful affection.

The education of any civilized gentleman in those days used to go through three stages, page, squire,

knight, and at any rate the Wart had been through the
first two of these. It was rather like being the son of a
modern gentleman who has made his money out of
trade, for your father started you on the bottom rung
even then, in your education of manners. As a page,
Wart had learned to lay the tables with three cloths and
a carpet, and to bring meat from the kitchen, and to
serve Sir Ector or his guests on bended knee, with one
clean towel over his shoulder, one for each visitor, and
one to wipe the basins. He had been taught all the
noble arts of servility, and, from the earliest time that
he could remember, there had lain pleasantly in the end
of his nose the various scents of mint—used to freshen
the water in the ewers—or of basil, camomile, fennel,
hysop and lavender—which he had been taught to strew
on the rushy floors—or of the angelica, saffron, aniseed,
and tarragon, which were used to spice the savouries
which he had to carry. So he was accustomed to the
kitchen, quite apart from the fact that everybody who
lived in the castle was a friend of his, who might be
visited on any occasion.

Wart sat in the enormous firelight and looked
about him with pleasure. He looked upon the long
spits which he had often turned when he was smaller,
sitting behind an old straw target soaked in water, so
that he would not be roasted himself, and upon the
ladles and spoons whose handles could be measured in
yards, with which he had been accustomed to baste the
meat. He watched with water in his mouth the arrangements for the evening meal—a boar's head with a
lemon in its jaws and split almond whiskers, which
would be served with a fanfare of trumpets—a kind of
pork pie with sour apple juice, peppered custard, and
several birds' legs, or spiced leaves sticking out of the

top to show what was in it—and a most luscious-looking frumenty. He said to himself with a sigh, "It is not so bad being a servant after all."

"Still sighing?" asked Merlyn, who had turned up from somewhere. "As you were that day when we went to watch King Pellinore's joust?"

"Oh, no," said the Wart. "Or rather, oh yes, and for the same reason. But I don't really mind. I am sure I shall make a better squire than old Kay would. Look at the saffron going into that frumenty. It just matches the fire-light on the hams in the chimney."

"It is lovely," said the magician. "Only fools want to be great."

"Kay won't tell me," said the Wart, "what happens when you are made a knight. He says it is too sacred. What does happen?"

"Only a lot of fuss. You will have to undress him and put him into a bath hung with rich hangings, and then two experienced knights will turn up—probably Sir Ector will get hold of old Grummore and King Pellinore—and they will both sit on the edge of the bath and give him a long lecture about the ideals of chivalry such as they are. When they have done, they will pour some of the bath water over him and sign him with the cross, and then you will have to conduct him into a clean bed to get dry. Then you dress him up as a hermit and take him off to the chapel, and there he stays awake all night, watching his armour and saying prayers. People say it is lonely and terrible for him in this vigil, but it is not at all lonely really, because the vicar and the man who sees to the candles and an armed guard, and probably you as well, as his esquire, will have to sit up with him at the same time. In the morning you lead him off to bed to have a good sleep—as soon as he has confessed and heard mass and offered a candle with a piece of money stuck into it as near the lighted end as possible—and then, when all are rested, you dress him up again in his very best clothes for dinner. Before dinner you lead him into the hall, with his spurs and sword all ready, and King Pellinore puts on the first spur, and Sir Grummore puts on the second, and then Sir Ector girds on the sword and kisses him and smacks him on the shoulder and says, 'Be thou a good knight.'"

"Is that all?"

"No. You go to the chapel again then, and Kay offers his sword to the vicar, and the vicar gives it back to him, and after that our good cook over there meets him at the door and claims his spurs as a reward, and says, 'I shall keep these spurs for you, and if at any time you don't behave as a true knight should do, why, I shall pop them in the soup.'"

"That is the end?"

"Yes, except for the dinner."

"If I were to be made a knight," said the Wart, staring dreamily into the fire, "I should insist on doing my vigil by myself, as Hob does with his hawks, and I should pray to God to let me encounter all the evil in the world in my own person, so that if I conquered there would be none left, and, if I were defeated, I would be the one to suffer for it."

"That would be extremely presumptuous of you," said Merlyn, "and you would be conquered, and you would suffer for it."

"I shouldn't mind."

"Wouldn't you? Wait till it happens and see."

"Why do people not think, when they are grown up, as I do when I am young?"

"Oh dear," said Merlyn. "You are making me feel confused. Suppose you wait till you are grown up and know the reason?"

"I don't think that is an answer at all," replied the Wart, justly.

Merlyn wrung his hands.

"Well, anyway," he said, "suppose they did not let you stand against all the evil in the world?"

"I could ask," said the Wart.

"You could ask," repeated Merlyn.

He thrust the end of his beard into his mouth, stared tragically at the fire, and began to munch it fiercely.

chapter twenty-one

The day for the ceremony drew near, the invitations to King Pellinore and Sir Grummore were sent out, and the Wart withdrew himself more and more into the kitchen.

"Come on, Wart, old boy," said Sir Ector ruefully. "I didn't think you would take it so bad. It doesn't become you to do this sulkin'."

"I am not sulking," said the Wart. "I don't mind a bit and I am very glad that Kay is going to be a knight. Please don't think I am sulking."

"You are a good boy," said Sir Ector. "I know you're not sulkin' really, but do cheer up. Kay isn't such a bad stick, you know, in his way."

"Kay is a splendid chap," said the Wart. "Only I was not happy because he did not seem to want to go hawking or anything, with me, any more."

"It is his youthfulness," said Sir Ector. "It will all clear up."

"I am sure it will," said the Wart. "It is only that he does not want me to go with him, just at the moment. And so, of course, I don't go.

"But I will go," added the Wart. "As soon as he commands me, I will do exactly what he says. Honestly,

I think Kay is a good person, and I was not sulking a bit.''

"You have a glass of this canary," said Sir Ector, "and go and see if old Merlyn can't cheer you up.''

"Sir Ector has given me a glass of canary," said the Wart, "and sent me to see if you can't cheer me up.''

"Sir Ector," said Merlyn, "is a wise man.''

"Well," said the Wart, "what about it?''

"The best thing for being sad," replied Merlyn, beginning to puff and blow, "is to learn something. That is the only thing that never fails. You may grow old and trembling in your anatomies, you may lie awake at night listening to the disorder of your veins, you may miss your only love, you may see the world about you devastated by evil lunatics, or know your honour trampled in the sewers of baser minds. There is only one thing for it then—to learn. Learn why the world wags and what wags it. That is the only thing which the mind can never exhaust, never alienate, never be tortured by, never fear or distrust, and never dream of regretting. Learning is the thing for you. Look at what a lot of things there are to learn—pure science, the only purity there is. You can learn astronomy in a lifetime, natural history in three, literature in six. And then, after you have exhausted a milliard lifetimes in biology and medicine and theocriticism and geography and history and economics—why, you can start to make a cartwheel out of the appropriate wood, or spend fifty years learning to begin to learn to beat your adversary at fencing. After that you can start again on mathematics, until it is time to learn to plough.''

"Apart from all these things," said the Wart, "what do you suggest for me just now?''

"Let me see," said the magician, considering. "We have had a short six years of this, and in that time I think I am right in saying that you have been many kinds of animal, vegetable, mineral, etc.—many things in earth, air, fire and water?"

"I don't know much," said the Wart, "about the animals and earth."

"Then you had better meet my friend the badger."

"I have never met a badger."

"Good," said Merlyn. "Except for Archimedes, he is the most learned creature I know. You will like him.

"By the way," added the magician, stopping in the middle of his spell, "there is one thing I ought to tell you. This is the last time I shall be able to turn you into anything. All the magic for that sort of thing has been used up, and this will be the end of your education. When Kay has been knighted my labours will be over. You will have to go away then, to be his squire in the wide world, and I shall go elsewhere. Do you think you have learned anything?"

"I have learned, and been happy."

"That's right, then," said Merlyn. "Try to remember what you learned."

He proceeded with the spell, pointed his wand of lignum vitae at the Little Bear, which had just begun to glow in the dimity as it hung by its tail from the North Star, and called out cheerfully, "Have a good time for the last visit. Give love to Badger."

The call sounded from far away, and Wart found himself standing by the side of an ancient tumulus, like an enormous mole hill, with a black hole in front of him.

"Badger lives in there," he said to himself, "and I am supposed to go and talk to him. But I won't. It was bad enough never to be a knight, but now my own dear tutor that I found on the only Quest I shall ever have is to be taken from me also, and there will be no more natural history. Very well, I will have one more night of joy before I am condemned, and, as I am a wild beast now, I will be a wild beast, and there it is."

So he trundled off fiercely over the twilight snow, for it was winter.

If you are feeling desperate, a badger is a good thing to be. A relation of the bears, otters and weasels, you are the nearest thing to a bear now left in England, and your skin is so thick that it makes no difference who bites you. So far as your own bite is concerned, there is something about the formation of your jaw which makes it almost impossible to be dislocated—and so, however much the thing you are biting twists about, there is no reason why you should ever let go. Badgers are one of the few creatures which can munch up hedgehogs unconcernedly, just as they can munch up everything else from wasps' nests and roots to baby rabbits.

It so happened that a sleeping hedgehog was the first thing which came in the Wart's way.

"Hedge-pig," said the Wart, peering at his victim with blurred, short-sighted eyes, "I am going to munch you up."

The hedgehog, which had hidden its bright little eye-buttons and long sensitive nose inside its curl, and which had ornamented its spikes with a not very tasteful arrangement of dead leaves before going to bed for the winter in its grassy nest, woke up at this and squealed most lamentably.

"The more you squeal," said the Wart, "the more I shall gnash. It makes my blood boil within me."

"Ah, Measter Brock," cried the hedgehog, holding himself tight shut. "Good Measter Brock, show mercy to a poor urchin and don't 'ee be tyrannical. Us be'nt no common tiggy, measter, for to be munched and mumbled. Have mercy, kind sir, on a harmless, flea-bitten crofter which can't tell his left hand nor his right."

"Hedge-pig," said the Wart remorselessly, "forbear to whine, neither thrice nor once."

"Alas, my poor wife and childer!"

"I bet you have not got any. Come out of that, thou tramp. Prepare to meet thy doom."

"Measter Brock," implored the unfortunate pig, "come now, doan't 'ee be okkerd, sweet Measter Brock, my duck. Hearken to an urchin's prayer! Grant the dear boon of life to this most uncommon tiggy, lordly measter, and he shall sing to thee in numbers sweet or teach 'ee how to suck cow's milk in the pearly dew."

"Sing?" asked the Wart, quite taken aback.

"Aye, sing," cried the hedgehog. And it began hurriedly to sing in a very placating way, but rather muffled because it dared not uncurl.

"Oh, Genevieve," it sang most mournfully into its stomach, "Sweet Genevieve,

> Ther days may come,
> Ther days may go,
> But still the light of Mem'ry weaves
> Those gentle dreams
> Of long ago."

It also sang, without pausing for a moment between the songs, *Home Sweet Home* and *The Old Rustic Bridge by the Mill*. Then, because it had finished its repertoire, it drew a hurried but quavering breath, and began again on *Genevieve*. After that, it sang *Home Sweet Home* and *The Old Rustic Bridge by the Mill*.

"Come," said the Wart, "you can stop that. I won't bite you."

"Clementious measter," whispered the hedge-pig humbly. "Us shall bless the saints and board of governors for thee and for thy most kindly chops, so long as fleas skip nor urchins climb up chimbleys."

Then, for fear that its brief relapse into prose might have hardened the tyrant's heart, it launched out breathlessly into *Genevieve,* for the third time.

"Stop singing," said the Wart, "for heaven's sake. Uncurl. I won't do you any harm. Come, you silly little urchin, and tell me where you learned these songs."

"Uncurl is one word," answered the porpentine tremblingly—it did not feel in the least fretful at the moment—"but curling up is still another. If 'ee was to see my liddle naked nose, measter, at this dispicuous moment, 'ee might feel a twitching in thy white toothsomes; and all's fear in love and war, that we do know. Let us sing to 'ee again, sweet Measter Brock, concerning thic there rustic mill?"

"I don't want to hear it any more. You sing it very well, but I don't want it again. Uncurl, you idiot, and tell me where you learned to sing."

"Us be'nt no common urchin," quavered the poor creature, staying curled up as tight as ever. "Us wor a-teuk when liddle by one of them there gentry, like, as it might be from the mother's breast. Ah, doan't 'ee nip our tender vitals, lovely Measter Brock, for ee wor a proper gennelman, ee wor, and brought us up full comely on cow's milk an' that, all supped out from a lordly dish. Ah, there be'nt many urchins what a drunken water outer porcelain, that there be'nt."

"I don't know what you are talking about," said the Wart.

"Ee wor a gennelman," cried the hedgehog desperately, "like I tell 'ee. Ee teuk un when us wor liddle, and fed un when us ha'nt no more. Ee wor a proper gennelman what fed un in ter parlour, like what no urchins ha'nt been afore nor since; fed out from gennelman's porcelain, aye, and a dreary day it wor whenever us left un for nought but wilfulness, that thou may'st be sure."

"What was the name of this gentleman?"

"Ee wor a gennelman, ee wor. Ee hadden no proper neame like, not like you may remember, but ee wor a gennelman, that ee wor, and fed un out a porcelain."

"Was he called Merlyn?" asked the Wart curiously.

"Ah, that wor is neame. A proper fine neame it wor, but us never lay tongue to it by nary means. Ah, Mearn ee called to iself, and fed un out a porcelain, like a proper fine gennelman."

"Oh, do uncurl," exclaimed the Wart. "I know the man who kept you, and I think I saw you, yourself, when you were a baby in cotton wool at his cottage. Come on, urchin, I am sorry I frightened you. We are friends here, and I want to see your little grey wet twitching nose, just for old time's sake."

"Twitching noase be one neame," answered the hedgehog obstinately, "and a-twitching of that noase be another, measter. Now you move along, kind Measter Brock, and leave a poor crofter to teak 'is winter drowse. Let you think of beetles or honey, sweet baron, and flights of angels sing thee to thy rest."

"Nonsense," exclaimed the Wart. "I won't do you any harm, because I knew you when you were little."

"Ah, them badgers," said the poor thing to its stomach, "they go a-barrowing about with no harm in their hearts, Lor bless 'em, but doan't they fair give you a nip without a-noticing of it, and Lor bless 'ee what is a retired mun to do? It's that there skin of theirs, that's what it be, which from earliest childer they've been a-nipping of among each other, and also of their ma's, without a-feeling of anything among theirselves, so natural they nips elsewhere like the seame. Now my poor gennelman, Measter Mearn, they was allars a-rushing arter his ankels, with their yik-yik-yik, when they wanted to be fed like, those what ee kept from liddles—and, holy church, how ee would scream! Aye, 'tis a mollocky thing to deal with they badgers, that us may be sure.

"Doan't see nothing," added the hedgehog, before the Wart could protest. "Blunder along like one of they ambling hearth rugs, on the outsides of their girt feet. Get in their way for a moment, just out of fortune like, without nary wicked intention and 'tis snip-snap, just like that, out of self-defence for the hungry blind, and then where are you?

"On'y pleace us can do for un," continued the urchin, "is to hit un on ter noase. A killee's heel they neame un on ter scriptures. Hit one of they girt trollops on ter noase, bim-bam, like that 'ere, and the sharp life is fair outer him ere ee can snuffle. 'Tis a fair knock-out, that it is.

"But how can a pore urchin dump un on ter noase? When ee ha'nt got nothing to dump with, nor way to hold 'un? And then they comes about 'ee and asks 'ee for to uncurl!''

"You need not uncurl," said the Wart resignedly. "I am sorry I woke you up, chap, and I am sorry I frightened you. I think you are a charming hedgehog, and meeting you has made me feel more cheerful again.

You just go off to sleep like you were when I met you, and I shall go to look for my friend badger, as I was told to do. Good night, urchin, and good luck in the snow.''

"Good night it may be,'' muttered the pig grumpily. "And then again it mayern't. First it's uncurl and then it's curl. One thing one moment, and another thing ter next. Hey-ho, 'tis a turvey world. But Good night, Ladies, is my motter, come hail, come snow, and so us shall be continued in our next.''

With these words the humble animal curled himself up still more snugly than before, gave several squeaky grunts, and was far away in a dream-world so much deeper than our human dreams as a whole winter's sleep is longer than the quiet of a single night.

"Well,'' thought the Wart, "he certainly gets over his troubles pretty quickly. Fancy going to sleep again as quick as that. I dare say he was never more than half-awake all the time, and will think it was only a dream when he gets up properly in the spring.''

He watched the dirty little ball of leaves and grass and fleas for a moment, curled up tightly inside its hole, then grunted and moved off toward the badger's sett, following his own oblong footmarks backward in the snow.

"So Merlyn sent you to me,'' said the badger, "to finish your education. Well, I can only teach you two things—to dig, and love your home. These are the true end of philosophy.''

"Would you show me your home?''

"Certainly,'' said the badger, "though, of course, I don't use it all. It is a rambling old place, much too big for a single man. I suppose some parts of it may be a thousand years old. There are about four families of us in it, here and there, take it by and large, from cellar to attics, and sometimes we don't meet for months. A crazy old place, I suppose it must seem to you modern people—but there, it's cosy.''

He went ambling down the corridors of the enchanted sett, rolling from leg to leg with the queer badger paddle, his white mask with its black stripes looking ghostly in the gloom.

"It's along that passage," he said, "if you want to wash your hands.''

Badgers are not like foxes. They have a special midden where they put out their used bones and rubbish, proper earth closets, and bedrooms whose bedding they turn out frequently, to keep it clean. The Wart was charmed with what he saw. He admired the Great Hall most, for this was the central room of the tumulus—it was difficult to know whether to think of it as a college or as a castle—and the various suites and bolt holes radiated outward from it. It was a bit cobwebby, owing to being a sort of common-room instead of being looked after by one particular family, but it was decidedly solemn. Badger called it the Combination Room. All round the panelled walls there were ancient paintings of departed badgers, famous in their day for scholarship or godliness, lit from above by shaded glow-worms. There were stately chairs with the badger arms stamped in gold on their Spanish leather seats—the leather was coming off—and a portrait of the Founder over the fireplace. The chairs were arranged in a semi-circle round the fire, and there were mahogany fans with which everybody could shield their faces from the flames, and a kind of tilting board by means of which the decanters could be slid back from the bottom of the semi-circle to the top. Some black gowns hung in the passage outside, and all was extremely ancient.

"I am a bachelor at the moment," said the badger apologetically, when they got back to his own snug room with the flowered wallpaper, "so I am afraid there is only one chair. You will have to sit on the bed. Make yourself at home, my dear, while I brew some punch, and tell me how things are going in the wide world."

"Oh, they go on much the same. Merlyn is well, and Kay is to be made a knight next week."

"An interesting ceremony."

"What enormous arms you have," remarked the Wart, watching him stir the spirits with a spoon. "So have I, for that matter." And he looked down at his own bandy-legged muscles. He was mainly a tight chest holding together a pair of forearms, mighty as thighs.

"It is to dig with," said the learned creature complacently. "Mole and I, I suppose you would have to dig pretty quick to match with us."

"I met a hedgehog outside."

"Did you now? They say nowadays that hedgehogs can carry swine fever and foot-and-mouth disease."

"I thought he was rather nice."

"They do have a sort of pathetic appeal," said the badger sadly, "but I'm afraid I generally just munch them up. There is something irresistible about pork crackling.

"The Egyptians," he added, and by this he meant the gypsies, "are fond of them for eating, too."

"Mine would not uncurl."

"You should have pushed him into some water, and then he'd have shown you his poor legs quick enough. Come, the punch is ready. Sit down by the fire and take your ease."

"It is nice to sit here with the snow and wind outside."

"It is nice. Let us drink good luck to Kay in his knighthood."

"Good luck to Kay, then."

"Good luck."

"Well," said the badger, setting down his glass again with a sigh. "Now what could have possessed Merlyn to send you to me?"

"He was talking about learning," said the Wart.

"Ah, well, if it is learning you are after, you have come to the right shop. But don't you find it rather dull?"

"Sometimes I do," said the Wart, "and sometimes I don't. On the whole I can bear a good deal of learning if it is about natural history."

"I am writing a treatise just now," said the badger, coughing diffidently to show that he was absolutely set on explaining it, "which is to point out why Man has become the master of the animals. Perhaps you would like to hear it?

"It's for my doctor's degree, you know," he added hastily, before the Wart could protest. He got few chances of reading his treatises to anybody, so he could not bear to let the opportunity slip by.

"Thank you very much," said the Wart.

"It will be good for you, dear boy. It is just the thing to top off an education. Study birds and fish and animals: then finish off with Man. How fortunate that you came! Now where the devil did I put that manuscript?"

The old gentleman scratched about with his great claws until he had turned up a dirty bundle of papers, one corner of which had been used for lighting something. Then he sat down in his leather armchair, which had a deep depression in the middle of it; put on his velvet smoking-cap with the tassel; and produced a pair of tarantula spectacles, which he balanced on the end of his nose.

"Hem," said the badger.

He immediately became paralysed with shyness, and sat blushing at his papers, unable to begin.

"Go on," said the Wart.

"It is not very good," he explained coyly. "It is just a rough draft, you know. I shall alter a lot before I send it in."

"I am sure it must be interesting."

"Oh no, it is not a bit interesting. It is just an odd thing I threw off in an odd half-hour, just to pass the time. But still, this is how it begins.

"Hem!" said the badger. Then he put on an impossibly high falsetto voice and began to read as fast as possible.

"People often ask, as an idle question, whether the process of evolution began with the chicken or the egg. Was there an egg out of which the first chicken came, or did a chicken lay the first egg? I am in a position to say that the first thing created was the egg.

"When God had manufactured all the eggs out of which the fishes and the serpents and the birds and the mammals and even the duck-billed platypus would eventually emerge, he called the embryos before Him, and saw that they were good.

"Perhaps I ought to explain," added the badger, lowering his papers nervously and looking at the Wart over the top of them, *"that all embryos look very much the same. They are what you are before you are born—and, whether you are going to be a tadpole or a peacock or* a cameleopard or a man, when you are an embryo you just look like a peculiarly repulsive and helpless human being. I continue as follows:

"The embryos stood in front of God, with their feeble hands clasped politely over their stomachs and their heavy heads hanging down respectfully, and God addressed them.

"He said: 'Now, you embryos, here you are, all looking exactly the same, and We are going to give you the choice of what you want to be. When you grow up you will get bigger anyway, but We are pleased to grant you another gift as well. You may alter any parts of yourselves into anything which you think would be useful to you in later life. For instance, at the moment you cannot dig. Anybody who would like to turn his hands into a pair of spades or garden forks is allowed to do so. Or, to put it another way, at present you can only use your mouths for eating. Anybody who would like to use his mouth as an offensive weapon, can change it by asking, and be a corkindrill or a sabre-toothed tiger. Now then, step up and choose your tools, but remember that what you choose you will grow into, and will have to stick to.'

"All the embryos thought the matter over politely, and then, one by one, they stepped up before the eternal throne. They were allowed two or three specializations, so that some chose to use their arms as flying machines and their mouths as weapons, or crackers, or drillers, or spoons, while others selected to use their bodies as boats and their hands as oars. We badgers thought very hard and decided to ask three boons. We wanted to change our skins for shields, our mouths for weapons, and our arms for garden forks. These boons were granted. Everybody specialized in one way or another, and some of us in very queer ones. For in-stance, one of the desert lizards decided to swap his whole body for blotting-paper, and one of the toads who lived in the drouthy antipodes decided simply to be a water-bottle.

"The asking and granting took up two long days—they were the fifth and sixth, so far as I remember—and at the very end of the sixth day, just before it was time to knock off for Sunday, they had got through all the little embryos except one. This embryo was Man.

" 'Well, Our little man,' said God. 'You have waited till the last, and slept on your decision, and We are sure you have been thinking hard all the time. What can We do for you?'

" 'Please God,' said the embryo, 'I think that You made me in the shape which I now have for reasons best known to Yourselves, and that it would be rude to change. If I am to have my choice I will stay as I am. I will not alter any of the parts which You gave me, for other and doubtless inferior tools, and I will stay a defenceless embryo all my life, doing my best to make myself a few feeble implements out of the wood, iron and the other materials which You have seen fit to put before me. If I want a boat I will try to construct it out of trees, and if I want to fly, I will put together a chariot to do it for me. Probably I have been very silly in refusing to take advantage of Your kind offer, but I have done my very best to think it over carefully, and now hope that the feeble decision of this small inno-cent will find favour with Yourselves.'

" 'Well done,' exclaimed the Creator in delighted tones. 'Here, all you embryos, come here with your beaks and whatnots to look upon Our first Man. He is the only one who has guessed Our riddle, out of all of you, and We have great pleasure in conferring upon him the Order of Dominion over the Fowls of the Air, and the Beasts of the Earth, and the Fishes of the Sea. Now let the rest of you get along, and love and multiply, for it is time to knock off for the week-end. As for you, Man, you will be a naked tool all your life, though a user of tools. You will look like an embryo till they bury you, but all the others will be embryos before your might. Eternally undeveloped, you will always remain potential in Our image, able to see some of Our sorrows and to feel some of Our joys. We are partly sorry for you, Man, but partly hopeful. Run along then, and do your best. And listen, Man, before you go . . .'

" 'Well?' asked Adam, turning back from his dismissal.

" 'We were only going to say,' said God shyly, twisting Their hands together. 'Well, We were just going to say, God bless you.' "

"It's a good story," said the Wart doubtfully. "I like it better than Merlyn's one about the Rabbi. And it is interesting, too."

The badger was covered with confusion.

"No, no, dear boy. You exaggerate. A minor parable at most. Besides, I fear it is a trifle optimistic."

"How?"

"Well, it is true that man has the Order of Dominion and is the mightiest of the animals—if you mean the most terrible one—but I have sometimes doubted lately whether he is the most blessed."

"I don't think Sir Ector is very terrible."

"All the same, if even Sir Ector was to go for a walk beside a river, not only would the birds fly from him and the beasts run away from him, but the very fish would dart to the other side. They don't do this for each other.''

"Man is the king of the animals.''

"Perhaps. Or ought one to say the tyrant? And then again we do have to admit that he has a quantity of vices.''

"King Pellinore has not got many.''

"He would go to war, if King Uther declared one. Do you know that Homo sapiens is almost the only animal which wages war?''

"Ants do.''

"Don't say 'Ants do' in that sweeping way, dear boy. There are more than four thousand different sorts of them, and from all those kinds I can only think of five which are belligerent. There are the five ants, one termite that I know of, and Man.''

"But the packs of wolves from the Forest Sauvage attack our flocks of sheep every winter.''

"Wolves and sheep belong to different species, my friend. True warfare is what happens between bands of the same species. Out of the hundreds of thousands of species, I can only think of seven which are belligerent. Even Man has a few varieties like the Esquimaux and the Gypsies and the Lapps and certain Nomads in Arabia, who do not do it, because they do not claim boundaries. True warfare is rarer in Nature than cannibalism. Don't you think that is a little unfortunate?''

"Personally,'' said the Wart, "I should have liked to go to war, if I could have been made a knight. I should have liked the banners and the trumpets, the flashing armour and the glorious charges. And oh, I should have liked to do great deeds, and be brave, and conquer my own fears. Don't you have courage in warfare, Badger, and endurance, and comrades whom you love?"

The learned animal thought for a long time, gazing into the fire.

In the end, he seemed to change the subject.

"Which did you like best," he asked, "the ants or the wild geese?"

chapter twenty-two

King Pellinore arrived for the important week-end in a high state of flurry.

"I say," he exclaimed, "do you know? Have you heard? Is it a secret, what?"

"Is what a secret, what?" they asked him.

"Why, the King," cried his majesty. "You know, about the King?"

"What's the matter with the King?" inquired Sir Ector. "You don't say he's comin' down to hunt with those demned hounds of his or anythin' like that?"

"He's dead," cried King Pellinore tragically. "He's dead, poor fellah, and can't hunt any more."

Sir Grummore stood up respectfully and took off his cap of maintenance.

"The King is dead," he said. "Long live the King."

Everybody else felt they ought to stand up too, and the boys' nurse burst into tears.

"There, there," she sobbed. "His loyal highness dead and gone, and him such a respectful gentleman. Many's the illuminated picture I've cut out of him, from the Illustrated Missals, aye, and stuck up over the mantel. From the time when he was in swaddling bands, right through them world towers till he was a-visiting the dispersed areas as the world's Prince Charming, there wasn't a picture of 'im but I had it out, aye, and give 'im a last thought o' nights.''

"Compose yourself, Nannie," said Sir Ector.

"It is solemn, isn't it?" said King Pellinore, "what? Uther the Conqueror, 1066 to 1216."

"A solemn moment," said Sir Grummore. "The King is dead. Long live the King."

"We ought to pull down the curtains," said Kay, who was always a stickler for good form, "or half-mast the banners."

"That's right," said Sir Ector. "Somebody go and tell the sergeant-at-arms."

It was obviously the Wart's duty to execute this command, for he was now the junior nobleman present, so he ran out cheerfully to find the sergeant. Soon those who were left in the solar could hear a voice crying out, "Nah then, one-two, special mourning fer 'is lite majesty, lower awai on the command Two!" and then the flapping of all the standards, banners, pennons, pennoncells, banderolls, guidons, streamers and cognizances which made gay the snowy turrets of the Forest Sauvage.

"How did you hear?" asked Sir Ector.

"I was pricking through the purlieus of the forest after that Beast, you know, when I met with a solemn friar of orders grey, and he told me. It's the very latest news.''

"Poor old Pendragon," said Sir Ector.

"The King is dead," said Sir Grummore solemnly. "Long live the King."

"It is all very well for you to keep on mentioning that, my dear Grummore," exclaimed King Pellinore petulantly, "but who is this King, what, that is to live so long, what, accordin' to you?"

"Well, his heir," said Sir Grummore, rather taken aback.

"Our blessed monarch," said the Nurse tearfully, "never had no hair. Anybody that studied the loyal family knowed that."

"Good gracious!" exclaimed Sir Ector. "But he must have had a next-of-kin?"

"That's just it," cried King Pellinore in high excitement. "That's the excitin' part of it, what? No hair and no next of skin, and who's to succeed to the throne? That's what my friar was so excited about, what, and why he was asking who could succeed to what, what? What?"

"Do you mean to tell me," exclaimed Sir Grummore indignantly, "that there ain't no King of Gramarye?"

"Not a scrap of one," cried King Pellinore, feeling important. "And there have been signs and wonders of no mean might."

"I think it's a scandal," said Sir Grummore. "God knows what the dear old country is comin' to. Due to these lollards and communists, no doubt."

"What sort of signs and wonders?" asked Sir Ector.

"Well, there has appeared a sort of sword in a stone, what, in a sort of a church. Not in the church, if you see what I mean, and not in the stone, but that sort of thing, what, like you might say."

"I don't know what the Church is coming to," said Sir Grummore.

"It's in an anvil," explained the King.

"The Church?"

"No, the sword."

"But I thought you said the sword was in the stone?"

"No," said King Pellinore. "The stone is outside the church."

"Look here, Pellinore," said Sir Ector. "You have a bit of a rest, old boy, and start again. Here, drink up this horn of mead and take it easy."

"The sword," said King Pellinore, "is stuck through an anvil which stands on a stone. It goes right through the anvil and into the stone. The anvil is stuck to the stone. The stone stands outside a church. Give me some more mead."

"I don't think that's much of a wonder," remarked Sir Grummore. "What I wonder at is that they should allow such things to happen. But you can't tell nowadays, what with all these Saxon agitators."

"My dear fellah," cried Pellinore, getting excited again, "it's not where the stone is, what, that I'm trying to tell you, but what is written on it, what, where it is."

"What?"

"Why, on its pommel."

"Come on, Pellinore," said Sir Ector. "You just sit quite still with your face to the wall for a minute, and then tell us what you are talkin' about. Take it easy, old boy. No need for hurryin'. You sit still and look at the wall, there's a good chap, and talk as slow as you can."

"There are words written on this sword in this stone outside this church," cried King Pellinore piteously, "and these words are as follows. Oh, do try to listen to me, you two, instead of interruptin' all

the time about nothin', for it makes a man's head go
ever so.''

''What are these words?'' asked Kay.

''These words say this,'' said King Pellinore, ''so
far as I can understand from that old friar of orders
grey.''

''Go on, do,'' said Kay, for the King had come
to a halt.

''Go on,'' said Sir Ector, ''what do these words
on this sword in this anvil in this stone outside this
church, say?''

''Some red propaganda, no doubt,'' remarked Sir
Grummore.

King Pellinore closed his eyes tight, extended his
arms in both directions, and announced in capital letters, ''Whoso Pulleth Out This Sword of this Stone
and Anvil, is Rightwise King Born of All England.''

''Who said that?'' asked Sir Grummore.

''But the sword said it, like I tell you.''

''Talkative weapon,'' remarked Sir Grummore
sceptically.

''It was written on it,'' cried the King angrily.
''Written on it in letters of gold.''

''Why didn't you pull it out then?'' asked Sir
Grummore.

''But I tell you that I wasn't there. All this that
I am telling you was told to me by that friar I was telling
you of, like I tell you.''

''Has this sword with this inscription been pulled
out?'' inquired Sir Ector.

''No,'' whispered King Pellinore dramatically.
''That's where the whole excitement comes in. They
can't pull this sword out at all, although they have all
been tryin' like fun, and so they have had to proclaim

a tournament all over England, for New Year's Day, so that the man who comes to the tournament and pulls out the sword can be King of all England for ever, what, I say?"

"Oh, father," cried Kay. "The man who pulls that sword out of the stone will be the King of England. Can't we go to the tournament, father, and have a shot?"

"Couldn't think of it," said Sir Ector.

"Long way to London," said Sir Grummore, shaking his head.

"My father went there once," said King Pellinore.

Kay said, "Oh, surely we could go? When I am knighted I shall have to go to a tournament somewhere, and this one happens at just the right date. All the best people will be there, and we should see the famous knights and great kings. It does not matter about the sword, of course, but think of the tournament, probably the greatest there has ever been in Gramarye, and all the things we should see and do. Dear father, let me go to this tourney, if you love me, so that I may bear away the prize of all, in my maiden fight."

"But, Kay," said Sir Ector, "I have never been to London."

"All the more reason to go. I believe that anybody who does not go for a tournament like this will be proving that he has no noble blood in his veins. Think what people will say about us, if we do not go and have a shot at that sword. They will say that Sir Ector's family was too vulgar and knew it had no chance."

"We all know the family has no chance," said Sir Ector, "that is, for the sword."

"Lot of people in London," remarked Sir Grummore, with a wild surmise. "So they say."

He took a deep breath and goggled at his host with eyes like marbles.

"And shops," added King Pellinore suddenly, also beginning to breathe heavily.

"Dang it!" cried Sir Ector, bumping his horn mug on the table so that it spilled. "Let's all go to London, then, and see the new King!"

They rose up as one man.

"Why shouldn't I be as good a man as my father?" exclaimed King Pellinore.

"Dash it all," cried Sir Grummore. "After all, damn it all, it is the capital!"

"Hurray!" shouted Kay.

"Lord have mercy," said the nurse.

At this moment the Wart came in with Merlyn, and everybody was too excited to notice that, if he had not been grown up now, he would have been on the verge of tears.

"Oh, Wart," cried Kay, forgetting for the moment that he was only addressing his squire, and slipping back into the familiarity of their boyhood. "What do you think? We are all going to London for a great tournament on New Year's Day!"

"Are we?"

"Yes, and you will carry my shield and spears for the jousts, and I shall win the palm of everybody and be a great knight!"

"Well, I am glad we are going," said the Wart, "for Merlyn is leaving us too."

"Oh, we shan't need Merlyn."

"He is leaving us," repeated the Wart.

"Leavin' us?" asked Sir Ector. "I thought it was we that were leavin'?"

"He is going away from the Forest Sauvage."

Sir Ector said, "Come now, Merlyn, what's all this about? I don't understand all this a bit."

"I have come to say Good-bye, Sir Ector," said the old magician.

"Tomorrow my pupil Kay will be knighted, and the next week my other pupil will go away as his squire. I have outlived my usefulness here, and it is time to go."

"Now, now, don't say that," said Sir Ector. "I think you're a jolly useful chap whatever happens. You just stay and teach me, or be the librarian or something. Don't you leave an old man alone, after the children have flown."

"We shall all meet again," said Merlyn. "There is no cause to be sad."

"Don't go," said Kay.

"I must go," replied their tutor. "We have had a good time while we were young, but it is in the nature of Time to fly. There are many things in other parts of the kingdom which I ought to be attending to just now, and it is a specially busy time for me. Come, Archimedes, say Good-bye to the company."

"Good-bye," said Archimedes tenderly to the Wart.

"Good-bye," said the Wart without looking up at all.

"But you can't go," cried Sir Ector, "not without a month's notice."

"Can't I?" replied Merlyn, taking up the position always used by philosophers who propose to dematerialize. He stood on his toes, while Archimedes held tight to his shoulder—began to spin on them slowly like a top—spun faster and faster till he was only a blur of greyish light—and in a few seconds there was no one there at all.

"Good-bye, Wart," cried two faint voices outside the solar window.

"Good-bye," said the Wart for the last time—and the poor fellow went quickly out of the room.

chapter twenty-three

The knighting took place in a whirl of preparations. Kay's sumptuous bath had to be set up in the box-room, between two towel-horses and an old box of selected games which contained a worn-out straw dart-board—it was called fléchette in those days—because all the other rooms were full of packing. The nurse spent the whole time constructing new warm pants for everybody, on the principle that the climate of any place outside the Forest Sauvage must be treacherous to the extreme, and, as for the sergeant, he polished all the armour till it was quite brittle and sharpened the swords till they were almost worn away.

At last it was time to set out.

Perhaps, if you happen not to have lived in the Old England of the twelfth century, or whenever it was, and in a remote castle on the borders of the Marches at that, you will find it difficult to imagine the wonders of their journey.

The road, or track, ran most of the time along the high ridges of the hills or downs, and they could look down on either side of them upon the desolate marshes where the snowy reeds sighed, and the ice crackled, and the duck in the red sunsets quacked loud on the winter air. The whole country was like that. Perhaps there would be a moory marsh on one side of the ridge, and a forest of a hundred thousand acres on the other, with all the great branches weighted in white. They could sometimes see a wisp of smoke among the trees, or a huddle of buildings far out among the impassable reeds, and twice they came to quite respectable towns which had several inns to boast of, but on the whole it was an England without civilization. The better roads were cleared of cover for a bow-shot on either side of them, lest the traveller should be slain by hidden thieves.

They slept where they could, sometimes in the hut of some cottager who was prepared to welcome them, sometimes in the castle of a brother knight who invited them to refresh themselves, sometimes in the firelight and fleas of a dirty little hovel with a bush tied to a pole outside it—this was the sign-board used at that time by inns—and once or twice on the open ground, all huddled together for warmth between their grazing chargers. Wherever they went and wherever they slept, the east wind whistled in the reeds, and the geese went over high in the starlight, honking at the stars.

London was full to the brim. If Sir Ector had not been lucky enough to own a little land in Pie Street, on which there stood a respectable inn, they would have been hard put to it to find a lodging. But he did own it, and as a matter of fact drew most of his dividends from that source, so they were able to get three beds between the five of them. They thought themselves fortunate.

On the first day of the tournament, Sir Kay managed to get them on the way to the lists at least an hour

before the jousts could possibly begin. He had lain
awake all night imagining how he was going to beat the
best barons in England, and he had not been able to eat
his breakfast. Now he rode at the front of the cavalcade, with pale cheeks, and Wart wished there was
something he could do to calm him down.

For country people, who only knew the dismantled
tilting ground of Sir Ector's castle, the scene which
met their eyes was ravishing. It was a huge green pit in
the earth, about as big as the arena at a football match.
It lay ten feet lower than the surrounding country, with
sloping banks, and the snow had been swept off it. It
had been kept warm with straw, which had been cleared
off that morning, and now the close-worn grass sparkled green in the white landscape. Round the arena
there was a world of colour so dazzling and moving
and twinkling as to make one blink one's eyes. The
wooden grandstands were painted in scarlet and white.
The silk pavilions of famous people, pitched on every
side, were azure and green and saffron and chequered.
The pennons and pennoncells which floated everywhere
in the sharp wind were flapping with every colour of
the rainbow, as they strained and slapped at their flag-
poles, and the barrier down the middle of the arena
itself was done in chessboard squares of black and white.
Most of the combatants and their friends had not yet
arrived, but one could see from those few who had
come how the very people would turn the scene into a
bank of flowers, and how the armour would flash, and
the scalloped sleeves of the heralds jig in the wind, as
they raised their brazen trumpets to their lips to shake
the fleecy clouds of winter with joyances and fanfares.

"Good heavens!" cried Sir Kay. "I have left my
sword at home."

"Can't joust without a sword," said Sir Grummore. "Quite irregular."

"Better go and fetch it," said Sir Ector. "You have time."

"My squire will do," said Sir Kay. "What a damned mistake to make! Here, squire, ride hard back to the inn and fetch my sword. You shall have a shilling if you fetch it in time."

The Wart went as pale as Sir Kay was, and looked as if he were going to strike him. Then he said, "It shall be done, master," and turned his ambling palfrey against the stream of newcomers. He began to push his way toward their hostelry as best he might.

"To offer me money!" cried the Wart to himself. "To look down at this beastly little donkey-affair off his great charger and to call me Squire! Oh, Merlyn, give me patience with the brute, and stop me from throwing his filthy shilling in his face."

When he got to the inn it was closed. Everybody had thronged to see the famous tournament, and the entire household had followed after the mob. Those were lawless days and it was not safe to leave your house —or even to go to sleep in it—unless you were certain that it was impregnable. The wooden shutters bolted over the downstairs windows were two inches thick, and the doors were double-barred.

"Now what do I do," asked the Wart, "to earn my shilling?"

He looked ruefully at the blind little inn, and began to laugh.

"Poor Kay," he said. "All that shilling stuff was only because he was scared and miserable, and now he has good cause to be. Well, he shall have a sword of some sort if I have to break into the Tower of London.

"How does one get hold of a sword?" he continued. "Where can I steal one? Could I waylay some knight, even if I am mounted on an ambling pad, and take his weapons by force? There must be some sword-smith or armourer in a great town like this, whose shop would be still open."

He turned his mount and cantered off along the street. There was a quiet churchyard at the end of it, with a kind of square in front of the church door. In the middle of the square there was a heavy stone with an anvil on it, and a fine new sword was stuck through the anvil.

"Well," said the Wart, "I suppose it is some sort of war memorial, but it will have to do. I am sure nobody would grudge Kay a war memorial, if they knew his desperate straits."

He tied his reins round a post of the lych-gate, strode up the gravel path, and took hold of the sword.

"Come, sword," he said. "I must cry your mercy and take you for a better cause.

"This is extraordinary," said the Wart. "I feel strange when I have hold of this sword, and I notice everything much more clearly. Look at the beautiful gargoyles of the church, and of the monastery which it belongs to. See how splendidly all the famous banners in the aisle are waving. How nobly that yew holds up the red flakes of its timbers to worship God. How clean the snow is. I can smell something like fetherfew and sweet briar—and is it music that I hear?"

It was music, whether of pan-pipes or of recorders, and the light in the churchyard was so clear, without being dazzling, that one could have picked a pin out twenty yards away.

"There is something in this place," said the Wart. "There are people. Oh, people, what do you want?"

Nobody answered him, but the music was loud and the light beautiful.

"People," cried the Wart, "I must take this sword. It is not for me, but for Kay. I will bring it back."

There was still no answer, and Wart turned back to the anvil. He saw the golden letters, which he did not read, and the jewels on the pommel, flashing in the lovely light.

"Come, sword," said the Wart.

He took hold of the handles with both hands, and strained against the stone. There was a melodious consort on the recorders, but nothing moved.

The Wart let go of the handles, when they were beginning to bite into the palms of his hands, and stepped back, seeing stars.

"It is well fixed," he said.

He took hold of it again and pulled with all his might. The music played more strongly, and the light all about the churchyard glowed like amethysts; but the sword still stuck.

"Oh, Merlyn," cried the Wart, "help me to get this weapon."

There was a kind of rushing noise, and a long chord played along with it. All round the churchyard there were hundreds of old friends. They rose over the church wall all together, like the Punch and Judy ghosts of remembered days, and there were badgers and nightingales and vulgar crows and hares and wild geese and falcons and fishes and dogs and dainty unicorns and solitary wasps and corkindrills and hedgehogs and griffins and the thousand other animals he had met. They loomed round the church wall, the lovers and helpers of the Wart, and they all spoke solemnly in turn. Some of them had come from the banners in the church, where they were painted in heraldry, some from the waters and the sky and the fields about—but all, down to the smallest shrew mouse, had come to help on account of love. Wart felt his power grow.

"Put your back into it," said a Luce (or pike) off one of the heraldic banners, "as you once did when I was going to snap you up. Remember that power springs from the nape of the neck."

"What about those forearms," asked a Badger gravely, "that are held together by a chest? Come along, my dear embryo, and find your tool."

A Merlin sitting at the top of the yew tree cried out, "Now then, Captain Wart, what is the first law of the foot? I thought I once heard something about never letting go?"

"Don't work like a stalling woodpecker," urged a Tawny Owl affectionately. "Keep up a steady effort, my duck, and you will have it yet."

A White-front said, "Now, Wart, if you were once able to fly the great North Sea, surely you can co-ordinate a few little wing-muscles here and there? Fold your powers together, with the spirit of your mind, and it will come out like butter. Come along, Homo sapiens, for all we humble friends of yours are waiting here to cheer."

The Wart walked up to the great sword for the third time. He put out his right hand softly and drew it out as gently as from a scabbard.

There was a lot of cheering, a noise like a hurdy-gurdy which went on and on. In the middle of this noise, after a long time, he saw Kay and gave him the sword. The people at the tournament were making a frightful row.

"But this is not my sword," said Sir Kay.

"It was the only one I could get," said the Wart. "The inn was locked."

"It is a nice-looking sword. Where did you get it?"

"I found it stuck in a stone, outside a church."

Sir Kay had been watching the tilting nervously, waiting for his turn. He had not paid much attention to his squire.

"That is a funny place to find one," he said.

"Yes, it was stuck through an anvil."

"What?" cried Sir Kay, suddenly rounding upon him. "Did you just say this sword was stuck in a stone?"

"It was," said the Wart. "It was a sort of war memorial."

Sir Kay stared at him for several seconds in amazement, opened his mouth, shut it again, licked his lips, then turned his back and plunged through the crowd. He was looking for Sir Ector, and the Wart followed after him.

"Father," cried Sir Kay, "come here a moment."

"Yes, my boy," said Sir Ector. "Splendid falls these professional chaps do manage. Why, what's the matter, Kay? You look as white as a sheet."

"Do you remember that sword which the King of England would pull out?"

"Yes."

"Well, here it is. I have it. It is in my hand. I pulled it out."

Sir Ector did not say anything silly. He looked at Kay and he looked at the Wart. Then he stared at Kay again, long and lovingly, and said, "We will go back to the church."

"Now then, Kay," he said, when they were at the church door. He looked at his first-born kindly, but straight between the eyes. "Here is the stone, and you have the sword. It will make you the King of England. You are my son that I am proud of, and always will be, whatever you do. Will you promise me that you took it out by your own might?"

Kay looked at his father. He also looked at the Wart and at the sword.

Then he handed the sword to the Wart quite quietly.

He said, "I am a liar. Wart pulled it out."

As far as the Wart was concerned, there was a time after this in which Sir Ector kept telling him to put the sword back into the stone—which he did—and in which Sir Ector and Kay then vainly tried to take it out. The Wart took it out for them, and stuck it back again once or twice. After this, there was another time which was more painful.

He saw that his dear guardian was looking quite old and powerless, and that he was kneeling down with difficulty on a gouty knee.

"Sir," said Sir Ector, without looking up, although he was speaking to his own boy.

"Please do not do this, father," said the Wart, kneeling down also. "Let me help you up, Sir Ector, because you are making me unhappy."

"Nay, nay, my lord," said Sir Ector, with some very feeble old tears. "I was never your father nor of your blood, but I wote well ye are of an higher blood than I wend ye were."

"Plenty of people have told me you were not my father," said the Wart, "but it does not matter a bit."

"Sir," said Sir Ector humbly, "will ye be my good and gracious lord when ye are King?"

"Don't!" said the Wart.

"Sir," said Sir Ector, "I will ask no more of you but that you will make my son, your foster-brother, Sir Kay, seneschal of all your lands?"

Kay was kneeling down too, and it was more than the Wart could bear.

"Oh, do stop," he cried. "Of course he can be seneschal, if I have got to be this King, and, oh, father, don't kneel down like that, because it breaks my heart. Please get up, Sir Ector, and don't make everything so horrible. Oh, dear, oh, dear, I wish I had never seen that filthy sword at all."

And the Wart also burst into tears.

chapter twenty-four

Perhaps there ought to be a chapter about the coronation. The barons naturally kicked up a fuss, but, as the Wart was prepared to go on putting the sword into the stone and pulling it out again till Doomsday, and as there was nobody else who could do the thing at all, in the end they had to give in. A few of the Gaelic ones revolted, who were quelled later, but in the main the people of England and the partizans like Robin were glad to settle down. They were sick of the anarchy which had been their portion under Uther Pendragon: sick of overlords and feudal giants, of knights who did what they pleased, of racial discrimination, and of the rule of Might as Right.

The coronation was a splendid ceremony. What was still more splendid, it was like a birthday or Christmas Day. Everybody sent presents to the Wart, for his prowess in having learned to pull swords out of stones, and several burghers of the City of London asked him to help them in taking stoppers out of unruly bottles, unscrewing taps which had got stuck, and in other household emergencies which had got beyond their control. The Dog Boy and Wat clubbed together and sent him a mixture for the distemper, which contained quinine and was absolutely priceless. Lyo-lyok sent

him some arrows made with her own feathers. Cavall
came simply, and gave him his heart and soul. The
Nurse of the Forest Sauvage sent a cough mixture,
thirty dozen handkerchiefs all marked, and a pair of
combinations with a double chest. The sergeant sent
him his crusading medals, to be preserved by the na-
tion. Hob lay awake in agony all night, and sent off
Cully with brand-new white leather jesses, silver varvels and silver bell. Robin and Marian went on an expedition which took them six weeks, and sent a whole
gown made out of the skins of pine martens. Little
John added a yew bow, seven feet long, which he was
quite unable to draw. An anonymous hedgehog sent
four or five dirty leaves with fleas on them. The Questing Beast and King Pellinore put their heads together
and sent some of their most perfect fewmets, wrapped
up in the green leaves of spring, in a golden horn with
a red velvet baldrick. Sir Grummore sent a gross of
spears, with the old school crest on all of them. The
cooks, tenants, villeins and retainers of The Castle of
the Forest Sauvage, who were given an angel each and
sent up for the ceremony in an ox-drawn char-à-banc
at Sir Ector's charge, brought an enormous silver model
of cow Crumbrocke, who had won the championship
for the third time, and Ralph Passelewe to sing at the
coronation banquet. Archimedes sent his own great-
great-grandson, so that he could sit on the back of the
King's throne at dinner, and make messes on the floor.
The Lord Mayor and Aldermen of the City of London
subscribed for a spacious aquarium-mews-cum-menag-
erie at the Tower in which all the creatures were
starved one day a week for the good of their stomachs
—and here, for the fresh food, good bedding, constant attention, and every modern convenience, the

Wart's friends resorted in their old age, on wing and foot and fin, for the sunset of their happy lives. The citizens of London sent fifty million pounds, to keep the menagerie up, and the Ladies of Britain constructed a pair of black velvet carpet slippers with the Wart's initials embroidered in gold. Kay sent his own record griffin, with honest love. There were many other tasteful presents, from various barons, archbishops, princes, landgraves, tributary kings, corporations, popes, sultans, royal commissions, urban district councils, czars, beys, mahatmas, and so forth, but the nicest present of all was sent most affectionately by his own guardian, old Sir Ector. This present was a dunce's cap, rather like a pharaoh's serpent, which you lit at the top end. The Wart lit it, and watched it grow. When the flame had quite gone out, Merlyn was standing before him in his magic hat.

"Well, Wart," said Merlyn, "here we are—or were—again. How nice you look in your crown. I was not allowed to tell you before, or since, but your father was, or will be, King Uther Pendragon, and it was I myself, disguised as a beggar, who first carried you to Sir Ector's castle, in your golden swaddling bands. I know all about your birth and parentage and who gave you your real name. I know the sorrows before you, and the joys, and how there will never again be anybody who dares to call you by the friendly name of Wart. In future it will be your glorious doom to take up the burden and to enjoy the nobility of your proper title: so now I shall crave the privilege of being the very first of your subjects to address you with it—as my dear liege lord, King Arthur."

"Will you stay with me for a long time?" asked the Wart, not understanding much of this.

"Yes, Wart," said Merlyn. "Or rather, as I should say (or is it have said?), Yes, King Arthur."

EXPLICIT LIBER PRIMUS

a note about the production
of this book

The typeface for the text of this special edition of *The Sword in the Stone* is Perpetua, designed in 1932 by the British artist Eric Gill. The text was photocomposed at Time Inc. under the direction of Albert J. Dunn and Arthur J. Dunn.

✕

The paper, TIME Reading Text, is from The Mead Corporation, Dayton, Ohio. The cover stock is from The Plastic Coating Corporation, Holyoke, Massachusetts.